HAVE YOU SEEN THE HORIZON LATELY?

HAVE YOU SEEN THE HORIZON LATELY?

BY

JAMIE S. RICH

AN ONI PRESS PUBLICATION
PORTLAND, OREGON

cover and interior illustrations by Joëlle Jones
cover colors and book design by Keith Wood
edited by Maryanne Snell & James Lucas Jones
copyediting by Lynn Adair

Published by Oni Press, Inc.
Joe Nozemack, publisher
James Lucas Jones, editor in chief
Randal C. Jarrell, managing editor
Douglas E. Sherwood, editorial assistant
Jill Beaton, editorial intern

ONI PRESS, INC.
1305 SE Martin Luther King Jr. Blvd.
Suite A
Portland, OR 97214
USA

www.onipress.com
www.confessions123.com

First edition: August 2007
ISBN 1-932664-73-7

1 3 5 7 9 10 8 6 4 2
PRINTED IN CANADA.

For Joëlle

"And like the leaves on the trees,
like the carpenter's son,
Like the planes and the trains and the lives that were young,
he's gone
and it feels like the words to a song"

— Brett Anderson

"Remember how ephemeral is this earth!"

— Sir Galahad's last words,
Le Morte D'Arthur by Sir Thomas Malory

1.

"Who are you?"

"I'm Julia."

"That doesn't explain anything. Are you American? Your accent—"

"Yes."

"What are you doing here?"

"In Beijing?"

"You've come to the wrong place."

"No, I haven't."

"Wherever you think you've ended up, you're not there."

"I am."

The girl stepped forward, up onto the front step of the house, putting her on level ground with the man. He was standing in the crack of the door, having only opened it part way. The sun was shining down from behind her, and it was making him squint. Behind him, the interior of the house was dark. His greasy bangs were hanging in front of his eyes, casting a shadow against his forehead. His hair had once been dark black, but it was now marbled with streaks of gray. He was only thirty, but anyone would have been forgiven for thinking he was much older.

"You're Percival Mendelssohn," the girl, Julia, said. She felt a sudden surge of energy as she said it, as if everything inside of her was pushing the words out of her mouth.

"Who?" the man asked. No hesitation. Not even a flinch. If the name registered, he wasn't showing it.

The man was sizing her up. The alleyway outside of his home was only a little over six feet wide, so it was impossible for them not to feel close, even with a door between them. The girl was pretty, in her early twenties. She had jet black hair—the color reminded him of his own at that age—cut in a bob, à la Louise Brooks. But instead of the translucent white of a girl from the Weimar Republic, her skin was brown, almost chestnut. Her face was oval shaped, her nose a little wide (but not too much), her eyes dark. If he had to guess, this Julia was Filipino, which only deepened the question.

How had a college-aged Filipino American ended up on his doorstep in China?

"You know who," Julia insisted, "because you're *him*. I know what Percival Mendelssohn looks like."

"You're saying I resemble this person?"

"Don't act so offended. Percival Mendelssohn is handsome. You used to look a lot healthier, though."

The man was only wearing a bathrobe—navy blue, silk. Comparing his wardrobe to hers, feeling the draft from inside the house, only made him feel more out in the open. A white sheet lay on the floor behind him, discarded in haste.

He snickered derisively. "I'm sure I don't know what you mean," he said. "I guess I'm flattered, but you're wrong. Statistically, there are only so many combinations of features that make up a face, so odds are that a couple of people are going to look a little bit alike."

"You see," Julia said, "that logic...you sound just like him."

"Or you're desperate to hear his words in mine."

"That sounds like him, too."

The man groaned. "This could go on all day. You could make that claim about everything I say."

Julia stepped forward again, moving closer to him. She was dressed entirely in black: a charcoal long-sleeved shirt, leather belt, skinny-fit pants with white vertical stripes, and a long scarf wrapped around her neck, an end dangling over each shoulder. The scarf was dark gray with flecks of silver, the lightest piece of her outfit. Her shoes were black and had thick, clunky soles, and when she walked, they made a sound on the sidewalk. The man recoiled from the noise and began to shut the door. "Wait!" Julia shouted, and she jumped back completely off the step. "Don't go! Don't lock me out!"

He froze.

"I've come a long way for this. A long way around the world. It took a lot of maneuvering and a lot of faith. I bet my entire education on a rumor just because I wanted to talk to you."

"You wanted to talk to this Percival person."

"Whatever. I wanted to talk to *you*. I wanted you to teach me, to explain things to me."

The girl sounded desperate. The expression on her face told him this was her last shot. She was begging.

"I'm not a teacher, nor am I an explainer," he said. "I'm just a man living in Beijing with his lover. I'm sorry, your gamble was a stinker. You bet on a loser."

He shut the door. Julia jumped a little in her skin when she heard the click of the lock. Small particles of stone tumbled down from the roof, loosened by the way the closing door shook the structure of the house, and the way the tiny pebbles bounced on the ground made her think of pearls from a destroyed necklace. Or rice at a wedding.

*

Val had two bags of groceries in his hand when he stepped into the entryway. He shut the door behind him and started to walk back into the house.

"Is she still out there?"

The voice startled Val. He was not used to his employer being in this part of the house and so had not looked when he had come in, but there in the shadows, the man sat with his back to the wall, hugging his knees to his chest.

"Percival? What are you doing there?"

"Don't call me that. She might hear you."

"The goth girl? Who is she?" Val saw the bedsheet on the floor and nudged it with his foot.

"I don't know, Val," Percival snapped, "but she knows who *I* am. What is she doing here? You have to get rid of her."

Val nodded. "It won't be a problem."

*

The house—traditionally known as a *siheyuan*—covered the entire block. It was the main building on this tiny street, and it could only be accessed through a complex navigation of other small streets. These alleys were called *hutongs*, and, as a result, the houses were often referred to by the same name. The design of the structures had been patterned after the layout of the Emperor's palace, and so was as old as Chinese history. In the modern age, a siheyuan was considered a relic, and most were being torn down and replaced by newer styles of apartments. Beijing was a big city, though, and it would take a long time to renovate the whole of it. The walls of the building were long and smooth, made of gray stone, with criss-cross patterns carved along their length. The roof was covered in old, clay tiles that had turned green with age. A pointed canopy jutted out above the rest of the house, marking the entrance. The south doorway was the only way into the house, a mirror of how China's imperial palace, the Forbidden City, can also only be entered from the south. The doorway was the last remaining ornamental fixture of this home. The stone planters that flanked the walk-up were now empty except for some remaining dirt and a few stray pieces of litter. There were no trees or bushes, only random weeds that had found their way through the concrete. Likewise, the front step had long since lost any of its decoration. Jagged stones on either side were all that remained of the original statuary, and these pieces served as a bad omen for the house. The sculptures that had been there were good luck charms strategically placed to protect the home and ward off bad spirits. Their removal had been intentional.

By contrast, the door still had some of its original ornamentation. Its wood was dark green, like a healthy leaf, and the frame and decorative trim were a beautiful scarlet. The paint was chipping, but the depth of the color was holding strong, looking more alive than the man's skinny fingers when he had hooked them around the door jamb like a gnarled claw. His skin was pale, and the bones of his knuckles were visible through it. It was as if when he touched the wood, it drained all of his blood into the doorframe. Its red was really his red, his inside had colored its outside. Just past the tips of his fingers was the edge of the *kanji* that was painted across the door, covering both halves. It was a *chengyu*, a blessing placed on the house. The girl wasn't so fluent in Mandarin that she could make it all out, but she got enough of it to recognize the phrase.

"Flowing water never goes bad, our doorways never gather termites."

Judging by the fuzzy edges of the lettering, Julia assumed it had been put there by the previous owner. If it hadn't been, if it had instead been chosen by the man who had greeted her, she wasn't exactly sure what his intention was in choosing it. The proverb meant that people needed to constantly move forward or life would pass them by. Its closest English equivalent was, "A rolling stone gathers no moss." Whether it was ironic because the life inside had come to a full stop or the man she had come to find was only there as one part of some bigger journey was something Julia intended to find out, but right then, only he knew for sure.

The girl was walking the edge of one of the empty planters when the door opened again and Val emerged from the house. He walked straight to her, his shoulders back, his gaze forward. Julia saw how determined he was trying to make himself look, and so she stopped her balancing act and stood still, straddling one corner with her feet spread across perpendicular sides. The planter was maybe a foot wide, and there was just a crack between it and the siheyuan. From the opposite end, where she was standing, she could just about lean across and touch the flank of the building on the opposite side of the hutong. It was taller than the little house, eclipsing it by three stories. Its windows peered down on the alley, but they all looked like they were empty, their glass black with grime.

Julia looked past Val. The door was shut tight again. She could not see him, but the man she believed to be Percival Mendelssohn was spying on her through a crack in the wall.

"Mr. Rossi has sent me to ask you to leave his property." Val spoke clearly and plainly. He was not interested in excess, nor did he wish to be misunderstood.

"Who are you? His lover?"

She said the last word like it was a taunt.

"That's none of your concern," Val replied icily.

"He said he lived with his lover."

Julia gave the word "lover" the same loaded delivery.

Val gestured back toward the siheyuan. "Mr. Rossi owns this entire quadrangle. Whom he lives with and what he does is no one's business but his own. We've asked you politely to go. Will you comply?"

"Moraldo Rossi," Julia said. She rolled the name around in her mouth, bounced it off her tongue. "Mora*lll*do *Rrr*rossi. I looked him up. They always said that when Percy was found, he'd be hiding under a pseudonym based on some person or character who ran away. It's because of how he tried to cover his tracks, taking that flight under the name 'George Willard.' I mean, come on? *Winesburg, Ohio*, that was a little obvious. It's not like everyone didn't already know how he stayed in hotels under the name 'Sherwood Anderson,' so that was barely trying. Did you know there's a whole website devoted to possible Percival Mendelssohn aliases? I think you were last spotted in Stockholm, when he was calling himself 'Harold Lime.'"

"It's clear, Miss, that you live a healthy fantasy life."

"Maybe that's what caused you to get more elaborate this time. Moraldo Rossi was Fellini's assistant director on *I Vitelloni*. I didn't see how that made sense at first, but then I read that Rossi was originally going to play his namesake, the character of Moraldo, in that film. Moraldo is the one who gets out of town at the end, who leaves it all behind. Just like George Willard at the end of *Winesburg*. You guys are sneaky."

"You being a smartass isn't going to be appreciated by anyone."

This curt response sucked the buoyancy right out of the girl, and she dropped off the planter to the ground. "You're right," she said. "It's probably not the right tactic. I have the utmost respect for Mr. Mendelssohn, and I don't want him to think otherwise."

Julia tilted to look past Val, and shouted at the green and red door, "I'm sorry, Mr. Mendelssohn!"

Inside, Percy jumped back from the hole he had been spying through. For a second, he thought she could see him.

"I really am! I meant no disrespect!"

Val took a step to his left, positioning himself in front of her again. "Mr. Rossi appreciates your apology," he said, "and he appreciates the trauma you may be caused by your *mistake*. But it is a mistake."

"If you say so, Val," Julia said. "That's right. I know your name, too. I told you I did my research."

"My name is unimportant."

"Maybe so, but I'm still not leaving. Go ahead and call the police. I'm sure the man who's in there that you say isn't in there won't mind the publicity that will come with it."

The two stared at each other a few moments, waiting to see who would blink first. It was Val. He nodded, spun on his heel, and went back inside. As soon as the door was locked again, Percy leapt from his hiding spot and grabbed Val by the shoulders. "What are you doing? You can't just leave her there!"

"What else can we do? We're going to have to wait her out."

"I don't think she's going to leave."

"Either way, you should move to the back of the house. I don't want her hearing you talking to me out here."

Percy looked around the room. His hands moved nervously, like he had misplaced something and was trying to remember where—or even what—it was. "Yes," he said, seemingly directed at no one. "I shall stay in my room until further notice."

Val placed a steadying hand on Percy's arm. "I think that would be wise," he said. "This nervous energy isn't good for you. Let me worry about this."

Taking a deep breath through his nose, Percy composed himself and disappeared through a sliding door into the main house. From there, he would go through the west wing, through the kitchen and Val's quarters, rather than take his usual path through the central courtyard. It seemed unwise to go outside, even if it was enclosed within the quadrangle. One never could tell what might be passing overhead on a day like today when everything was so exposed.

a.

"WALKING WITH A GHOST: THE CURIOUS CASE OF PERCIVAL MENDELSSOHN"

From the October 2004 issue of Houdini *magazine*

by
Denton Haines

It was five years ago this month that the greatest literary mystery of the 1990s capped the 20th century, when Percival Mendelssohn—arguably the most famous writer of his generation even if he wasn't the most widely read—left his home in Connecticut and disappeared with too many traces to count. The impetus for his departure was clear: his wife, Iris Mendelssohn-Tierney, had taken her own life the night before. The reasons this would cause the gossip-column favorite to flee are up to conjecture; the speculation on what happened next is vast, murky, and self-reflexive. Only Elvis has topped Mendelssohn's ability to be spotted in more places than he could possibly be, but unlike Elvis, given that there is no grave, no body, no evidence at all that Percival Mendelssohn isn't still alive, one or more of these sightings might actually be true.

Percival Mendelssohn was only twenty-three years old when he walked away from his rather glamorous life. A prodigy, he began publishing his first philosophical articles and short stories when he was in high school—which he finished two years ahead of schedule. As his output grew, so did his fame, and his books delighted some critics while infuriating others. One detects a whiff of jealousy amongst his peers, because very few writers in history have achieved the kind of fame Mendelssohn did. Like a latter-day Fitzgerald or Capote, though, much of that fame was for his partying skills and hobnobbing with celebrities. The famous and the infamous liked having him around to treat them to pearls of his wisdom, dispensing bons mots about how they should live their lives. Percival Mendelssohn was more than willing to oblige, trotting out his talent like an organ grinder's monkey to dance for nickel-sized crackers topped with caviar.

Though Tierney attended most of the same social functions as her husband, it was always noted that she didn't have quite the same relish for it. The two of them were high school sweethearts, and by all accounts, she only had eyes for him. The same could not be said for Percival. He had scandal enough for both of them. Distinguishing between his actual affairs and those that were merely apocryphal would be as difficult as unraveling the mystery of his disappearance, and there is only room for one of those topics in this article; however, Mendelssohn's wandering tastes do go to motive, both for Tierney's suicide and Percival's subsequent flight. He was allegedly philandering at the same time his beloved was bleeding to death.

*

There are currently three active websites devoted to keeping track of the movements of Percival Mendelssohn since November 1, 1999. Any Internet search engine will turn up hundreds of reported sightings, but one really need only navigate these three pages: He Is Nowhere Dead, Percival's Other Streets, and the much less clever-clever (and unsurprisingly, the most informative) Percival Mendelssohn Tracker. The devoted webmasters dogmatically catalogue any and every anecdote of someone spotting the elusive author anywhere in the world. The Tracker (www.percytracker.com) even rates each story for its possible validity, ranging from "Myth" to "Maybe" to "My George, We Have Him!" The fact that there are only three of the latter category amongst nearly 150 entries lends the Tracker its air of believability and is a testament to how seriously the site's curator, George Rawlings, takes his job.

"I've been a Percival fan since I was in high school, and I read *One*," Rawlings says. "It really grabbed me. People like to call it depressing, that it somehow promotes a doomed worldview, but I find it liberating. I want to know what happened to the man who gave so many of us the key to our lives. Did his fall apart? Or did he find new answers?"

Rawlings' motivations for keeping up with the Mendelssohn legend are pretty common among the writer's fans. They want to know where their hero went, and they want to know why. In reading their testimonies or talking to them, you will find that their slavish devotion to the man's work is the one thing that is keeping the myths of his exile from eclipsing the realities of his printed output. It's almost like when he fell off the planet, Percival Mendelssohn stopped time, and his acolytes are now stuck in the mindset he left them in. Likewise, new fans are caught up in a similar time warp. While the point of philosophy is to provide a springboard into a new way of tackling life, Mendelssohn fans become fossilized in their thinking. They need their hero to come back and dig them up, brush off the dust, and point the way to evolving past this.

Some speculate that this is all part of some grand plan on behalf of Percival Mendelssohn—particularly those who question his real abilities as a writer. He never really had to deliver the goods in print because all along he had designs to create a cult of personality around himself. They see him as a Hemingway who didn't have the talent, and so is just left with the bullfighting and elephant killing.

Such petty gripes about prose quality are easy to dismiss, but the notion that Mendelssohn had been planning to fly the coop for some time is not so easy to shake. The first evidence is the work he left behind, including a childhood story that has surfaced called "Cat on a Hot TV," predicting a crotchety version of the elderly author that has removed himself from all human contact, and his famous novella, *I Was Someone*

Dead, about a man named Hieronymus Zoo who bought himself an island and left the world to pursue a vocation as a hermit. Those who make Mendelssohn lore their pastime are quick to point out that in both stories, someone unexpectedly finds the hermit and thrusts him back into the land of the living. Never mind the conflicting outcomes. While Hieronymus Zoo finds love over the rainbow, the Percival Mendelssohn stand-in from the earlier story pummels the intruder to death with a book. The author kills his fan with the only real thing connecting them.

Again, this could all be by design, a contradiction contained in Mendelssohn's self-heralded "Gemini nature." Anyone who is going to seek out Mendelssohn has to want it badly enough that he or she is prepared to risk death, just like one of the heroes of the author's allegories. Hieronymus Zoo must slay a scary monster before he can have true love. One should also remember that the name Percival is derived from one of the knights who seeks the Holy Grail. Mendelssohn's mother is a distant relation of Sir Thomas Malory, and Percival and his two half brothers—Tristan Scott, the famous cult musician, and Lancelot Scott, who enjoys a minor career in Portland, Oregon, performing music under the name J. Cricket—were all christened from the Round Table. Thus Mendelssohn placed a high value on the importance of quests. (The Scott Family declined to comment for this article, maintaining the silence they established when this whole mess started.)

Nothing supports his possible desire for this kind of speculation more than how Mendelssohn actually organized his disappearance. Despite the tragic event that was the catalyst for his going through with it, the fact that he apparently had multiple identities already set up, thus enabling him to travel undetected, lends a lot of weight to the theory that he would have hightailed it out of real life eventually. The names he chose for these identities are even more telling. All of them have a story foundation that involves leaving one life for another, and while some of the aliases have possible suicidal outcomes, none are definite, giving hope that Percival Mendelssohn is still alive.

*

The string of allusions begins with the cab ride that Mendelssohn, along with his personal assistant, Val Stuart, took from a grocery store parking lot hours after authorities had left his house with the body of Iris Tierney. Mendelssohn and Stuart abandoned Percival's car at around the same time a yellow cab picked up two passengers and took them to the airport. The call was made under the name George Willard, the hero of Sherwood Anderson's *Winesburg, Ohio*, which is credited with ushering American literature into the 20th century. *Winesburg, Ohio* is a collection of short stories about the titular small town, and most of them feature George Willard. Like any young man of his age, Willard wants to leave his home and find his place in the world. The final story of the cycle, "Departure," has him doing just that, sneaking out of Winesburg for parts unknown.

Sherwood Anderson was often cited by Percival Mendelssohn as one of his greatest influences. His favorite story was one called "Tandy," in which a small-town girl meets her true love in the guise of a traveler breezing through Winesburg. Fate has it that their ages are too far apart for them to ever be together, and he moves on, but not before she insists on changing her name to mold her identity to meet his image of her. Of equal fascination to Mendelssohn, though, is the story of Anderson himself. Anderson abandoned his family and a straight job in his mid thirties to become a writer. The legend goes that one day he just got up from behind his desk, walked out of the workplace, and never looked back. Mendelssohn regularly spoke of his admiration for the strength it must have taken to pursue such an action.

The fact that he adopted this moniker is pointed to by many as his signal to the world that he was getting the hell out of Dodge. What he did next is believed to be either an attempt to stoke the flames of speculation or exactly what it appears to be on the surface: a man of means using those means to cover his tracks.

Once they were at the airport, Stuart and Mendelssohn visited every ticket counter and booked flights to various locations around the world—all under different names. For each individual flight, the pair presented passports, driver's licenses, credit cards, and other forms of identification to support their aliases—and also similar documents to hide Val's identity (though these were usually less clever, often using Val's real name combined with the name of Mendelssohn's given alias, passing him off as some kind of relative; so, for instance, he was both Val Willard and Stuart Anderson). One pair of tickets was bought under both Mendelssohn's and Stuart's real identities. They were for a flight to Los Angeles, Percival's hometown.

The other tickets that day would establish the bulk of the list of monikers that would crop up time and time again in future reports among Percy watchers. In addition to George Willard and Sherwood Anderson, they are:

• Ambrose Bierce, the Civil War-era reporter, horror writer, and author of *The Devil's Dictionary*, who crossed the border into Mexico in 1913 and was never seen again; showing at least some sense of humor in this activity, Mendelssohn put this alias on a 747 to Mexico City.

• B. Traven was like Bierce in that he hid out in Mexico. He retreated from the U.S. due to his irascible political viewpoints and his strong adherence to Communism. He is most famous for writing the source material for *Treasure of the Sierra Madre*, and in a twisted pun, this version of Percival Mendelssohn was shipped off to Sierra Leone.

• Richard Edwards/Richey James, the real name and the stage name for the lyricist and rhythm guitarist of a Byronic rock band from Wales called the Manic Street Preachers. In 1995, Edwards abandoned his car on a bridge in England and vanished. While there have been claims among his fans that they have seen him in various places, none have been verified. This new version of Richard Edwards went back to Wales, while the invented Richey James went to Bangkok, where his band had enjoyed a particularly debauched tour at one time.

• Weldon Kees, a little known poet from the '40s who also abandoned his car on a bridge—the Golden Gate Bridge in San Francisco, CA, in 1954. He was said to also be a fan of Bierce, and there have been at least two reports of people running into him in years since, including one in Mexico. Mendelssohn seized on the other, though, and sent his version of Kees to New Orleans.

• Harold Lime, the formal name of Harry Lime, the antihero of Graham Greene's novel and screenplay *The Third Man*. Immortalized on screen by Orson Welles, Lime was a bad dude who faked his own death to avoid prosecution. Mendelssohn sent Harry to Vienna, where he originally made his ill-gotten fortune selling medicine on the black market.

• Jerome Salinger, a reference to J.D. Salinger, another famous author who withdrew from public life and has refused all contact. He was another big influence on Mendelssohn, and he and his brothers used to imagine they were like Salinger's Glass family, a collection of gifted yet strange children. Jerome flew back to the New Hampshire hideaway where he has been holed up since the mid-'60s.

• Hieronymus Zoo. Percival sent his own character to an island in the Caribbean. This island, though, had people on it, which made it vastly different than the last island this fictional doppelganger visited.

George Willard, ironically, was sent back to Ohio, and one wonders what he would have made of Cleveland. Sherwood Anderson was sent back to Paris, where he could rejoin the spirits of the expatriate writers he inspired.

Of course, no one knows which one of these men may have actually been Percival Mendelssohn. There are a lot of hazy facts surrounding the flight manifests and the check-in processes. The airlines believe that someone got on almost every plane in each instance that a ticket was purchased, a feat of obfuscation that would probably stump even a seasoned debunker like our own mascot, Houdini. If the truth ever is found out, smart money says that none of these known identities was the one used. Mendelssohn and Stuart most likely took a trip under names no one would recognize so as not to call attention to their real destination.

*

Which leaves us with, where has Percival Mendelssohn been seen since?

Surprisingly, one of the most popular stories is one that Rawlings has taken the utmost care to disprove on his site. "The most common one we hear is that a collegiate backpacker spotted Percy in Morocco, where he was playing a guitar for spare change," Rawlings said. "This seems ludicrous, because he would never be out in public performing, that's not what this is about. It takes on an even more interesting hue when you realize that it's actually a mixed-up version of a story about Richey James from the Manic Street Preachers. He was supposedly spotted playing on the streets of Sri Lanka."

So, what are the three "My George!" stories on Percy Tracker?

Third from the top of absolute belief is Percy living as Harold Lime in Stockholm. In a twist worthy of Lime's creator, Graham Greene, this character made flesh is said to be a roving bookseller, hawking bootleg editions of famous literary works from a rickety cart he pushes through the Swedish streets. With the purchased book, you also receive his long-winded, detailed opinions on the prose. A Mendelssohn reader first became wise to this disguise when they were buying a copy of the man's final novel, *The Other Side of the Street*. Before handing it over, the bookseller gave his usual analysis and, as he did so, absent-mindedly opened the novel and signed it. Only, he signed it

"Percival Mendelssohn," rather than "Harold Lime," the name on his cart and that he stamps on the inside front cover of all of his books. When he finished, the bookseller froze and stared in shock at what he had done. The buyer snatched the novel from his hands, and Lime began ranting and raving until the buyer ran off.

Rawlings claims to have seen the actual book, though most people have only seen one of the dubious scans of the autograph that float around on the Internet. The identity of the alleged owner is a closely guarded secret. Some fans still make a pilgrimage to Stockholm and occasionally make claims of tracking down Lime/Mendelssohn. The more common wisdom is that if it really was the author, he disappeared as soon as his cover was blown.

The second story has another Orson Welles connection. In it, Percival Mendelssohn has changed his name to Gregory Arkadin, the lead character in Welles' crime film, *Mr. Arkadin*. In the film, an extremely wealthy man hides a shady past, one he claims not to remember. His amnesia extends to his given name. He is also known for throwing lavish masquerade parties, something this new Mr. Arkadin also does, having week-long revelries in a castle on the Spanish countryside. No one who has attended one of these soirees can make any claims to having seen their host's face: he never removes his own mask. It is said to be a featureless visage made of smoked plastic.

Again, Rawlings has tried to verify this myth on his own. He has traveled to Spain, where he claims to have found people who have attended an Arkadin gathering. He was not, however, able to secure an invitation for himself, and so he returned home empty-handed. Or did he? Some Internet chatter suggests Rawlings got an audience with the man himself and is keeping that info under his hat. "Patently false," Rawlings insists.

The top of the food chain of Percival Mendelssohn sightings, however, is positively mundane. In it, the writer has set up camp on a small island near Sweden, much like the one revered film director Ingmar Bergman lives on. While the specific island has never been established, one can often see the man who is purported to be Percival Mendelssohn at a coastal town buying supplies. He has adopted the rather simple handle of Percy Schutte, a play on the surname of his brothers, something he already did, once again, in his fiction. Hieronymus Zoo's grandfather was called Schutte.

Apparently, this one earns points both for its simplicity, its direct allusions to the written work, and the number of people who have verified it. It's said that if you do find the town where the man visits, the people there will not tell you anything about their famous citizen, choosing instead to close ranks and protect him. Similarly, those lucky Mendelssohn fans fiercely guard the exact location of this coastal village. You have to be part of the inner circle to be blessed with this knowledge. Rawlings claims to know, but he refuses to publish the name on his site because he doesn't want the seaside town flooded with Percy pilgrims. (He refused to divulge the name to me for the same reason, afraid I would publish it here for anyone to read.) Strangely, Rawlings claims to have not yet gone himself. "Some of my webmasters have," he said, "and I plan to as soon as I save enough money."

*

Unfortunately, as fascinating as the story is, it ends up being a whole lot of information adding up to nothing. The plot would make Raymond Chandler blush for being so labyrinthine while offering little by way of concrete explanation. Then again, I almost got the sense that was the point. In talking to Rawlings and the other devoted followers of Percival Mendelssohn, I got the sense that maybe more than they want life lessons from their rock star philosopher, they want to maintain the culture they have established around hunting for him. Like *Star Trek* fans who accept ever-diminishing returns as the movie studios crank out yet another tired franchise, the Mendelssohn faithful would rather the myths keep churning than be left with nothing at all.

It causes one to wonder, if Percival Mendelssohn is out there and watching the buzz that continues to circulate around his legend, is he amused by the grand and literary prank he pulled off, or does his analytical mind cause him to step back and ponder just what it all means? Like the unnamed hero at the end of his novel *One*, the now nameless author can look back over the course of his own life, and all the lives he affected on his search for self, and smile at the absurdity of it all. "*And in the end*," the book concludes, "*all he could carry with him was the laughter, the small chuckle born from a joke he had only told himself.*"

2.

As the sun set, it cast an orange netting over the hutong. The light trickled in through the alleyway entrance, the last reminder of the world Julia had come from. The street didn't continue on in this direction, instead it ended abruptly at a wooden fence. Once the sun was gone, it would be like the entrance was sealed. The vault door was closing, leaving them inside.

Which was really just a pile of wishful thinking on her part. Julia didn't want to go back, not without getting what she had come for. She sat on the rim of the planter. The thin ledge hurt her rear, and it was probably more comfortable on the steps, but she wanted to be somewhere they could see her or they might think she'd given up and left. On one hand, that could actually be good, causing them to drop their guard and open the door, but she had to give them credit for being smarter than that. They couldn't have remained undetected for over seven years if they weren't. Percival Mendelssohn had disappeared in 1999. He had become a ghost, a figment, a myth of smoke. All that was left of the man were stories.

She tried to imagine it. He'd waved goodbye to the police, watched them take away his wife's body, and then Percival was gone. He'd vanished under a haze of grief, cloaked in aliases, traveling on some kind of force of will, the desire not to be seen carrying him away.

Then again, he also had all the money in the world, and Julia bet that made things easier. She didn't have much money at all, and that had certainly presented obstacles to traveling across the globe, and she was even using her own name. Studying Asian literature had given her a bit of a safety net, but had her hunch not been right, had Percy not been in Beijing, then what? She had used her education, rolled the dice to get into a school program in China, gambling that he was there based on the fact that he had never been seen there. He'd been seen in Prague, Casablanca, Dublin, and Dallas, and places everywhere else in the world, but not Beijing. What made the city interesting, however, was that several people had thought they'd seen Val there. Val Stuart, who had been Percival Mendelssohn's personal assistant for three years prior to the disappearance, who had done everything for his employer back in the States and was as well known to Percy's hardcore fans as Percy was and yet virtually unknown to the general public. It made a perfect kind of sense to her that he'd be the one to be spotted, because he'd be the one out taking care of business while the real quarry stayed hidden. Her resolve wavered a little when she considered that if it was simple enough for her to figure out, then surely someone else had had the same thought before. Even so, it was important. She had to take the chance.

And here she was, staring at his front door. Trusting her instincts had paid off.

Wind was kicking up and blowing the fine gray dust that covered the ground around the alley. A thin brushing of it lay over Julia's dark shoes and clung to the hems of her pants. How had all this dust gotten into Beijing? What part of the world was eroding away?

Maybe it was Percy's dust, remnants of a past he'd let crumble.

Maybe she had been right and the rest of the planet, the place where the sun had been setting, was now gone, and this was the debris.

It had gotten dark, the hours had ticked by, and it was well past midnight before Val came out again. He had an apple in each hand. Without saying a word, he handed one to Julia and then sat down on the planter next to her. He took a bite of the other apple. It was crisp and loud. When she smelled the scent of the fruit, Julia realized she was incredibly starved. She hadn't eaten since breakfast. Food hadn't figured into her plans.

The apple tasted amazing.

As soon as her mouth was full, Val asked, "So, where do you think this is heading?"

"I don't know," she replied.

Val laughed. "Not so cocky now, eh? It could get real messy around here, you know."

"I don't want it to."

"Neither do we. Neither does Mr. Rossi."

"Mendelssohn."

"Just because you say something is another thing, doesn't mean it is."

"Neither does it mean it isn't." Julia was done with the apple. She looked around for where to put the core, and Val extended his hand, palm open. She placed the remains in it. "By that logic, too, just because you take someone like Percival Mendelssohn and say he's *The Third Man* or whatever, it doesn't change who he really is. You have no more power than I do."

Val took another loud crunch into his apple. "Let's say for the sake of argument, in this bizarre universe you've made up in your head, Moraldo Rossi really was this other person you said he is, what then?"

Julia's stomach rumbled. Now that she had eaten a little, she had grown more hungry, and her body wasn't afraid to tell her. She clutched her belly with her forearms and looked down at the ground, embarrassed. "I just want to spend time with him," she said, "to talk to him."

"What for? Have you ever considered that this person you're looking for is merely a man, just like any other?"

"But he isn't!" Julia exclaimed. She looked at this accuser, this person who had been Percy's confidante—she knew this man knew better. "You of all people, you can't tell me he's just the same as everyone else. His writing, you know his writing, it's helped so many people. It saved my life!"

"Well, you still have that then, don't you?"

"Yes, I do. I do. But he went away, and it was like he took a lot of that with him, and it all stopped. His words stopped, but my life kept going, and I need to know why he stopped because I don't know what to do next."

Val nodded. He chewed at his bottom lip and it made the whiskers just underneath stand up, like a beetle kneeling down on its front legs and sticking its tail in the air to protect itself.

"That's fascinating, but it still doesn't mean that Moraldo Rossi is Percival Mendelssohn."

The man stood again and went back inside, carrying the apple cores with him.

*

As the night wore on and grew darker, Julia began to hear creatures scuttling back and forth on the tile roof of the hutong. When she looked up, she thought she saw movement, but wasn't sure. It made her doubt that she heard any sound at all.

Then one of the rooftop creatures turned its head, and the light from the distant street corner, or perhaps the moon, caught one of its eyes and it lit up like a green flare. From lime to orange to a slow fade, the tracer lingering. There was definitely something up there. Julia had heard it, and now she had definite evidence of it.

She only needed a better look, and then she'd know what it was.

*

Just after 3:00 a.m., Percy began his regular tour of the house. This was his routine, traveling through his own space while the rest of the world slept. Generally, he did so with very little clothes on. At the most, he wore his boxer shorts, but usually nothing—just a white bed sheet wrapped around his frail shoulders, draped over his body like a cape. Tonight, though, knowing there was a spy at his door, he had put on his pajamas. They were long sleeved, with a full pant leg, and had white with blue pinstripes. Percy still had the sheet, but it wasn't the same. The pajamas were warm, the sheet made him warmer, and the heat was confining.

Val was sitting in the entryway, keeping vigil—except his head was down. His chin rested on his chest, his eyes were closed. Percy thought he had padded in silently, like a night prowler or a spectral vision that could travel undetected, but as soon as he was in the room, Val lifted his head.

"Is she still out there?" Percy asked.

"Yes, she is," Val said. "I thought we agreed I'd come get you when she left?"

"I was bored. How convinced is she?"

"It's blind faith at this point, but she's done her homework."

"If she makes it to morning, give her breakfast."

"What? Why?"

"If she makes it to morning, there's no going back. We'll never change her mind, so we had better start being nice to her."

Val rubbed his hand over his chin, and the sound of his fingers over his stubble dug into Percy's ears like a metal pin. Percy didn't like rough noises. *This is what it must sound like for one insect to eat another,* he thought, and he shuddered.

"But if we feed her," Val said, "isn't that practically a confirmation? I still think we should deny, deny, deny."

Percy looked at the door, almost like he could see through it to the girl. Val wasn't exactly wrong, but Percy didn't know how to make his assistant understand why his way was less wrong. His words were out of shape, he couldn't rally them to his defense the way he always had before.

"Maybe it's just instinct," he said. "Maybe I understand what it's like to want something to be true so badly that nothing will shake your belief that it is."

After he said it, Percy reached out and touched the door. As soon as he felt the wood, though, he asked himself why he had done it. What had he expected, to feel her breathing on his skin? To send her a signal?

He wrapped the sheet tighter around his neck, pressing his Adam's apple back into his throat. If he could wrap himself completely in the fabric, he could freeze his existence right there and prevent any more of it from getting away. Like a paper finger trap where the more you struggled, the tighter it got. Like quicksand.

Percy said nothing more, and he resumed his walk. He passed from the entryway to the room immediately inside, crossing to the sliding door that opened out into the courtyard. The paper windows made a rattling sound. Percy held still until it stopped. It was reflex. Even after three quarters of a decade away from other people, he still couldn't shake the late-night fear that he might wake someone up.

The sky was clear, the air crisp. He immediately wished again that he didn't have this shirt, didn't have these pants. He longed to feel the chill over all of his body, not just his face. The breeze crackled on his cheeks like he was being tickled by the fingers of an electric anemone. He sat on the steps and looked at his courtyard garden. He and Val had let it get overgrown. The grass was too tall, the fountain in its center had grown over with algae since being turned off, the trees on either side were stooping under the weight of their leaves. It was of no consequence to him. Let the imperfection exist, otherwise what good had it been to jump out of modern life's endless pursuit of precision.

The grass rustled. There was something out there. More than one something, actually. Percy's cats were also out for their evening strolls. One of them meowed, but Percy could not see which one. "I bet that's you, Gawain," he said. "I can tell by your voice. What vermin have you found for me this evening?"

There was more noise above him, little footfalls on the roof, and he could sense movement over his head. A sleek calico dropped down on the path in front of him, sliding in the gravel. The cat sat and faced Percy, puffing out his chest before yawning and licking his lips.

"Oh, Roland!" Percy laughed. "So daring! Have you been keeping guard for me tonight? The enemy rests at our gates, you know. If she storms our walls, there may be casualties."

Roland approached his master and pushed one shoulder against Percy's shins before immediately turning around and rubbing past the man in the other direction. Percy reached down and scratched the cat under his chin. Roland lifted his head in response, eyes closed tight. He was purring.

"You know, Roland, when they asked the men who built the atomic bomb how they could live with themselves after creating something so deadly, all of them, down to a man, responded that they were scientists.

The use of any particular discovery was not their problem, otherwise they might be persuaded to abandon their mission and never see what would happen once all the elements were brought together. Yet, do you really think none of them ever stopped to think about what *might* be done with this 'discovery'? Did they really sleep easy knowing the world might destroy itself because they just *had* to see how atoms smashed together?"

Roland didn't answer but kept accepting the scratching. The grass was still rustling, and four more cats emerged. It was as if they had seen the attention Roland was getting and jealously wanted their own. A scrawny boy was the most aggressive, climbing up on Percy's lap and stretching across his thighs. He had a white underbelly but was gray with black stripes on top. In the center of his back was a green spot, about the size of a half dollar. "My goodness, Gawain," Percy said. "You just can't let anyone else have a good tickle without getting in on it!"

Percy looked at the other three cats. "Bors, Tristan, Galahad," he said, acknowledging each one. "Where are the others?"

Tristan, a light-orange tabby with extra long whiskers and wild hair on his cheeks and dome, meowed in response, as if to say, "Nowhere!"

"Too true," Percy answered. "You are here, and you are enough for me to handle at this moment. I've only got two hands."

Lying back on the steps, Percy stretched his arms out at his sides. Gawain dug his claws into Percy's pajamas, barely pricking his skin, leery of being rocked off, but once Percy was settled, the cat began to knead at his legs to soften up the bed. The other cats followed suit, climbing up on their master. Except for Roland, who went and lay down next to Percy's left hand and began to lick the man's palm. The cat's tongue was coarse, and his breath was hot, but Percy appreciated the gesture.

"Have you ever seen such a sky?" he asked them.

One of the cats meowed.

"No, Bors, neither have I."

*

Julia started to doubt whether she could last. She wanted to stay awake in case something happened, and the Beijing pavement wasn't an inviting place to take a nap, anyway. As the night wore on, however, she found it difficult to fight her body's desires. First her head began to droop, then her whole body. She jerked awake two, three, four times—to be honest, she'd lost count. She was having the standard falling-asleep dream, the one where you see yourself as falling and feel like you're tumbling down. Julia was having visions of herself walking, usually back to her dorm at the Chinese university, and her feet would slip out from under her and she'd hang suspended in the air. She wasn't upright, but she wasn't dropping either, and her slumbering body, under the impression that she was about to hit cement, would wake up, catching her and putting her back on her feet again.

She wasn't sure how long she had been out when the rain woke her up, but it was nearly 4:00 a.m. Summer in the area could be like that: flash showers that hit out of nowhere and are gone just as fast as they came. It hit her hard and cold, like the pressure had been building in the sky and the fabric of the atmosphere ripped, releasing the entire rainstorm at once. Julia jumped to her feet—once more catching and righting herself—and dashed into Percy's doorway. The overhang didn't protect her completely, but just enough. She looked up, searching for the tear in the sky. Some of the raindrops looked as fat as apples. Who was shaking the tree to knock them loose?

Julia was definitely awake now. There was no fear of falling asleep again. Leaning her back against the door, she wondered if either of the men inside was losing any sleep because of her. The way she was feeling at the moment, she didn't think it likely. She felt too small to even register. If any of her friends or family knew why she had really come to China, they'd think she was insane, particularly if they saw her this dirty and soaked through. She couldn't say she would blame them, but she also dismissed the notion of "crazy." Someone had dumped a big bucket of rain on her and washed her illusions away. Life itself was crazy, and the maddest act of all was to try to straighten it out.

Which was exactly what she was in China to do, so Julia decided she must be nuts after all.

Something brushed against her calves, and Julia nearly jumped backward through the door. She gasped and was just about to scream but bit her lip before it came out. A cat was on the porch with her. It was black, and it had a mangled tail. Half of it was gone, and what was there had a kink three-quarters of the way up. Its hair was mangy and matted with rain. Julia could hear it purring as it worked its way back and forth across her legs.

Crouching down, Julia scratched the top of the cat's butt. It dipped down frontward, extending its rear in the air, but then whipped around and bumped its forehead into Julia's hand. She rubbed the cat's skull, moving under its chin and scratching. The cat tilted its head back, giving her fingers more access, and the purring picked up speed and volume. "You like that, don't you?" she asked. "That's some motor you have on you."

The cat was squinting, and so she didn't see until it opened its eyes to look at her that its right eye was gone. Only an empty socket remained, mostly closed over and protected by fur. The left eye was a gorgeous jade with a dark sliver for its pupil.

Julia raised her hand up to her mouth and spit on her thumb. She then opened her other hand and turned the palm up. She dug the wet thumb into her palm. It was a superstition her mother taught her. It wasn't Filipino, but something she had learned in America. Julia's uncle was doing field work and one of the farmers taught it to him, and he taught it to his sister, who then passed it on to her daughter. One-eyed cats were lucky, and Julia had wished on it. Of course, she asked that it would really be Percival she had found and that he would eventually let her inside to talk. She wasn't positive that counted as one wish, but she'd take the chance.

"It's you that was watching me earlier," Julia said. "Have you been here all night? You're my little *maneki neko*, aren't you?"

The cat banged the top of its head against the inside of her wrist. She peered under its tail and saw that it was a him. "My sweet little boy."

The rain had passed, so Julia scooped the cat up into her arms and carried him over to the planter. He struggled a little, but once Julia let him adjust his position so that he was lying across her forearm, his front legs dangling over either side, he seemed comfortable with their arrangement. He raised his head high in the air as if he were a king being carried by his servants, paraded before his subjects.

Dawn was still an hour or two away from breaking, but the sky was starting to grow lighter. They'd gotten through the darkest patch of the night, and the world was clearing the way for morning.

Morning. Everyone would be awake...and then what?

Julia scratched that cat's cheek under his bad eye, and he got excited and clamped his teeth down on her hand. It stung for a second, but she saw him going for it and was able to brace herself rather than yank her hand away and scare the poor thing even worse. It wasn't like he broke flesh or anything, and within a couple of seconds he softened his bite, easing his teeth off her skin. The cat licked the spot of his attack, like he was trying to fix the damage he had done.

"Who are you?" she asked him. "Do you live with Percy?"

The only answer she received was more licking.

If this fuzzy boy had indeed been watching her all night, it made her wonder again if the other boys had been watching her, as well. (She thought of them as boys, but was being facetious. They weren't boys. Particularly not that weirdo Val. And she was getting old enough now that the distinction between boys and men, women and girls, was all getting a little too clear. Eventually she would have to drop the ambiguity and choose which side of the line she wanted to be on. Was that maybe part of why she was here?) While she didn't imagine herself scary, to pretend that the situation wasn't possibly frightening to them would have been stupid. Unless this had happened before and they had ways of handling it. Would they eventually decide she had to be dealt with and orchestrate a little disappearance of her own?

Then again, if this was Percy's cat, then Percy couldn't be so bad, because boys (and men) who were into cats were usually all right by her. If only she could know for sure, if she could get some glimpse inside the house and see what was going on, she would feel better. When she imagined things between them, she imagined that she and Percy were pretty much the same, and if they were both up late at night, they'd be passing the time in the same way. She chose to believe it, and it made her feel calm.

*

And, of course, she was right, even if she had no way of knowing.

---

b.

"*Meanwhile....*"

Percival held up his hands, creating the approximate shape of a magazine using his thumbs and forefingers as the frame.

"That's what we'll call it! *Meanwhile....* With three dots."

He was beaming, pointing out each period with a poke of his finger. He imagined this was how Walt Disney felt when he conceived of *Steamboat Willie*. This was something new, inventive. This would change the world.

He imagined the scandal when he won the Nobel Prize for Literature that year. He was only eight. Could the world of letters hardly stand it?

"I don't get it," Lancelot said. He lifted the black mask that was wrapped around his head away from his eyes, as if that was somehow obscuring his brother's point.

Percival's first response was, "Lance, you're ten. Do try to keep up with the pack," but he kept that to himself, much like he kept most of his first responses to himself. Lancelot already felt a persistent sting because he and Percival were in the same class at school, and it was never good to remind him that his younger brother was smarter than he was.

"It's a story thing," Percival said. "It's like, when you switch scenes, it says 'Meanwhile...' to let you know that you're looking in on something already happening. This magazine is going to let people in on what we're doing. It says we're already in motion."

The three boys had stashed themselves in the oversized closet that served as their toy chest and clubhouse. Tristan was visiting less and less now that he was thirteen and in junior high, but Percival had insisted he be there for the announcement of the new Scott family project. The closet had been their secret hideaway for many years. There was even a small record player set up inside it. Percival was playing his copy of Franz Liszt's *Faust* symphony. It was a double record that came in a box with a lurid painting of the doomed Doctor and his demonic temptations on the lid. Percival never missed a chance to indulge his sense of the dramatic, and he wanted the other boys to feel that they were entering into an unholy pact. This was literature, it was important. It was *deadly* important.

Even if the atmosphere in the closet was really one of play.

For instance, Lancelot had been wearing the mask over his eyes because in the clubhouse he was in his secret identity of Touché, a swashbuckling adventurer and gentleman thief. All the boys had adopted different identities, guises to be worn when out of sight from parental eyes. Tristan imagined himself as Shortwave, a wisecracking criminal who could control the very fabric of sound, from creating ear-deafening shrieks through vibrations in the air or tuning in a radio station with his teeth.

Percival's alter ego was a little less lighthearted. He was Cur, a hulking, animal-like man who lived by his heightened senses and natural instinct. When necessary, Cur got what he wanted through violence. Adopting this persona was a way for the youngest of the group to see himself as bigger than his half brothers, who, whether they knew it or not, had a bond that made Percival feel like he was always playing catch-up. It also allowed him fantasies where he could fight bullies all on his own, he didn't need Lancelot coming to his rescue. No one was a match for Cur! Not even Lancelot and his hot temper.

"I've got it all planned out," Percival said. "Everyone will contribute something, it's going to be a group effort. I've already got my story underway, it will be the centerpiece."

In the end, that story would be the only piece of any great length to be completed for the magazine. Although the other boys agreed—albeit reluctantly on Lancelot's part—like so many of their group schemes, interest would be lost before the magazine would ever come together. Lancelot didn't write anything for Percival at all, and it really wasn't clear what he had been doing with his time. For his part, Tristan turned in a couple of poems, most of them rewrites of favorite songs, borrowing the rhythm and structure of the lyrics to stuff like the Cure's "Plainsong," now retitled "Chansonplain." He even sketched a picture of a man walking into a massive ocean to go with it. Tristan's efforts for the magazine were recycled in more ways than one. He was trying to start a band and had been working on these as songs for himself. Truth be told, as much as the boys wanted to work as a unit, they were much better on their own.

Percival's story was called "Cat on a Hot TV." In it, Percival imagined a future vision of himself. He would become a reclusive old man living in a gothic mansion on a hill. He had moved there after the last of his loved ones had died, when society no longer had anything to offer him. The house was described in ornate detail, full of sharp angles, sheer surfaces, a barren landscape, and a spiked, iron fence. Eighty-six-year-old Percival lived there alone except for a Siamese cat. They watched movies together, listened to music, and read books.

"Cat on a Hot TV" opens as a relative he never knew existed finds Percival. He's a bastard son of Lancelot's. At one point, Percival toyed with the idea of the relative being a child he had fathered himself, but instead made his senior incarnation a virgin, like the knight for whom he was named.

This newly arrived nephew is the narrator of the story, and the prose style was inspired by some of the manic first-person tales of Edgar Allen Poe. "*There*," it begins. "*Just up there. That's where he lives. You cannot possibly imagine how long it took me to find him. You cannot fathom the number of houses that fit the description I was given. Mansions like this exist all across this country. They are all the same, standing off by themselves in the middle of an otherwise mundane suburb. I have already visited many. Each one had a path much like the one I walked on to get here, stretching from an old, rundown gate to his crumbling front door. One solitary path, and one path only, up each hill to these grotesque homes.*

"*As I knocked on this particular door, a strange notion struck me, a long lingering doubt became a conscious thought. Though each house had been a mirror image of the other, from the basic description to the lonely path, the way the dark clouds hovered overhead, down to the way the sound echoed from within when the door knocker was used, this time I could sense that things were different. I had finally found the right one.*

"He stood in the doorframe wearing a black robe and a green fez. The man was quite small, and yet he still seemed larger than all the pictures I had seen of him from his younger years. The sides of his hair, or that which was not covered by the fez, were black as pitch, and the color melded with the darkness of the room behind him, causing his head to look as if it were sinking away into its opaque surroundings.

"Yes, I thought that it could be him, but I was only sure when I saw the Siamese cat striking a pose on his shoulder, perched above me, examining me coldly with its haunted eyes.

"Finally, the man spoke. 'Who are you, boy?'"

After a convoluted explanation of his lineage and much cursing against the boy's "immoral" father, Old Percival admits to being who he is and invites his nephew inside. The prose continues its descent into deeper shades of purple:

"He turned and walked inside, his cat jumping from his shoulder. I followed close behind, treading the murky corridor, until we came to a rather large room. It was dimly lit with one small lamp, its shade pointed to the ceiling, laboring to keep one last scintilla of hope alive. There was a desk and one solitary chair shoved against the far wall. It was piled with papers that had been tossed into one hulking mess, and there was also a white typewriter. I could hear its faint humming. To the left of the desk was a grand bookshelf. The printed volumes it housed were astronomical in number. In front of it was an old mattress with a green sheet and a few blankets, and straight in front of that, against the right wall, was a television and a VCR. Video tapes were scattered on the floor around it."

Old Percival begins to taunt the boy, asking questions about his life and his mother. The boy hasn't amounted to much, and it was his mother's dying wish that he find his uncle in order to get a piece of the man's great fortune. Before Old Percival had retreated to his castle, he had written many successful books and gained world renown. Surely there was some money left? As if presenting evidence that all is not as one might imagine, Old Percival removes his fez, revealing that he is balding. The boy has what is described as a "*repugnant reaction*," but Old Percival's response is even more repugnant, as he disparages the boy's mother, his own, and really, all mothers. "'*As you know, it is the female who passes the bald gene on to her child. My mother just so happened to see fit to tell my DNA to spit all the hair from the top of my skull. She wanted me to be a shedding old fool.*'"

Finally, once he is done grilling the boy, Old Percival lets him speak. "'*Don't you get lonely here?' I asked. 'Don't you need any companionship?'*

"*He pointed to his cat. 'I have Seymour,' he laughed.*

"'*Don't you have any old friends you want to see again?'*

"'*To a degree. I watch one of my favorite old movies or read a beloved fiction, and I remember the joy it brought me the first time I saw it, and those memories serve.'*

"*He turned from me and withdrew a copy of* The Picture of Dorian Gray *from his bookshelf. His face hardened, the lack of light casting a mysterious shadow over his features. 'If I begin to think of my actual life, I just shove it out of my mind. I'd rather build a brand new world from images that others have left me, from books and film.'*

"*I leaned back on the mattress. A broken spring stuck in my back, poking me through the sheet. Everything was so weird. I had just met my uncle, and yet the conversation we were having was opening up doors that should have remained sealed. It was almost like he was leading me to something, and I felt compelled to follow, to inquire with more questions. 'What do you plan to do here?'*

"'*To live out my life,' he said. There was a glint of hellfire in his eyes. 'My passions, my pain. I plan to leave very easily and quietly. I want to be* found *dead, like discovering a lost treasure. Until my departure, though, I'll keep writing, leaving behind an eloquent will and testament, as well as a couple hundred manuscripts. It will be beautiful.'*

"*He tucked the book under his arm. I looked once more to his little brown desk and the scads of paper on top of it. 'How can you write so much?' I asked. 'Don't you have to live to have experiences to reproduce?'*

"*He laughed loudly in my face. 'Why? I've never used real experiences before. Living alone allows for such wild thoughts to run through my mind, reality is no longer necessary. You'll see. My stories are something entirely otherworldly now. Self-imposed confinement is the best thing that ever happened to me.'*

"*I looked away. Seymour was sitting on top of the television. He licked his paw and looked down at me, his cat eyes resembling those of a hungry vulture. 'It all sounds so perfect,' I said, 'it can't possibly work.'*

"He looked at the bookshelf once more. 'Oh, but it is,' he said, his voice growing tense. 'It's perfect to the last detail, not counting the one where a fool like you shows up at my door.'"

The story turns even more macabre as Old Percival removes a heavy copy of *The Devil's Dictionary* from his bookshelf and strikes the boy across the head with it. The decrepit writer delivers multiple blows, each one a different book, grim things by Poe and Lovecraft.

It was here that the real Percival, the young Percival, the actual writer, had concocted what he thought to be his most delicious twist. You don't know until the very end of "Cat on a Hot TV" that you are reading the tale of a dead man! His explanation is coming from beyond the grave!

"*Seymour jumped from the TV as the last book, a volume of Greek tragedies where relatives turned on one another for selfish gain, was risen above my uncle's head. The tome came down and went up again, then came down once more. The face of the man holding it distorted and twisted with each blow. With every hit of every book I heard the smashing of bone and I saw blood squirting into the air.* My bone! My blood!

"*The strikes just kept coming, until eventually I was dead.*"

The aborted publication of the first issue of *Meanwhile...* and the completion of "Cat on a Hot TV" had been a part of Percival Mendelssohn's life two decades prior to his meeting Julia Jiménez in Beijing.

3.

Morning came, finally, and sitting on the steps of the house, Julia found herself lost in a waking reverie. She remembered being eight years old and going with her Papa to horse auctions. She didn't really find the outings very interesting, as she didn't have the love of horses her father had. In truth, horses scared her. He saw their wild, untamed nature as freedom, a symbol of a passionate spirit let loose; she saw them not as a symbol, but as something large and uncontrollable that could crush her.

Papa always dreamed of owning his own horses, but that wasn't really feasible for a working immigrant in Stockton, California. So, a lot of weekends, he'd drive down to Salinas and see the horse shows and dream that one day maybe he'd buy one. From the first time he took Julia, she had found it to be dreadfully boring. She hated sitting there all day, staring at one horse after another. They all looked the same to her. Once, there was an old, black poodle hanging around the stables, and she wanted to play with it. When her father's head was turned, she left the spectator bleachers and chased after the dog. It ran away from her, ducking under the stands, and she followed. When she caught the poodle, Julia wrapped her arms around it and sat down in the dirt and the trash that everyone had been dropping from up above. When Papa found her, he was very angry, and he scolded her. Julia understood now that he was probably scared when he discovered her missing, but at the time, it had traumatized her. Papa never hit her, so raising his voice became like violence for his daughter. It hurt more than any simple slap of the hand.

So, the next time Papa wanted her to go, Julia refused. The old man kept asking for a while, but she kept saying no; pretty soon, he just went on his own without ever bringing it up. As Julia got older, it made her sad. She realized she could be spending those Saturday afternoons with her dad if she really wanted to. He looked so shocked when she told him. "Really?" he asked. "You want to go with me?"

"Yes, Papa. I want to go see the horses."

He packed them both a lunch for the day. He made hot dog sandwiches—the links sliced down the middle and placed flat on the bread with big chunks of American cheese and too much mayonnaise. Eating them was like biting through a gooey brick—but that was her Papa's way of doing things, and she still had him make lunch whenever she visited home.

The horse shows still bored her—Julia just couldn't muster up the appropriate level of appreciation, no matter how hard she tried—but that didn't stop them from being good days. It was more about sitting in the cheap seats with her father, who to her was as large and magnificent as any horse but one she could admire without any fear of being crushed. These were some of the only times she could spend alone with him, and, rarer still, times she could see him truly happy as he enjoyed the creatures that inspired such awe.

After that first Saturday back, Papa had started asking if Julia wanted to go with him again. Julia went the second time, and even though she didn't go every time, Papa kept asking and didn't take it personally when she had to refuse. She was getting older and other commitments were emerging as she entered her preteen years. That was all fine, though, because the damage of that first rejection had been undone.

If only the rest of life's trouble spots were that easily smoothed over....

Julia was startled when the door opened and Val emerged. His appearance broke the string of memory that had wrapped itself around her. Val was carrying a tray of food. Julia spotted the tall glass of orange juice and immediately felt relief at the back of her throat. There was also a silver carafe that she prayed was full of coffee.

She stood as Val sat the tray on the steps next to her. The little black cat had tucked himself into the corner of the doorway, and upon hearing all of this activity, he hissed at the man. Val sneered back at him.

Julia crossed her arms, almost hugging herself, something she did when she was nervous. Biting her lip, she pondered what she should do. Would Val tell her the food was hers? Should she take it if he offered? Should she just reach for it right then and there and not worry?

She could smell all the smells. The fresh fruit cut up and mixed together in a bowl, the granola, and the mini pitcher of cream. There were also cubes of sugar, and the carafe was definitely filled with coffee. There was no mistaking the aroma as it twisted around the perfume of the mangoes, berries, and oranges.

"Mr. Rossi thought you might be hungry," Val said.

Oh, thank goodness!

"That's very sweet of him," Julia replied.

"Yes, it is. Personally, I didn't think it was a good idea. You don't need the encouragement."

Julia laughed. "Oh, you're a bulldog, you." She knelt down and poured herself a cup of coffee. The mug was white and had red kanji printed on the outside. "日出." *Sunrise.*

Julia balanced some berries on a crispy piece of miniature toast. "Where is your Mr. Rossi at this time of morning? Someone with a coffee cup as optimistic as this should be out greeting the day."

"Mr. Rossi works at night, and he has gone to bed. I hope you will respect that and keep the peace."

"Yes, peace." Julia winked.

"I'm being quite serious. I expect you'll eat your breakfast and go?"

"I expect since you made that statement like it was a question, you know I won't. Perhaps instead you can schedule an audience for myself with Percival and Señor Rossi for when they are up and about."

Val gave her a hard look, and Julia wondered if it was the face someone made when they were intending to punch another person. She'd never been hit, so she didn't know. Thankfully, the man just nodded to her and went back inside.

Truth be told, Julia was surprising herself with her aggressiveness. She wasn't used to standing her ground. If it worked, she'd have to be this stubborn more often. It seemed amazing to her that something as simple as not taking "no" for an answer would be a lesson that would come to her so late in life. It seemed so easy that everyone should have been doing it. Then again, maybe that was the problem. Like how she had found Percy, it was so simple, most people didn't think it was true.

Imagine if she had known this in ninth grade when Jason Rice had tried to cheat off of her in health class and they got caught. She told the teacher that she had not helped Jason, that when he asked her for the answers, she told him to shut up. Jason even backed her up on it. He wasn't a big enough jerk to try to drag her down with him. "It's true," he said. "She wouldn't tell me anything." The teacher refused to believe them, though, and Julia quickly crumbled and accepted the detention. What kind of stand would she have really had to take to bat the false accusation down? Nah, it probably wouldn't have worked. Innocent people go to jail claiming they're innocent all the time. So do guilty people. That's why no one believes anybody.

The morning was starting to warm up. It was going to be a clear, bright day. At the moment, there was shade, but by midday, the sun would be directly overhead, and the alley would light up like a chicken roaster. If Percy didn't let her in by then, she might end up a pile of charred bones on the dusty road. Over time, she'd be gone altogether, just a black stain from her burnt remains, a smear of ash the only reminder she had ever been alive.

But that was the sort of worried thinking that made most people lose their resolve. That was taking "no" for an answer.

She wouldn't.

*

Val had not been lying. Percival regularly stayed up all night, finally collapsing as dawn broke and sleeping the day away. Intermittently, he would wake up and read for a while or scribble unfinished thoughts in his notebook, pet one of the many cats that might be napping in the room with him, whatever would pass the time until he was ready to doze off again. He kept Chinese choral music playing on his stereo, lullabies mostly. One of his favorites was "Kitty, Stop Meowing." He didn't understand the lyrics, he had never learned the language, but the title was cute and the melody soothing. The voices rolled into the song like wind, and when he heard them, he imagined them blowing through the streets of the city, bending around corners and ferreting cats out of alleyways. It stops being a request for the kittens to be quiet but serves as a sort of Pied Piper melody, luring the animals toward something more grand, some grassy field somewhere with a gentle river and plenty of bugs and rodents for them to eat. There was one phrase that sounded to his American ears like they were singing, "*Holy night, holyyyyy night*," and there was something holy about this gathering of cats. He knew in Malaysia that cats were believed to carry one's soul out of Hell and toward Heaven. So, too, this feline tune directed them all to paradise. Percy also remembered a Thai story about an ancient temple where a gathering of a hundred cats took a giant golden goblet that had been owned by the Buddha and protected it from Burmese invaders. They hooked their tails together and wove them through the goblet's handles. Man's strength is no match for a cat's. An army of flesh can do nothing against a conglomerate of fur. His own cats were proof of that. His Knights Templar, they barred the outside world from his door.

Percival kept a handful of books in his room, and he read them over and over to get himself through the dark days. He had more books, and he would read those at other times, but they were kept outside of his private space, away from his interior vigil. The books in his room were his most beloved: *Winesburg, Ohio*, his fascination with which was famous; *Tender is the Night*; *The Pursuit of Love* coupled with *Love in a Cold Climate*; and of course, *Le Morte D'Arthur*, his connection back to home. His mother, Gwendolyn Malory, was a distant descendent of Sir Thomas Malory, and all three of her sons had been named for knights from her favorite stories. In some ways, she had doomed them to their characters, the way giving Bill Clinton a middle name of Jefferson suggested one day he would be president, or naming your daughter Sky would cause her to end up spacey. What was neat for them when they were kids eventually became a burden.

(Percy's middle name was Thomas, also for Malory, which was Tristan's middle name. Lancelot's middle name was James, for his father, James Scott, now deceased. Percy's father was Keith Mendelssohn.)

The books Percy kept in his room were meant to bring him comfort. They were all romantic stories about boys going on quests and love affairs with highs of incredible ardor and lows of great tragedy. He fancied they all had characters who tried their best to get things right but often failed. Occasionally, he might bring in one of the volumes of C.S. Lewis' *Chronicles of Narnia* because they had been favorites of his as a child. He liked tales of children who were part of something larger that they had no power over but that pushed them to be greater than they realized they could be. Lewis' use of spiritual subtext had also greatly influenced him and was something Percy had always wanted to emulate in his own fiction. There were also heavier volumes in his main library, theological and philosophical texts, more involved novels and great works of literature, and collections of mythology from around the world. He was, at present, re-reading *Journey to the West,* China's greatest legend. He liked studying the foundation of the country's beliefs through its most important manuscripts because even if he never ventured beyond his home, he should at least be in tune with what was resonating in the soil under his feet.

His bedroom collection—the Anderson, Fitzgerald, and Mitford books—were the sort of books Percy wished he could write. He had stumbled with allegory, and looking back, he saw that it had proved a realm beyond his abilities. He needed to understand the real world first, where the heart was the most important instrument at a man's disposal. He wanted to write beautiful stories about lovely people struggling to be together. If he could sort it out on paper, then maybe he could get it right in the flesh. Set the heart straight before worrying about the soul.

Since coming to China, the writings he engaged in, the scribbled thoughts he could never complete, were his attempts to write these novels. Sometimes what he wrote was just an idea for a story, other times he would attempt to outline something, and on even rarer occasions, he would attempt actual prose. He never got very far before becoming frustrated with it. Two-and-a-half pages was his record. It just never came out right, and that was another reason to stay where he was, locked in his house. He could not leave there until he understood why it was wrong.

Except it was a fool's errand. He would never get it right, would never allow himself, because he didn't really want to leave. He had found where he belonged. In case he forgot that, he had another book. A photo album.

The first few pages were filled with pictures of his family. He particularly liked one of his mother from when she was nineteen. It was a classic portrait, her hair was up in a kind of beehive and she had on heavy eyeliner. Her dress was light lavender, and around her neck, she had a white choker with a black cross at its center. She was smiling, and it didn't look like it had been posed, because there was something else in her eyes: the sparkle of real laughter. He fantasized that somebody said something funny to her and the photographer caught her when her guard was down. Or better yet, she was thinking of the life that was in front of her, and it had lit a fire inside of her. At the time of the picture, his mother was already a year into her relationship with James Scott (he had been her freshmen year English Literature professor!) and deeply in love. It was that feeling, that expression on his mother's face, that Percy wanted to write about. He wanted to look at the thread of her life and how it connected to everyone else, the way she bound them together. It was why he was so fascinated with the names she had given them. It was like she had handed out pieces of a puzzle, giving each a single clue to a greater mystery, so that together they might unlock it. Each character was essential to the overall myth.

After the pictures of the family—of mother, father, brothers—the rest of the book was devoted to one person: Iris. Percival's wife.

All the pages had pictures of her. He was in some of them with her, but he had covered his face with correction fluid in all of them. He wanted the photos to reflect his absence. He hadn't been there, he was never present. Iris had hung her love on nothing, had groped for affection in an empty space. Then she had left him, and he had left the world. If she wasn't going to live in it, neither would he.

*

Val returned an hour later. Julia had kept her dishes stacked on the serving tray, arranged for easy retrieval. She watched him as he walked over and silently bent to gather the remains of her breakfast. She had eaten everything, except for three dates that had been in with the fruit. She didn't like dates. Their sweet gooiness made her back teeth hurt.

"Thank you," Julia said, and she smiled. The sun was above them, and she had to shield her eyes to look at Val. He maintained his silence, even when the cat hissed at him again on his way back inside.

Val did, however, do something.

Or, more precisely, he didn't do something.

Val didn't close the front door.

Julia couldn't believe it. It must have been intentional. Everything had been too precise up until that point, there was no way that she could believe Val would suddenly become so careless. Not after nearly eight years of living underground. The door was open because he wanted it open.

At first, Julia stood slowly, her arms folded. She stepped toward the opening with caution, but then she realized caution was not something she could afford. Get through the door, don't give Val time to change his mind. The black cat bobbed his head up and down as she approached, excited by her sudden movement. He meowed, mucous around his hollow eye glistening in the sun. Once Julia was through the door, he followed. He made a little hop over the piece of wood that ran across the bottom of the frame. It was an old Chinese tradition. Ghosts don't have feet, and if they can't step over the barrier, then they can't enter your house. The cat, however, had no such impediment. He brushed his body past her shin before standing in the entryway, waiting for her and on guard against what might lie beyond. "Is it a trap?" Julia whispered. "Are Percy and Val going to leap out and grab me?"

If so, they were waiting until she got deeper inside. The front of the siheyuan was completely still. The first door she encountered was a sliding door, and it had also been left open a crack, just enough so she could see the fissure from where she was standing but not enough to be spied from the street. She took it as her hint of where to go next.

The Beijing dust was still on Julia's clompy black shoes. Not wanting to track it inside, she crouched down and undid her laces. Ten holes in all, five on each side, the mouth of the shoe extending up over her ankles, protecting them. Once her feet were out, her stripy socks were exposed, and Julia felt vulnerable. Shoes stave off worldly dangers—like horses, for instance!—that might be larger and heavier than you. Your feet keep you upright and mobile, and if your toes were smashed, you'd be taken down. Part of why Chinese people took their shoes off indoors—whether explicitly intended or no—was that a home is meant to be secure. Forgetting the dirt, Julia couldn't go halfway. She had to enter Percival Mendelssohn's home like she belonged there, like she was safe.

Through the next door—which had another ghost barrier, one last defense against the malevolent spirit world—Julia entered the front room of the siheyuan. This was usually the main hall, a place for greeting guests and relaxed evenings. There were no lights on, the only illumination coming through the windows on the opposite wall. Through them, Julia could see the courtyard. The windows were high, though, so she could really only see pieces of trees. These framed segments looked to her like brush paintings done in extreme close-up, obscuring the full details even when it was obvious there was something more to be seen.

The room itself was relatively bare. There wasn't even a rug on the smooth, tiled floor. Julia thought if she stretched out her arms as far as she could, placing one hand on the far wall, her other hand would reach the center of the room; if she could duplicate herself, the other Julia could touch her palm to the original Julia's, and her free hand would reach the entrance they had both come through. There were two small tables flanking a door that led to the courtyard. A houseplant was in a burgundy vase on the left table, and it looked like it needed some care. Many of its leaves were browning and dying and needed to be picked off. The right-hand table was empty.

Even if the plant was neglected, the rest of the room was not. It was immaculately clean—no dust, no spots on the window. If it weren't for that, she wouldn't have thought anyone lived there. If appearances were deceiving and the home had been entirely abandoned, the deserters had at least paid through on their maid service.

Julia walked through to the door opposite, where the cat had already gone. He was pushing his head against the wood, like he was anxious for her to open it, but when she approached, he stepped back from the door and hissed. “Are you trying to warn me against something?” she asked. “Or telling me to keep going forward?”

The cat meowed at her, showing his yellow teeth, and then banged his skull on the door once more. Its knob was old, with little flecks of green paint on the metal where it connected to the wood. The brass façade on the knob itself was starting to peel, and it had turned a dull brown. Julia put her hand on it and paused. She didn’t want to place too large an importance on the moment, but the first two doors had been left open for her. This one she was opening herself.

As soon as she cracked an opening, the cat ran through, a cry trailing behind him. She followed him into another dark room. As her eyes adjusted, she saw that it had been lightly stocked with ornate, hard-backed chairs. They seemed much too tall for such a small room. Every space in the house was likely going to be cramped, maybe twelve feet wide at the most. She was through and into another passageway on her right in just a couple of short steps. Turning that corner put her into a whole other side of the quadrangle. There was no door on the frame, so the cat was already disappearing into the light beyond it.

Julia, on the other hand, lingered. The air smelled like pine, but not like real pine, more like some kind of cleanser. Underneath it, she detected a whiff of wet newspaper. Val was probably trying to mask the latter scent with the former. It was unpleasant and reminded Julia of the garage in her house back in California. Specifically, the corner in the back everyone avoided, where the water heater had leaked onto a bunch of boxes of her old baby clothes. They were all scared to touch the cardboard because it looked like the boxes would disintegrate with the slightest pressure.

This third room also had a plant. It was hanging from the ceiling in a wire cradle, and its tendrils dangled toward the floor. Most of them were stripped of their leaves, and any that remained looked humiliated and dead. It seemed to Julia that at some point either Val or Percy had tried to spruce up the place, but they’d long since given up, leaving only the stalks and the stench of something defeated.

A crunching noise traveled in from the next room over. It sounded like someone was walking across gravel. Julia finally stepped through the doorway the cat had vanished into. This new room was well-lit, its windows perfectly positioned to let in the afternoon sun. There was also an electric lamp on top of a small, old-fashioned icebox that cast its glow in a corner the sun didn't reach. Based on the icebox and the exposed sink that hung on the wall next to it, Julia quickly surmised that this was the kitchen. Tables pushed against the wall served as countertops, and there was also a small stove—everything taking up an entire half of the room, leaving just enough space for one person to pass between it and the long, wooden table under the windows on their way trough. Val was sitting at the head of the table where the light began to taper off, silently chopping vegetables. Green onions, carrots, and peppers were all spread out in front of him, and he was slicing them with a large knife. As he'd finish each vegetable, he'd lift his cutting board and push the pieces into a wide-mouthed mixing bowl. His board had one corner broken off of it.

The one-eyed cat was at the foot of the table eating dry cat food out of a silver metal bowl. His chewing was the gravel sound Julia had heard. He looked up at Julia and meowed a greeting, little crumbs of food falling out of his mouth.

"Lancelot seems to like you," Val said.

"Is that his name, then?" Julia nervously reached over and gripped her left forearm, pushing it against her body without really realizing she was doing it.

"Yes. You'll find we have quite a few cats around here. You've somehow befriended the least agreeable of the lot."

"How did he lose his eye?"

"We don't know, he came to us that way. He gets into a lot of fights. I'd guess he met someone with swifter claws than his own."

Lancelot picked up a couple of pieces of food and carried them to the other side of the room. He dropped them in front of the refrigerator before finishing them off.

"I think he knows we're talking about him," Julia said.

Val was working on the carrots. They were harder than the peppers, and so the chopping was louder. Julia couldn't help but think it was intentional. Was he trying to intimidate her?

"You need to understand some ground rules," he said.

"Okay."

Julia pulled out a chair and sat at the center of the table. Its surface was cold, but surprisingly smooth. The way the grain looked, she thought it would be rougher.

"You're familiar with a quadrangle house?" Val asked.

"Uh-huh."

"Then you know that the back of the house faces north, away from the Palace, and that part of the house is usually used for storage and things."

"Right."

"Well, in this house, it's reversed. The head of the household, Mr. Rossi, stays back there. You are forbidden from going to the back of the house."

Oh, so they were still pretending it wasn't Percy. *How long is this charade going to continue?*

"Preferably, you will remain at the south of the building. You can travel to either the east or west sides, but stay toward the front. Do you have any idea how long you're intending to stay with us?"

"Um, no...I mean, that depends."

"On what?"

"A lot of things."

"Well, now that you're in, you're in. If you step back out that front door, it will be locked to you forever." Val lifted the cutting board and dumped the chopped carrot into the bowl. He rose and went to the ice box, opening the door and taking out a slab of tofu that was sitting on a plastic plate. "I haven't quite worked out where we're going to keep you," he said.

"I'm easy," Julia replied. "I don't need much."

Val sat back down. He sliced the tofu brick down the middle and moved one half to his cutting board. His hands moved swiftly, dicing the white gel into cubes. "That's good, because you're not going to *get* much. As you can see, we live rather bare."

Julia nodded.

"Once the sun sets, you'll be required to remain indoors. Mr. Rossi enjoys his garden at night, and you are to have no contact with him. There is a library in the northeast corner of the house, and you're not allowed in there after dark, either. You can access it during the day, but I want you to clear it with me first. In general, I'd like to be aware of your whereabouts at all times."

"Exactly why am I here, then?"

"That's what I'd like to know."

"I didn't mean it that way. I mean, why are you letting me come inside if you're just going to confine me to the front of the house?"

"Because containment is the preferred method for dealing with a disease."

Julia blushed. She didn't know why that made her embarrassed. It was rather insulting. She should have been mad. "I'm not a disease."

"That's your perspective."

"What if I don't like these rules of yours?"

"Then you're free to walk out the way you came."

Val looked at her coldly. Julia wanted to ask him if he'd ever told a joke in his life.

Instead, she decided to try a gambit.

"I understand that I can't talk to Moraldo Rossi, but what if I cross paths with Percival Mendelssohn? Can I talk to him?"

Val stood, loudly shoving his chair backward. "You've heard the terms," he said. "Take them or leave here."

Taking deliberate strides, Val turned and went to the door at the back of the room. He didn't look back at Julia as he exited, not to see how she was reacting or to give her a final warning; instead, he slammed the door with great force, and that left impression enough.

*

When Percy roused himself late that afternoon, he spent nearly an hour in bed reading Baudelaire and waiting for the sun to set. Gawain was sleeping at his feet, purring contentedly, and Percy saw no reason to disturb his slumber. The tranquility lasted until Val knocked on the door. It was his usual time, and Gawain recognized the sound even in his sleep. The cat jumped from the bed, but then stopped at the foot of it to lick his paw.

"Sir? Are you awake?" Val asked, poking his head through the door.

"Yes, yes. Val, listen to this. '*From heights I contemplate the roundness of the world/ And don't search any longer for a sheltering lee./ Avalanche, in your crush will you not swallow me?*'" Percy clutched the book to his chest. He smiled, but more to himself than an outward projection. "Isn't that extraordinary?"

"It's a well-crafted line, sir, yes."

"You're being terse, Val. Why are you being terse?"

"It's the girl, sir."

Percy sat up. "Oh? Is she still here?"

"I have her confined to the front of the house."

"You finally gave in and let her inside, eh?"

"I'm afraid so. I still think it's a mistake."

"You know why they say 'the jig is up,' Val?"

"It means the dance is over."

Percy gasped in mock drama. "Ah, you knew that! Most people, they've never actually thought about it. They just *say* it."

"Are you trying to tell me that this jig is up, sir?"

Val rarely showed any emotion around Percy. He tried to keep things as even keel as possible around his chief, and his chief knew it. Once, Percy said to him, "You know, Val, I often think you see me as some deranged flower girl who dances around the house sprinkling pieces of egg shells from a basket, blanketing the floor in white."

"I take that to mean I'm acting like I must walk on them, is that correct, sir?"

"Oh, Val...." Percy clucked his tongue at hearing Val's flat tones ebb into droll ones, the aural equivalent of rolling one's eyes.

That was also how Val sounded when he said the word "jig."

"In a matter of speaking," Percy explained. "This particular jig may be over, but the band may play again, and I'd like to have a friendly partner for the next number."

"You're stretching the analogy rather thin, sir. And I must say, you're being rather calm about this."

Without Val mentioning it, Percy had already noted that his response to Julia's arrival was rather queer. Hearing her knocking on his front door had made him extremely nervous, and yet he had opened the door anyway, something he never did. People rarely came by the siheyuan, and when they did, it was usually someone who had turned the wrong way or a peddler, people easily shooed away. Val had grown quite good at it, in fact. If Val wasn't there, Percy would ignore their knocking until the strangers went away.

But yesterday, Julia had knocked and Percy had answered. It was a rash decision, one he regretted the moment he undid the lock. Yet, he turned the knob and opened the door and for whatever reason he had done so, Percy had to live with it.

"I suppose you're right," he said. "Give me time, I'm sure I'll become the usual anxious mess I always am."

Val looked at him with an arched eyebrow.

"Oh, come now, that's some of my trademark wit, Val. I'm a crack-up in the right circles."

"I'm sure." Val smiled dryly.

"That's my boy."

Val opened the door again and scooted Gawain out. "I'll leave you to your day, sir. You know where to find me."

And servant followed feline from the bedroom.

Shutters had been placed over the windows in Percy's bedroom to block out the light. Percy opened them to check the sky. The sun was setting, disappearing off the edge of his eye line. He stood there, naked, and watched the last tendrils of the day dragging across his garden. Some of the cats were already on the prowl. Guinevere was sitting in the empty pond cleaning herself as the glow of the magic hour illuminated her luxurious white fur.

Across the way, the sliding door was open, and Julia was resting her shoulder against the jamb. He thought she looked pretty there, and he admired the sculpted curves of her cheeks. She also had attractive lips, like two pieces of candied marshmallows. It looked like she was watching the sunset, too. Percy found it strange that he was spying on her again. She had come to his home to take a peek at his life, but he was beating her to the punch every time.

As he watched, Val appeared in the doorway and snapped his fingers at her. "It's getting dark," he said, and then he gestured over his shoulder with his thumb. "Get inside and close this door."

Julia didn't say anything, but even from a distance, it was clear she didn't like Val, even if she was going to do what he'd ordered. The door was shut and they were both gone; even so, Percy stood for several minutes and stared at the space Julia had left empty.

Eventually, he turned away from the window and slumped down to the floor of his bedroom. He placed his cheek against the cold tile, the top of his head butted up to the wall. He could hear things moving down in the earth underneath the floor, feel the vibrations of the lives that existed beyond his own. It was as close as he wanted to get. He tried to turn his despair to counter-vibrations and return the signal the world was beaming in at him, but he had nothing to give. He had drained all the energy from his sadness long ago. That's what made it so easy to remain.

Without lifting his head, Percy reached behind him and pulled the sheet from his bed. He wrapped it around himself like one would enfold a precious statue being prepared for shipment. He was going out.

Every room in the house was connected. Had it not been before, Val had gone in after they had moved here and made sure each room had two doors, making it possible to walk a complete circle around the interior of the home. Percy's bedroom had the door that Val had come in through, as well as an exit on the other side of the room, past the shuttered windows. It emerged into what had been a closet but was now a sort of hub for movement in the north side of the house. It was Percy's passageway to either his bathroom or, if he turned to the right, the outside garden.

The evening air was crisp, and it tickled the flesh he still had exposed, stippling his skin. He knew he should have worn his pajamas, but he didn't want to be stifled again. Besides, the sensation reminded him of how Iris had always liked it when he'd gotten goose bumps. She'd run her palm over the fine hair standing up on his arms and tell him it made her think of a field of dandelions when they were white and about to scatter their seed. The hair would bend to her touch like electricity in a Tesla coil. She would blow in his ear sometimes, her breath sending a rushing tickle through his nervous system, and it would make him tingle, and Iris would get the reaction she wanted. "You're inflating me," he'd say.

"You're my own personal party streamer. My New Year's Eve horn."

Percy would toot for her, be her toy. He loved Iris so much, and looking back, he still felt his trumpeting was a good way to express that. Had she noticed the effort? Surely she must have known how he felt. He thought she had.

But then she went away from him and he was left to wonder, to ask those questions you don't ask when it's all good because you have convinced yourself that it is good and that the answers are self-evident. He was there, he was tooting like a trumpet, he was loving her—but had he really done enough to tell her? Obviously not. Had he loved her enough? He thought so. But then, it could have been his failing. Maybe if he'd loved her more, he'd have grasped her in time, put his hand on her arm, and caught her, stopped her, saved them.

Galahad let out a loud shriek. It was a high-pitched meow that then settled into a low growl. Lancelot had his jaws around Galahad's neck and was pinning the other cat down. Galahad was an overweight, gray longhair, and was bigger than the black one-eye, but he must have been taken unaware and had capitulated to his meaner foe.

The fight snapped Percy from his reminiscence, and he moved quickly, whipping one end of the sheet so that it cracked over Lancelot's head. The cat let go of Galahad and jumped back, dodging the snipe. He raised his back haunches and hissed at Percival. The man cracked his whip again, and Lancelot retreated.

Percy scooped up Galahad. He sat back down and held the chubby feline in his lap. There was a little blood on his neck, but just a drop or two. Only one of Lancelot's fangs had broken skin, but the move had likely been more about immobilizing Galahad than causing any real damage. "You're all right," Percy cooed, and he scratched the cat behind his ear. Properly soothed, Galahad began to purr.

Guinevere was still in the pond. She had lain down on her side, but she was watching them. Gawain, Roland, and Tristan were padding around in the overgrown grasses, curious as to what the fuss was about. Bors, a tomcat with a white underbelly and gray-and-black striped top, was rolling around in the dirt of one of the pathways, twisting this way and that on his back.

Percival's court was at the ready.

Suddenly, Gawain jumped and twisted around in the air. As he landed, he stiffened his legs and stuck his tail straight up. He was on alert.

"What do you see?" Percy asked.

Gawain meowed. Percy followed the direction of the cat's gaze.

Julia could be seen in one of the house windows. She was trying to hide herself, only half of her face was visible, but she was watching them.

Percy was embarrassed. He hadn't minded her seeing him with his cats, he even noted their trading the spy role back and forth, like their own game of cat and mouse. He just didn't know how long he had been the mouse, and he didn't like the idea that she might have seen him sad, that her eyes had intruded on his melancholy. He dumped Galahad from his lap and stood, flicking his wrap once more in a motion of dismissal. He went back into his room and slammed the door behind him. He then went to his windows and slammed the shutters, blocking the girl from his sight.

Even so, they each remained on the other's mind.

---

c.

"What did you do to your hair?" her mother had asked by way of a greeting. "You look like a boy."

It was Julia's first trip home from college. She had held off coming back all semester, returning only for the winter break when she either had to leave or pay an extra dorm fee that she knew her parents would never pony up. When at home, her mother had opposed any desire Julia had to get her hair cut short. "Not as long as you're under my roof," the older woman would tell her. "Your hair is so beautiful, why do you want to destroy it like that?"

Julia was attending Lewis & Clark College in Oregon, a decent school that wasn't too far away but far enough that there was no way she could commute or be expected to return home too often. That was her choice; her majoring in pre-law was her parents'. It was their one condition for letting her go away. If she wanted to fritter her life away on her ridiculous interests in Asian books and art, then she could start off at the nearby community college and pay her own way; however, if she accepted their urgings to become a lawyer, to make something of herself beyond what anyone in her family had known, they had scrimped and saved a college fund over the past eighteen years that would now be hers. If she rejected their offer, then there was a vacation in Hawaii awaiting Mom and Papa. It was her choice.

She took the deal, because she *had* to get out of there. It didn't matter how. Besides, the ins and outs of the academic system baffled her parents. They didn't notice her slyly inserting a minor into her application form. Major in law, minor in comparative literature. When it came time to craft her schedules, the law courses would be full up, much harder to get into because there were far more practical-minded students at a fine institution like Lewis & Clark than there were silly dreamers who wanted to spend their days between the pages of a book. By the time she had fulfilled most of her literature requirements and switched her major officially, it would be too late for her parents to do anything about it.

Getting out of California and away from the family home was as liberating as she had expected. Her dorm room was small and her roommate a strange girl from the Midwest with freckles and tangled hair who told bad jokes while sitting on her bed underneath her posters for Julia Stiles movies—but these were fair trade-offs. She made two vows to herself before she left. The first was that she would not eat fried rice for the entire semester. She was sick of her mother's endless variations on the rather simple dish, the worst being the addition of corn and tomato sauce. Her father joked that it was an Iowan-Italian take on a Filipino tradition. Her mother got angry and told him if he was happy having the same thing night after night she was fine with it and she'd put no effort into making him anything special at all. Papa felt guilty and he ate an extra helping, and so that particular culinary monstrosity was destined to return to their table again and again.

The second vow was that she would get her hair cut short the very first chance she got. She had pictures of Louise Brooks and Twiggy and Mia Farrow in *Rosemary's Baby*, and she took them with her to the salon to show the man with the scissors what she wanted. "Oh, sweetheart," he said in a lilting accent, "you didn't need to bring me pictures for *that*. I've got you covered."

Watching him cut away her long, dark tresses, Julia felt like her skin could finally breathe. A million tiny mouths opened on the back of her neck and took a huge gulp of air all at once. Sweet freedom!

Her hairdresser had made it look so easy, it convinced Julia that revolution was simple. One of her favorite passages from *One* was when the nameless main character was told by an elderly man he had met on the subway, "*I change my life every day. Nothing grand, just tiny acts. Like I might decide to try soy milk in my coffee, or I'll strike up a conversation with the handsome young man sitting next to me on my commute. It's not much, but it's enough to alter the course of my day, and when you add those days up, it's changed the whole of my life.*"

The next time her hair needed to be cut, Julia did it herself in the dormitory bathroom, leaving black shards of her independence in the porcelain sink. The lines were less even than the professional cut had been, but she felt that was even better. The style looked looser, more spontaneous, more modern. Its very impreciseness was a sign of her breaking out.

Julia's shag was indicative of the romantic time, her feelings of being on her own at last. She set her own rules, answered to no one else's sense of propriety. During the evenings, she would go down to the library when she had finished her regular studying—or sometimes before, only picking up her classwork after the library had closed, working late into the night to maintain her grades. She would disappear into the art section, going through books she was sure had not been touched by anyone in ages, poring over collections of Japanese wood blocks and fancy illustrated editions of classic Chinese texts, like the *I Ching* with gorgeous brush paintings, ornately designed and done entirely by hand. It was quiet and isolated, just her and what was on the paper. On weekends, she would take the bus into Portland and walk through downtown, looking at street performers and gutter punks by Pioneer Square, touring the aisles of Powell's Books, seeing movies and eating Thai or Indian food. Cultural things like plays and the ballet and the symphony and the museum all had student discounts, making her L&C ID a pass into a richer world than she had ever known. It was far more fulfilling than the rigorous step-and-repeat of weekends at home: the visits from the Villagrans on Saturdays (which eventually replaced her father's horse shows, though sometimes Papa would go to them with Mr. Villagran instead, leaving the wives to gossip and the children to play), and then on Sundays the family would go to church. After mass, they'd always eat at the same restaurant. It wasn't even a fancy restaurant, but a place that boasted of Texas-style hamburgers—meaning they were huge, and Julia had to cut hers in half because it was always larger than she could comfortably hold in both hands. A toy train ran around the perimeter of the room, on a track elevated above the diners, just below the ceiling. Before they brought out the food, they served bottomless baskets of pre-popped popcorn, the kind that came out of giant plastic bags three feet tall, and frosted mugs of soda. When she got older, Julia tried to rebel against this ritual. She wanted to be a vegetarian, but the burger joint had very little to offer on that front (no one would ever say what the french fries we cooked in), and she was convinced that the unlimited pop refills would completely destroy her skin.

At her luckiest on those high-school weekends, she'd get to go out on Friday nights. Usually it was to some carefully monitored "acceptable" event, but at least she wasn't in the house. She could work those events, anyway, and sneak away with her friends Melissa and Heather to go to the mall or the Taco Bell parking lot where all the other kids hung out. As long as they were at the pre-arranged pick-up place at the pre-arranged time, none of their parents were ever the wiser.

College weekends were entirely her own, they were there for her to do as she wished. Every time she came home late on a Saturday night to find a note from her roommate that her mother had called—or better yet, an answering machine message with some kind of disapproving "You're probably out partying" statement—it gave her a rush. Yes, she had been out, and she could have been partying if she had wanted to, and there was nothing they could do about it.

So, it was with dread that she boarded the train from Portland to Stockton to go home for break. She hadn't wanted this liberation to end. She had managed to stave off Thanksgiving by listing off a litany of tests she had to study for and papers she had to write. They were all real assignments; she just bunched them all together and neglected to mention that some had already passed.

Winter Break, though, really was a break. The lifeline snapped.

It had been Julia's idea to take the train. Not only would it take longer, delaying the agony, but she had an idealized vision of what it would be like. How romantic it would all be! She wasn't single-minded enough to insist that all her memories of home life were horrible. Her parents loved Alfred Hitchcock movies, and any time they were on TV, it was a family event. All three of them would gather in the living room and watch whatever was on offer, and this time the bottomless bowl of popcorn was freshly popped. One Father's Day, her dad had asked for a fancy machine that moved the kernels around in a wok, pushing them through the oil with a skinny arm that would keep them from burning or sticking to the bottom. He got a real kick out of firing it up, and he'd try all kinds of spices and garnishes to give them variety. These experiments were much more successful than her mother's assault on fried rice. He'd used seasoning salt, parmesan cheese, dipping caramel, and once he had even crushed a bunch of Oreo cookies and mixed in the crumbs.

These family entertainment nights gave Julia a notion of what trains were like. Hitchcock used trains for excitement, or so that people could connect. In *Shadow of a Doubt*, evil Uncle Charlie tried to push the niece who was his namesake off a train; in *Strangers on a Train*, the titular strangers hatched their murder plot in their anonymously numbered cars; Cary Grant met Joan Fontaine for the first time in *Suspicion* when both were traveling by train, and he canoodled with Eva Marie-Saint in a sleeper car once they had gone *North by Northwest*; and, of course, in *The Lady Vanishes*, Miss Froy defied all explanation and disappeared from a cross-country railer while it was still in motion. Julia had fantasies of orchestrating her own vanishing from the train on the way down to California. It would be so simple; since she'd be traveling alone, there'd be no one to notice. She'd get on the train in Portland and get off some time later, leaving her parents in Stockton waiting for her to detrain, wondering where she had gone.

Julia's train hadn't even left the station before all of her starry-eyed ideas were proven to be smoky myths. Though there was an empty seat next to her, the seats to the front and the left were both occupied by overwhelmed single mothers with two kids apiece. A couple of rows back, a morbidly obese man who had been complaining about standing in line to board for far too long was sitting by himself harrumphing and exhaling dramatically at regular intervals. The air was stale, and the pillow too small, and it hadn't occurred to Julia that these conditions would have to be endured for eighteen hours—sixteen more than if she had flown. To make matters worse, her laptop battery had decided to become useless all of a sudden and her screen blacked out after twenty minutes. She had expected that electrical outlets would be plentiful, but they came one per car, and the man who occupied seat fifty-five was not going to give it up. She could not catch up with her journaling or writing e-mails to her friends who had gone to other schools. She had a few hours of life left on her MP3 player, and that was going to have to suffice. Thankfully, she had brought along a copy of Percival Mendelssohn's *The Other Side of the Street*. If there was any one book that she thought could take her out of the space she was trapped in, that would be it. The novel started as the first step of a new journey:

"*It was late when Horatio arrived in the city. The bus left him alone on the curb, suitcase in his hand and around $300 in his wallet. He had no place to go, and the metropolis was already asleep, its doors shut tight for slumber. The streets were empty, wet with rain, and the neon lights were unlike anything Horatio had seen back home. A purple sign flashed 'PAWN,' and beyond it, the blinding red lights of a theatre marquee drew his eyes even as they squinted from the glare. The crimson bulbs ran in a circle around the sign, two at a time, one chasing the other. It seemed as good of a direction as any, so Horatio chose to follow it. Yet, even as he approached it, his hope that it would erase the life he was abandoning was overshadowed by the onslaught of memory the neon inspired.*"

Julia left Portland in the afternoon and arrived in Stockton early the following morning. Papa picked her up in his truck. He hugged her, but did not say anything about her appearance. It surprised her, because not only had she cut her hair, but she had lost around ten pounds and she looked a bit gaunt. He only wanted to know what she had seen on the train, saving the superficial judgments for later.

"I didn't see much that was very cool," she told him. "A lot of small towns, some fields of sheep. At one point we were passing by a lake that had some kind of processing plant next to it, and it was sucking a big hole out of the center of the water, like it was lake, lake, lake, then drop-off. But I couldn't get a good look at it. There was another train parked on the tracks between us and I could only see the water in the spaces between its cars!"

Her mother, on the other hand, did not disappoint. Julia had stepped in through the kitchen door, smiling sheepishly, suddenly flushed with emotion at having come home after so long, ready to be fussed over, ready to re-accept all that she had tried to deny....

"What did you do to your hair? You look like a boy."

"Nice to see you, too, Mommy."

Julia thought right then she knew what it was like to be that hole in the lake. Not just what it was like to be a fish swimming along that suddenly found itself tumbling to God knows where, but the hole itself. Her body was no longer a mass in space, it was suction.

All those months might as well have not existed. Julia's life at the Jiménez home picked up right where it left off. Her high-school friend Melissa was also home on break, and she was having a bunch of kids from school over to her house. Julia had wanted to go and reconnect with them all in person, but her parents quickly put the kibosh on that. "You just got back," Papa pleaded.

"But I want to see my friends."

"I know, but we want to see you."

"Do your friends pay your tuition?" her mother asked. "Do they pay your rent?"

"No," Julia answered, pouting. That was the end of that. It didn't matter that her parents were asleep by 11:00 and the party was likely still going. Julia had no way to get there, and she couldn't ask anyone to leave the fun to come pick her up.

Adding insult to injury, her parents informed her that she could not go out the next day, either. "It's Saturday," her mother had smiled, drilling a bony finger into Julia's shoulder, "and you know what that means."

"The Villagrans are coming over?"

"You betcha."

And why wouldn't they be? The Jiménezes and the Villagrans had spent practically every Saturday together for more than a decade.

"And guess what else?" her mother continued, her voice needling at Julia's brain. "You're not the only one at home."

Papa snorted. "Maybe Jules and Artie will finally make it official."

"You never know!" her mother shrugged demonstratively, pleased by her own cleverness.

The only thing official about it, Julia thought, *and the only thing I hate worse than being called Jules and being part of "Jules and Artie," is that bastard Arturo himself.*

*

Both of Julia's parents were part of the first generation of their families to be born in America, their parents having immigrated to the country when they were very young themselves. Their families were looking for a better life than the ones they could have in the Philippines. The two of them met at church as teenagers, and Joseph Jiménez did two things the day after he graduated from high school: he went out and got a full-time job, and he asked Maria Cruz to marry him.

Joseph worked hard in the asparagus fields, and in two years he had moved up to the manufacturing level, where he began to clean and sort. Three years later, he moved into packaging. It was there that Joseph met Arturo Villagran, Sr. They were both the same age, both from similar backgrounds. Though they attended the same Catholic church, they had never met before. They would soon find out that their wives had, though neither Maria nor Amelia had realized their husbands worked at the same place.

The Villagrans had a son who was nearly a year old, Arturo Jr.

Maria was expecting. She was in the middle of her second trimester. It was a difficult pregnancy, and Maria was ill more than was common. Amelia started to help her out and guide her toward the birth. Once Julia was born, Amelia would be of further assistance, passing on the knowledge she had learned with Little Artie and handing down things he no longer needed.

Joseph and Big Artie were easily the two hardest working men at the farm. They saw all the other immigrant workers, from Mexico and all over Asia, and they didn't understand why they weren't making more of the opportunity. A Mexican family, the Dos Pasoses, owned more than just the asparagus fields, and there were plenty of opportunities for management positions and better jobs as part of the overall Dos Pasos

Produce Company. If they were like Joseph and Big Artie, this was the first real chance anyone in their families had to move up in life. How could anyone blow that?

The two men started to spend every night after work at the bowling alley. There were old-fashioned pinball machines there, which both men preferred to the flashier video games. "This is something you control," Papa had explained to Julia once when he had taken her to play. "You choose how hard to pull the plunger, you slam the flippers and shake the machine. It takes skill and your own two hands, not a bunch of lights."

Maria and Amelia began to join the same groups at the church, as well. Just as their husbands criticized the men they worked with, the wives criticized the other women at the church for a litany of things, from the brazenness of their outfits to the level of their faith, and often the two were linked. No one was putting as much into the Catholic charities as they were, of that they were certain.

When the kids were younger, the two families got together on intermittent Saturdays, maybe once every month or two. They'd barbeque and talk, and usually end the night playing a card game called Rook that Julia never could understand but that had crows on the backs of the cards, which she always liked. The crow looked majestic to her, its claw extended, its beak open in a cry. When she was six, she would run around the table flapping her arms and cawing loudly. It always made Little Artie giggle.

As the children grew older, the get-togethers became more frequent, and by the time Arturo was ten and Julia was nine, they happened pretty much every Saturday. That was when the parents started referring to them as Jules and Artie, almost making it one word. *Jules'n'Artie*, like a creation spawned from an e.e. cummings poem. This was also when the mothers had started to hatch serious plans for the two to get married one day. Neither was old-fashioned enough to believe in arranged marriages, but they thought their children were so good together, it only seemed natural.

And, really, it probably wasn't that unreasonable a notion. The kids were practically best friends, enjoying playing together all day in the back yard. The weekends were the only times they saw each other, though, because they attended different grammar schools. As Julia would soon discover, things are often different in the rarefied world of family, away from the regular childhood social order of school and friends.

Sixth grade was an upgrade for Julia, the first year of junior high. Districting was slightly different, and the change meant she and Arturo—he hated the nickname just as much as she—were finally going to be at the same school. He had already been there a year and was in seventh grade, an important distinction, as he was quick to point out to her. "It's not baby school anymore," he told her on the Saturday before Labor Day, the day after which school would start. "It's different there. The grade numbers mean something."

Julia didn't really give it much thought. What really could it mean? Just that she would have a friend who was higher up than she was, and there was nothing wrong with that. Sure, she had noticed a subtle indifference creep into his demeanor over the previous year, but she figured that would all change when they were on equal footing again.

For a girl her age, the realities of romance hadn't really settled in yet. She had vague fantasies of being with Arturo in the future, but they weren't born of any real romantic feelings. They were part of very young dreams, of the abstract concepts of marriage that girls were often taught. When she was small, Julia held out that she might be a princess one day, and she concocted elaborate stories in which Arturo was the dark and handsome prince of another kingdom, and their parents were eager to put them together in order to forge an alliance between their territories. She would resist it, finding the private side of Prince Arturo to be rude and abrupt, nothing like the charming public face he showed her subjects. She had her eyes on the more suave, rebellious knights who weren't of her station but were passionate fighting men that could offer her excitement. In these roles she usually cast men from her mother's record albums: young, Brill-creamed images of Neil Diamond and Tom Jones. (She hadn't any concept that these men no longer looked like they did on their album covers, that most of those records preceded her birth by a couple of decades.) Sometimes those dangerous crooners would win out, and sometimes it would turn out that they were really the jerks, that Arturo was the hero, and he would swoop in at the last second to save her from whatever indignity they were seeking to inflict on her.

By sixth grade, though, when she was nearly twelve, Julia had discovered the books of Jane Austen. This made her private fantasies grow more sophisticated. Rather than medieval castles, she now envisioned society dances and picnics on a beautiful countryside. She was a witty girl, often too witty for most of the crowd, but that sullen and brooding Mr. Darcy would understand, or the staid Mr. Knightly would school her in how to better get along with those less fortunate than herself. Sometimes, Julia would try to live these fantasies, tossing out pithy one-liners at the dinner table that no one would understand. She would insist that her audience was just not as well-bred as she, so of course they did not get it. Her jests were beyond them. Years later, she would realize what stupid logic this was, that it was impossible to have better breeding than your parents, and that really her jokes just weren't funny.

There was no expectation of anything more than hanging out with her friend when she approached Arturo at school. Julia had no inkling that he would suddenly be her boyfriend or anything of that nature, she just thought they could have lunch together and stuff. On the first day, she found him in the far corner of the cafeteria with his friends. None of the boys were sitting on the benches, but they were all perched on top of the table instead. The boys were wearing sports jerseys, and one wore a headband and another a doo-rag. Arturo was wearing a shirt with the logo for the San Jose Sharks on it.

"Hey, Arturo," Julia said. "I didn't know you liked hockey."

Arturo didn't respond.

"Did you hear me?" she asked.

His friend with the doo-rag hit Arturo in the shoulder. "Yo, A," he said. "You know this girl?"

Arturo hissed. "I don't think so," he said. "She's under the mistaken assumption she knows me."

"What are you talking about?" Julia protested.

Arturo stood up on the table. He held his arms out, his hands pointed down. "Don't you understand, all the girls want to get to know *this*. Even the little freaky nerd ones."

All the boys laughed, and Arturo high-fived them one after the other before sitting down again, this time his back turned to Julia.

When Julia explained to Melissa what had happened, she said, "You gotta forget that boy. Him and those guys he hangs out with, they're jerks. They think they're all rap stars and are gonna play professional basketball, and they aren't talented enough to do either. They only care about hip-hop hoochie mamas who dress all slutty and stuff."

Julia didn't see why her taste in music or her clothes should matter to Arturo. It wasn't like they were going to be dating! So, she tried to confront him in the halls once, when he was away from his clique.

"What's the matter, Arturo? Why are you being so mean to me?"

"You don't get it do you? Just because our folks say we should be friends doesn't mean I have to be when they aren't around. I don't deal in goody girls like you."

Arturo was leaning in close to her, their noses almost touching. His voice was low, and as soon as one of his buddies appeared from around the corner, Julia realized it was because he didn't want anyone to hear. Then they'd see he actually knew her.

"Get away from me with your stank breath!" Arturo shouted, pushing her away.

"What's goin' on, A?" his friend asked.

"This dumb girl tried to kiss me, man, but she's got breath like fish sauce. Get out of here, flatty. When I want a surfboard, I'll call you, okay?"

"Dude, you called it. I got more tits than her."

Julia hauled her arm back and punched him in the stomach. Her fist felt small when it sank into his gut, and he barely flinched. Instead, Arturo and his friend just laughed more. Julia shoved past them and stormed away.

When the weekend rolled around, she asked her mother if the Villagrans were coming over again.

"Why wouldn't they? It's going to be Saturday!" her mother replied.

"I don't want them to. I hate that stupid Arturo!"

She then told her mother what had happened.

Mrs. Jiménez clucked her tongue and looked at her daughter sternly. "Well, maybe he has a point, dear," she said. "Maybe you're not trying hard enough. You *could* make yourself prettier, and you're probably just being overly sensitive anyway."

Julia couldn't believe it. How had it become *her* fault?

The next day, when the Villagrans showed up, Arturo acted no different than normal. He was his usual friendly self, all smiles when the adults were around, playing the good little boy. He wasn't even wearing one of his stupid sports shirts. Instead, he had a T-shirt with Tweetie Bird on it.

Julia's initial fantasies had been right. Prince Arturo was the two-faced cad she had cast him as, only there would be no happy ending where he revealed a kind inner soul and saved her from trouble. She no longer believed in that particular childish notion.

4.

Several days passed without Julia and Percival running into each other. She might catch a glimpse of him down the hall, the last flapping of his makeshift outfit trailing behind him as he turned out of sight, or maybe a quick flash through a window as he passed through the garden in the dead of night, but she kept her distance. She didn't want to rush him.

For his part, Percy sometimes spied on her the way he had that first day she had entered his house. He'd rise when he was expected to be sleeping and watch her from his room or from cramped hiding spots as she went about her day. She had started attending to his houseplants, watering them and removing dead leaves and moving them where they might get more light. It appeared to be her special project. Percy also noticed that Julia did a lot of reading, taking particular interest in his collection of Austen and the Bronte and Mitford sisters before settling on *Anna Karenina*. She was a fast reader, going through the books swiftly. If he had to guess by her choice of reading material, she was a girl who dreamed of having a life that was more passionate than the one she was living.

He wasn't too far wrong. In those early days, Julia felt as if she were in some kind of heaven in Percy's home. He had built a life of pure contemplation for himself. The siheyuan was a place where he (or now, she) could be alone and read and ponder over the words he (or she) was taking in. She could have done with more variety in his art books, though. The ones he had were all religious and depicted scenes from the Arthurian legends. She liked Catholic iconography, but after awhile, all the bleeding Jesuses and impaled Crusaders became a bit much. Julia needed more things to *look* at, but she also knew that even Heaven could not be perfect. Percy had taught her that. "*Perfection is in imperfection, as a life that cannot change is in itself flawed.*"

Her taking over the plants in the house filled some of that gap. She could watch them change and grow, a kind of living art. It also made her feel like she was earning her keep. She was already starting to formulate a game plan for getting that garden back into shape, too.

So, there was no shortage of things to occupy her time. There were, however, some amenities she was finding it hard to do without. It hadn't been her intention to come and stay. She didn't want a quick drive-by visit, but she expected to be able to come and go, and so she had shown up at his doorstep with only the clothes on her back. Val gave her access to one of the bathrooms, and it was stocked with soaps and shampoos, so she was able to keep her body fresh; her attire, on the other hand, was getting a little gamey.

"I need to go to my dorm and get more to wear," she said.

"If you do that, you can't come back."

"Come on!"

"I warned you about this. If you put one foot in, you can't leave one foot out."

"I'm not going to tell anyone. I'll be right back."

"You can't come back."

"Aren't I more dangerous if you banish me for good? Then I can go anywhere, tell anybody."

"We'll be gone before the first reporter rolls up to our door."

"That's ludicrous!"

"Is it? You don't know how many times we may have moved already. You'll come back to an empty house and the entire world will think you're crazy."

There was a closet just off of the kitchen with a small washer and dryer stacked on top of each other, like they might have in a hotel room. Julia used them every other day, stripping down and washing her clothes while she sat on the floor with her back to the machine and her feet on the door. There was no lock and she didn't trust Val not to come in. "There's something not right about that guy," she'd started muttering to herself every time he passed her in the narrow corridors. She was pretty sure he heard her when she said it, but she didn't care. His smarmy attitude made her want to get under his skin.

The only time Julia saw any compassion from Val was when he was talking about Percival. He still wouldn't mention the man by name, but he talked in roundabout ways that referenced specific details about their situation.

"You have to understand something," he explained to her. "In this house, it's 1999. Time stopped the day we left Connecticut. When you're within these walls, you can't talk about things that have happened in the world since then. If you slip, and we're lucky, whatever you say will be treated like science fiction."

"And if we're unlucky?"

"Someone might shatter."

All of Val's information about Percival ended ominously. Whatever he was warning her about was the Worst Thing Ever and All Creation Could Crack in Half! She imagined that the decision of what shoes to wear each day was met with dire importance. Choose wrong, and Val's feet may turn to dust!

After nearly two weeks, Julia started to go stir-crazy. The books and the plants could not counter the boredom of roaming the same hallways, avoiding rooms declared off limits, reporting her movements while dodging the very man she had come looking for. The only open space available to her was the sky as viewed from the courtyard, but even that was confining, like she could only peer out one window, only see outer space on TV when she knew there was a rocket ship out in the garage. It was fueled up and ready to go, but no missions were scheduled.

She and Percy needed to run into each other again.

*

It was just after 3:00 a.m. when Julia stopped pretending to sleep and snuck out of her room. Val had set up a cot for her in what she believed had previously been a storage closet on the east end of the house near the library. There wasn't much room for anything but her body, but it did have a light and a door, so she could find some peaceful solitude there.

Julia went into the library, taking great care not to make a sound. The smallest noise would be easy for either Percy or Val or any of the cats to detect. At that hour, the house was in a late-night limbo while the rest of existence was put on mute. Only the dead could speak because elsewhere the living slept. The library had one of the three sliding doors that opened onto the garden. It faced west, toward the kitchen. She opened it a crack, to see what she could see of the rest of the hutong. Roland was out stalking in the foliage, and Julia saw him pounce, catching whatever it was he was hunting. She thought maybe a bug.

The lights were on in the kitchen, and Val was moving around in there, momentarily appearing in the tiny windows as he went about his chores. When did he sleep? Julia had tried to figure out his pattern, but there didn't seem to be any. Whatever time she'd get up to check on him, Val was always awake and doing *something*, God knows what. How much was there really to take care of in this place?

Then Julia saw something in her peripheral vision. She thought it was in the back of the courtyard, near Percy's room, but when she looked, there was nothing there. Was it one of the cats, and it had ducked out of sight? She had tried cataloguing them in the time she had been there. In all, she'd counted eleven: Roland, Gawain, Galahad, Pendragon, Guinevere, Bors, Tristan, Yseult, Lancelot, Morgan (a black cat with white cheeks), Merlin (a white cat with black feet). Apparently, they had all been strays that Val had rescued and brought home on his master's request. Percy then tried to intuit what might be the appropriate Round Table moniker to fit their personalities. Sometimes he'd use physical details, like the green spot on Gawain's back. The discoloration was used as a play on the literary figure's nickname of "the Green Knight." In fact, it had been caused by motor oil. Val had found Gawain when he heard the poor kitten crying from under the hood of an abandoned automobile.

Lancelot had been given his name because of his ornery disposition—a dig at Percival's brother of the same name—and because on the day he was brought home, he had tried to usurp the King. Pendragon and Guinevere had been found as a couple, and they had the sort of feline bond that suggested they had grown up together, meaning they were possibly brother and sister. Pendragon was a long and skinny chocolate-point Siamese with fuzzy ears and long feet. His fur was dark from elbow to toe, with fluffy brown sleeves on top. Guinevere was a much subtler Siamese. Her fur was more fair, almost white. The two rarely separated.

Immediately upon being let loose in the garden, Lancelot had made his way over to the pair, who at the time were sleeping in a patch of sunshine. Guinevere's chin was resting on the center of Pendragon's back, and occasionally she would sleepily lift her head and lick a patch of his fur, working the same spot like she was trying to clear a persistent stain. Lancelot shoved his face in between them, rolling the girl cat off of the boy cat. The sudden ambush startled Pendragon, and he jumped to his feet, only to be greeted by a vicious hiss from the new kid in town. Backs were raised, challenging yowls issued, but before any blows could be struck, Val had jumped down on them and kicked Lancelot out of the way. "I had intended to put him in his place," Val told Julia, "but instead, I think I made a lifelong enemy."

It could have been Lancelot now skulking through the grass, it could have been any of them. Julia caught another glimpse, and she recognized the shape now—a large blob of white slinking between the trees near the master bedroom. It wasn't a cat at all, but her own personal phantom.

Julia opened the library door just enough so her body could fit through. She had turned off the lights in the room, so there was no fear of it spilling out and giving her game away; however, she knew that the wider she slid the door open, the louder and squeakier it got. Val would definitely notice it. There was no background noise to cover it up at three o'clock in the morning.

Once outside, Julia stayed on the edge of the garden, hiding in the shadows between the plants and the wall. There was just as much danger of alerting Percy as there was to alerting Val. Val would send her back to her room, and she would send Percy back to his.

Percy was, as per usual, wearing a loose toga made out of bed sheets, but he'd gotten used to covering more and had shorts and his long-sleeved pajama top underneath. He was walking around in circles on a small patch of garden, gesturing to various entities that did not appear to be there. This was one of the more productive ways he had of writing these days. Words came more easily than when he put pen to paper. He would speak the lines, acting them out if it was a story, or playing to an imaginary test audience—his cats, perhaps?—if it was an essay. Even if he was stuck for anything new, going back over his past work created an illusion of productivity. He'd take an old story and rewrite it, shifting the point of view around, trying different avenues, and look for cracks in the narrative he could exploit. In this case, he was chewing over a conversation from *One* where his hero was being confronted by a private detective in an overcoat who was trying to unravel the mystery of the man's background. He was insisting that he had discovered his subject's name, and the two were at a standoff. The detective wouldn't say who he thought the other man was, and the hero wouldn't give in and admit his identity in case it was a trick. "I know who I am," he kept saying. It was his staunchest defense.

"Do you?" the detective asked. "Because I'm not sure. Let's see if we can match the identity you think you have to the one I found for you."

Julia could make out some of the mumbled dialogue. She recognized the scene, she knew the cue.

"'You can tell me who you think you are,'" she said, "'but you'll still be who you are to me, and which one wins?'"

Startled, Percy jumped back and pressed himself flat against the house. Julia thought for a second he might actually smash through to the other side.

"I'm sorry," she said. "You thought you were alone. I should have been more subtle."

Percy stared at her a moment, like he didn't know who she was and was about to get mugged in his own home, but then a flash of recognition registered in his eyes. "You're that girl," he said.

"Yes, I'm Julia."

She held out her hand, but he didn't take it. He didn't even look at it.

"You answered my dialogue," he said. "I thought my characters had come to life."

Julia smiled. "But they *are* alive, Percival."

Finally, she was able to say one of the billion things she had always wanted to say to him.

"Yes, and I endlessly torment them. I expect one day they will rise up and kill me for the things I've put them through."

"But those things give them meaning."

"Wait," Percy said, shaking his head. "Who are you?"

Julia laughed. "We met before. I'm *Julia*. Or is this still the scene?"

Percy hadn't meant her name. He knew her name. It was a deeper question. He, of course, remembered who she was, he had been shadowing her, but he was taken off guard by her sudden appearance and he suddenly realized he knew nothing about her. "Why are you talking to me like this?" he asked.

"Like how? You mean here in the garden?"

"No, in these banalities. What do you want? It's like we're at a book signing and you've only got five seconds to say the most meaningful thing you can come up with."

Ouch. That stung.

"I'm sorry," she said.

Her deflated tone immediately let the air out of his defenses in turn. He shook his head. "No, it's me...."

"You're not wrong, Mr. Mendelssohn. It's not that different. It's like, I've been waiting forever to talk to you, and here I am, and there are so many things I've thought about, and yet I only have a precious few moments to impress you because Val might catch us and then he'll make me go away."

"And where would you go if he did?"

That seemed like a strange question, and Julia put it together with his previous question, and now she realized he was posing an existential riddle. She wanted to ask again if they were still playacting one of his fictions.

"I don't know. My first instinct would be to go back to my dorm and figure it out from there, but then maybe that's a waste of time, and I should maybe walk in the complete opposite direction until I find something else or tumble off the edge of China or something."

Percy had been standing on his tiptoes the whole time, still back against the wall, his arms stretched out and his palms flat against the house. He looked a little like a man who was trying to escape a flood, and the tide was rising against him and it was just a matter of time before he drowned. Only, now he lowered himself so that his feet were flat, and he let go of the wall. He pulled his sheet tighter around his body defensively, like he was entombing himself in a shroud. Behind it, he looked limbless and absent of detail.

He stepped closer to her. "That's it?" he asked, softening his voice. Julia thought he sounded intrigued. Or maybe amused.

"To be honest," Julia continued, meeting his approach with a step of her own, "I tried really hard not to think about what would happen next. I spent all my time focusing on finding you, and on getting myself here, I didn't want to jinx it by imagining an outcome. I wanted to let whatever happened surprise me."

"Even if it had gone poorly?"

"Ha! That I didn't want to think about at *all*."

The two of them were quite near to each other now. He could see the deep brown of her eyes. They were nearly black in the darkness, whereas to her, his green eyes looked like strange insects catching light in the night sky. She wasn't sure if it was the proximity or her confession, but she suddenly felt anxious, and though Julia didn't move away, she did retreat, shifting her attitude back. She crossed her arms so that she was hugging herself.

It undid whatever spell had been cast. Her nervousness made Percy nervous. He saw Galahad curled up inside a small cabinet next to his bedroom door. Percival used the feline as an excuse to turn away, and he scooped Galahad up and held him to his chest. The cat lay upside down, cradled in the man's hands. Percy scratched him under his chin. The fur there was a lighter gray than the rest of his charcoal body, and it looked like a little beard. Julia could hear the cat purr, and she moved closer to them, but instead of touching Percy, she put her hand on Galahad's belly, pushing her fingers through the thick fur. "You're a cute little chubb, aren't you?" she cooed.

Galahad squirmed in pleasure, excited to be doted on by two sets of hands. His body undulated like an S, like a dragon kite in a peaceful breeze.

Only Percy's hand moved away, as if flicked off by the wave of cat body. His brow had furrowed, his jaw stern. This sudden change in expression scared Julia a little. "I'm sorry, did I—?"

He cut her off by shoving the cat in her chest, forcing her to take Galahad in her arms. Without answering her unfinished question, Percy went back into his room, once more slamming the door behind him.

*

Julia had thought she had gotten in, but she was locked out again. She feared retribution. If she had angered Percy enough, he would complain to Val, and then Val would be on her. He would mete out some punishment, though his choices were thankfully limited. Sending her away would be the worst he could do, of course, and he could also try to confine her movements even further. Julia envisioned him as a sort of jailer, a creepy assistant to a Bluebeard Percival. Perhaps there was a secret basement to the hutong, and they had a dungeon where previous nosy admirers had been locked away.

But no retribution came. The next time she saw Val, they passed in the kitchen doorway. The man nodded to her, maybe even smiled vaguely. If Percy had mentioned the encounter to him, Val didn't let on. In her heart of hearts, Julia hoped that maybe she was being played, that she was being kept around for a specific purpose and had fallen right into their trap, and that was a little friendly smirk she had seen on Val, an unguarded signal of success.

As long as she was imagining, Julia thought it would be great to have a superpower where she could fly undetected through the house, passing through walls, floating above Val as he did chores, moving into Percy's room where she could watch him as he did whatever it was he did in there. At least that mystery would be solved! The only thing, though, was that even then she wouldn't be able to touch him, she'd still be distant and locked outside. Even worse, she'd have no way to tell what he was thinking. That was the real key. She could probably guess what he did locked away all day based on the sorts of things he kept around his home, but how he felt about her being there was another matter entirely. Forget the other powers, telepathy would be the real score.

Had she acquired this ability, Julia would have been both surprised and pleased at what she would have discovered. She was closer to unlocking the doors than she thought.

Julia's run-in with Percy had unnerved him. He had been jittery while talking to her, but that was to be expected; what he did not expect, however, was to find it a little bit thrilling. Talking with the girl had excited him, so much so that he couldn't stop thinking about it afterward. He had been trying to deny that he had been thinking about her even *before* they met up, telling himself that he was merely keeping tabs on her, but that defense was quickly crumbling. When he stopped kidding himself, he had to admit the most unnerving truth of all: since Julia had come into his house, he had often wished she would find him outside his room, coming upon him suddenly, and push herself in his direction.

Just as she had now done.

He often tried to deny these fantasies by unspooling them, tearing them down into versions where the outcome was not so nice. She would try extorting money from him or stab him in revenge of a sibling who had committed suicide and blamed one of Percy's books. By allowing for the darker option, he thought he was building evidence that he didn't care one way or the other about how he wanted such a meeting to go. He was merely hoping to get it over with.

Well, that was a paper tiger that could no longer stand. Though the girl inserting herself into his safe little world should have chilled him to the marrow, it had the opposite effect.

Something inside Percival Mendelssohn wanted Julia Jiménez there.

---

d.

MAN OUT OF TIME:
THE FINAL PERCIVAL MENDELSSOHN INTERVIEW

By
Chester Melville

I met Percival Mendelssohn several months before his disappearance. I was interviewing the twenty-three-year-old author for Vanity Fair. *The article was printed mere weeks after that fateful Halloween in 1999. It featured pieces of the interview as part of a larger work of journalistic prose. It presented the elements of a portrait I wanted to paint. However, taken as a whole, my conversation with him shows a more nuanced rendering, one unfiltered and without an outside point of view. The text is presented here in its entirety for the first time, and it broaches some chilling subjects in light of the tragedy that was to follow.*

Chester Melville: *You talk about suicide a lot? Why is that?*

Percival Mendelssohn: Well, it is man's most fundamental question, isn't it? How much of this life does he really want?

Most people would say that's morbid.

Yeah, so? Life is morbid. Everything is finite. We're all one breath away from being completely out of existence. *That*'s morbid. Why shy away from that? I'd say most people are dishonest.

What inspired this point of view?

As cheesy as it sounds, it was something I was born with. I've always had visions of my own death. It changes often. I guess there are times when a certain mode passes, it's no longer valid for me. Sometimes it's very abstract. When I was in elementary school, I used to draw pictures of myself impaled on a stony stalagmite that grew out of the sandbox.

Should people be expecting to read about your own death in the papers soon?

Well, no...and this is actually something I really hate talking about. Which I realize some people see as hypocritical.

Isn't it, though? You encourage others to take their own lives—

That's a complete falsehood, a complete misrepresentation of what I write about. Do you even read my books, or did you just read other articles about me to prepare for this? I mean, seriously. I've clearly stated time and time again, including in the text itself, that this idea, it's Camus' idea, and it's not "Go and die right now," it's "Explore the question." This is philosophy. It's rarely about flesh and blood, even when we talk about flesh and blood. It's metaphor. Like Camus, I believe that once you have accepted the imperfection of life, and the need to escape it, then you've already escaped. It's metaphorical suicide. The decision is the freeing key, and to actually do it is redundant.

It seems conflicting, though, when you talk about visions of your own death and things.

That's just something I live with. I've always been struck with my own mortality. I've always been very aware of it. A day doesn't go by that I don't imagine it. It comes like a flash, a quick image. I could be having a grand time, eating a wonderful meal, and all of a sudden, in mid-chew, I see myself with a gun in my hand, and I'm pointing it at my head. I don't even blink, you wouldn't know it if it happened right now. You'd have no idea that there was a flash in my mind and my blood on the wall.

But I don't like talking about it because guys in your profession, they can twist it. And it's also incredibly hard for the people around me. At best, I can hope they think I am being melodramatic. It's like I wrote in my story "Deep End," that yes, it is melodramatic, of course it is! *Life* is melodramatic. Next thing I know, I open up *Spin Magazine* and they're saying I'm a publicity monger talking about my suicide to sell books.

At worst, the people in my life feel there should be cause for concern. They read me saying, "I see myself dying by my own hand," and the next thing I know, my mom is calling wondering if everything is okay. When it's not about that at all. It's not.

The real conundrum here is how to even express oneself when it comes to suicide. Imagine this scenario: a boy goes to a holiday dinner. He doesn't know anyone there except for the girl that invited him, yet everyone else knows each other, they are carrying on conversations about things he knows nothing about. He's an outsider. Standing against the wall, he is overtaken by a sudden chill and the realization that when he leaves, he will go home and take his own life. He wants to go to his friend and tell her, ask her to stay with him, to not let him go, but he knows this will frighten her. He could try to explain to her that it's not going to happen, that he knows how to convince himself not to let it happen, and yet he knows he can't make her see that it doesn't make the urge any less real. The compulsion is the same, and he'd love to have support for it, but unless she is hiding the same secret shame he is hiding, he can never make her understand how he feels. It makes you more alone.

Then what's the goal here, if you can't talk about it? You want to reach out, but you won't trouble anyone. Aren't you the one, then, making it so melodramatic and alienating yourself from everyone else?

Possibly. But you have to understand, these dramas, this is how I cope. My line of thought, starting with Camus and the other existentialists, is to crack open the imperfection, to look at the struggle of modern life, and understand it. And by understanding and embracing our foibles, to reconcile ourselves with civilization, religion, everything, to step outside it and beat it. To say that this life is not worth living and rebuke it, that takes away its power to cripple you. You've shed it, and you've moved forward.

Is that just mumbo-jumbo? It reminds me

of the whole self-help industry.

I've been accused of that before. Maybe when you boil it down to a paragraph, sure. But what doesn't sound that way when stripped of the full level of thinking? If you take the thousands of years of theology that have gone into Christianity and just state the basic principle, all you have is a pop song. "All You Need Is Love." But would anyone accept that Christianity, despite being that simple, is really that simple?

Don't you worry, though, that you'll be lumped in with the television psychiatrics of your contemporaries?

No, because I don't measure myself against current writers. I don't want to be considered in any kind of league with them. I want to stand next to important writers. I can't get beyond the early 20th century, for the most part. Writers of my generation, they have it the wrong way around. Their values are mixed up. They're too self-conscious about their stabs at literary fame. And I can't stand their irony. They don't know what irony is. The version of irony that has been *de rigueur* in the late 20th century, this way the authors and artists play everything as if it doesn't matter, it's nothing. If you can't say what you mean, shut up. If you want irony, look at someone like Jean-Paul Sartre. His story "The Wall." That's my kind of irony.

What is your response to people who say suicide is the "coward's way"?

I say they are obviously someone who has held a razor in their hands and don't want to admit they didn't have the guts to go through with it.

That seems a little contradictory of your previous attitude.

Oh, such are the inconsistencies of the man with character!

What about violence? You seem to have that in common with your peers.

There is violence in all human stories.

Are you saying that violence is inevitable?

Pretty much. It serves a purpose on a character's journey. It's a wake-up, a savage reminder, the signal that he or she has done something wrong and punishment will be meted out. It snaps them out of their reverie. Think of it this way. You're asleep in a library, dreaming about the open book in front of you that you're drooling on. You're in the life of the mind. Suddenly, another person enters the library and slams a baseball bat down on the desk next to you. His violence wakes you up, takes you out of the life of the mind and puts you back in reality.

Many people go through life without ever

seeing violence once.

Many people go through life as dull works of fiction.

So, what role does the real world take in your work?

In the fiction, very little. In the essays, more, since they are about applications of a certain thought process in the real world. And really, the fiction is kind of the same. Metaphorical representations of a thought process and examples of how to apply it.

The thing is, though, when it comes down to *story*, I have no need for the real world. I live in the real world, I am opening up a book to experience another. It's why I often have a few scenes of an exaggerated reality, a hyper reality, in each story, to signal to the reader this is not a place you know, it's different.

I'll tell you who got it right in a contemporary context. Kubrick in *Eyes Wide Shut*, he got it right. We'll ignore the fact that his source material is older. In *Eyes Wide Shut*, he replicates a dream state. It's one of the few things I've seen that has deserved the Kafka-esque tag. Tom Cruise's character, the journey he goes on in that one night, if his world were the real world, it would never take place in such rapid succession. Since it's the life of the mind, however, his journey can be compressed. To move his hero from his starting point to his ending point, he has to line up these experiences in much closer proximity.

That being said, the real world is not as staid and normal as we expect. People who engage in the creation of fiction have some odd ideas about how things happen, how human beings act. Any scenario you can imagine *could* happen, and just may have already. Look at the number of outrageous acts that get reported in the newspaper every day, and then consider how many we probably never hear about. You hear writers and critics talk about how some fictional person may have "acted out of character," and it's complete crap. They've manufactured this idea that human behavior follows rules, when the truth is people are unpredictable, unreliable, inconsistent. How many times have you had a reaction to something that's happened to you and you have zero idea why you reacted the way you did? There is no way to write a false reaction, and to force a character to stick to one line of logic is not realism, it's bad writing.

Have you experienced violence in your life?

Of course. There are actually photos of the first time I was violently attacked.

How did that happen?

We were at some kind of amusement

park or fair when I was five or so. I was attacked by a monkey on our family vacation.

You're kidding.

No, it's true. They had this monkey out where people could feed it peanuts and stuff. There was a metal pole in the ground, and at the top of the pole, they had this round metal stanchion, almost like a funnel or an upside-down umbrella. The monkey was in the funnel, chained to its center, and he could run around the perimeter of this thing. I was on my father's shoulders, and I was reaching out, giving the monkey a peanut, when it suddenly jumped out and grabbed me by my hair. There was all this screaming, both the monkey and myself just wailing our guts out. It felt like it took forever for them to pull us apart. There are actually two photos. In the first, I am handing the monkey the nut, and everything is peaceful; in the second, he is fighting with me. More interesting, though, is to look at the crowd. My older brother Lance is there. In the first photo, he looks like he is winding up to throw something, and in the second he's laughing hysterically. I think he threw a peanut at the monkey and when it hit, that's when the monkey attacked. He sicced the monkey on me.

This is the brother who is James in The Other Side of the Street*?*

I wouldn't say that.

But you have said that.

I know, and it was misunderstood. I shouldn't have said it like that. It's not fair to say any one character is really any one person. It's fiction. He was understandably not very happy about it.

Well, James isn't your most endearing character. He's kind of a misogynist.

True. Though, I prefer to think of him as disillusioned, not as someone who actually hates women. More that his original conception of women was so high, there was no way for them to live up to it. He is a failure of ideals. People maybe focus a little too much on what those ideals are—or aren't, as the case may be.

What would you say is the biggest hurdle your writing career has ever faced?

People who don't believe in true love. You know, "I'd like your stuff more if it wasn't so romantic." It's very trendy to say you don't think anyone is meant to be together forever and have this sort of blasé view of all these relationships ending. To those people, I say why bother? What's the point of getting into a relationship fully accepting that it might fail? I believe that all we're searching for in this temporary life is a little permanence. That could be many things, but I can't see it being someone's work or job, for example. What a soul crushing notion! So, why not another person instead?

Yeah, you've taken a lot of heat for the direction your writing has taken in the last couple of years—or more specifically, the strictly philosophical writing. The fiction seems to have stayed its course while the essays have gone from, some say, deeper ruminations on spirituality and the role of the individual to being about relationships and love advice. Like I said earlier, things that sound remarkably like self-help.

It's not conscious. I didn't set out to do that.

You've been accused of such, though, of making a bid for more popularity.

That's just wrong. I follow my thoughts where they take me. It might make me more popular, but that's simply because love is perhaps the world's most popular concept and one that thinkers have neglected for a long time. This kind of criticism suggests that the only important questions to ask are ones about God and Heaven and man's moral compass, yet we spend more of our daily lives searching for some kind of companionship then we do wondering about the afterlife.

So, you're not merely trying to hang on to fame now that you have it.

Absolutely not.

Do you like being famous?

Of course! Who wouldn't? Granted, I'm not massively recognizable. I can usually buy groceries without anyone caring. But I'm not going to insult your readers by sitting here and whining about having lots of money and having the perks of celebrity. I think most people know that's utter crap. And really, in this day and age, we've all had plenty of warnings about the "price of fame." You know what you sign up for.

You've become a pretty regular talk-show staple, and I would argue that becoming that kind of personality causes you to run the risk of becoming just that: a personality whose artistic accomplishments become secondary to the image he or she has created on television. I'm thinking of people like Truman Capote and Orson Welles, and more recently Quentin Tarantino.

That's a fair concern, and I think with those examples, you are totally right. Their talent was supplanted by shtick. The thing that I would say makes me different—and I may be delusional, that may well be your follow-up—is that I've continued to work. Those three did not produce as much while they were visiting every TV couch available. Capote and Welles were struggling, and they tried to mask their inability to complete anything by becoming the party anecdote guys. Tarantino bought into something that was happening to him and lost focus, from what I can tell, and that's why he seems to have disappeared for all intents and purposes. Maybe he's pulled a Salinger? There are worse solutions one could come to.

Anyway, none of that has happened to me. I continue to write, to produce, and I see these talk shows as a multi-pronged tool for myself to road-test ideas, to continue to spread them, and to hone my craft in a conversational way, something I can bring to my writing, to make it more accessible.

Which, let's quit dancing around it, that's the real deal, isn't it? These "some people" who might say this or that about me, they object to my accessibility. They want philosophy to be this high thing that is out of reach for low people. It's a detestable idea, that somehow the common man should be barred from thinking. At the risk of sounding like an egomaniac, I've made it okay to be smart again, I've made thinking trendy. People are reading, they are talking about ideas, it will lead to a greater discourse with a larger slice of the population—why is that bad? It's a fear of class warfare, and really, if this is how the intellectual elite wish to portray themselves, if this is how they really think, maybe it's good that I'm handing people the tools with which they can demolish these institutions.

That's a pretty bold statement.

Yes, well, when you're apparently as shallow an intellect as I am, you can't help but resort to crassness. Bold is all I know. Broad adolescent concepts are my stock in trade. Isn't that what you're telling me?

You're mad at me? I'm here to discuss your work with you. I have to bring up the opposition.

And by opposing, end them. I know. Do you not want me to fight back?

Oh, no. This does make for better copy.

How self-serving and self-reflexive this is, then. To rail at the personality of this thing called "Percival Mendelssohn" while drawing it out so you can sell a magazine or two on the back of it.

This "thing"?

I don't know. Maybe since this is a conversation about ideas, it's best if we make the man in question an idea, too.

Irregardless, I was speaking sarcastically.

Were you? Because you went from defending the personality construct to referring to it as a "thing" in a matter of seconds.

You're reading too much into it.

Maybe. But maybe there is also another question there. I am not discrediting the honesty of the Percival Mendelssohn whom you present to the world, that you really mean it, but is it maybe like a suit of armor? Is there another Percival Mendelssohn behind it?

No, I present myself as who I am.

You save nothing for yourself?

Only in so much as not every thought I have and not everything I do is sufficiently interesting to share.

What of privacy?

I gave that up when I opened myself to the world.

That's a very progressive approach to celebrity.

I'm not a sitcom actor, I'm a thinker. I decided to share things I thought and felt, and that entered me into a pact with my audience. They expect something of me, and I have to give.

How much will be too much, though?

I've yet to find out.

Almost as if on cue, Percival Mendelssohn's personal assistant, Val Stuart, came over to us. "It's time to go," he told his boss, before turning to me. "Thank you, your time is up."

I would have kept the tape recorder running at that point, as I often find the good-byes useful. Even if I can't print everything said in the moments after an interview has ended, I often find it makes interesting color, even if just for myself, to remember exactly how we parted. This time, however, Val Stuart reached over and clicked the recorder off for me.

Mendelssohn rose from the table, reached across, and shook my hand. "It's been a pleasure," he said. I recall it because I thought he genuinely meant it. His smile said as much. For as contentious as it had gotten, it seemed he enjoyed the debate—surprising for a man who was so disdainful of having what he thought and why explained to him.

What I was most struck with was how much I liked the guy. On those talk shows he and I had discussed, he was often preening and self-involved. In my profession, I've met many people who are used to being told they are the smartest indivdual in the room, and they all tend to like it. That was not Percival Mendelssohn in person—which is another reason I choose not to believe that there aren't at least two versions of the man, if not more. The tail end of the conversation, when he switched so easily from being "on" to sincerely friendly was proof enough of that.

In other words, when we lost Percival Mendelssohn, we not only lost a fascinating mind, but I'd wager we lost a pretty nice fellow, as well.

---

e.

Percy hadn't really had any girlfriends before Iris. There had been flirtations, sure, and crushes galore. Girls noticed him, and they liked him because although shy, he could talk to them and, more importantly, he listened. In junior high, when they discovered he wasn't averse to writing notes, his popularity skyrocketed. Most of the other boys would only write back a couple of sentences, and usually there were more sentence fragments than complete ones. Percy would write the girls whole letters, often pertaining to things they may have talked about. "I've been thinking about what you said, Christina, and you're right to be mad at Jimmy. He's being really selfish about all of this. Your plans matter, too, and a football uniform doesn't trump that."

He was two years younger than everyone else in his class, having skipped ahead in elementary school. It didn't matter so much when it was just fifth grade because outside of class, he could just blend in with others his own age. It was only in middle school that kids really started to get all bent out of shape about who was in what grade and how old someone was. There were tables in the cafeteria reserved for cliques of different classes—not officially, of course, but not stopping the same kids from taking the same spots everyday was akin to an endorsement in that kind of environment. And a lunch table wasn't that far off from the faculty-endorsed 8th Grade Lawn. This was a whole open area between class buildings that the older kids had claimed. If sixth or seventh graders tried to cross it, they would be hazed, and the powers that be would make only a nominal effort to stop it.

Some kids were daredevils, and they would try to traverse the lawn. Lance was one of those. He'd start off on the edge, stepping slowly onto the grass, strolling at first. "The goal, you see, is to walk as far as you can," he had explained once when he was trying to get Percy to try it. "You only run when they start on you."

"Lance, this is stupid. Why are we doing this?"

"Because it's fun. Why does everything have to be so smart all the time?"

"I'm not as fast as you. If they catch me, those guys will kill me."

"No, they won't. I'm here. I'll pound 'em."

"I'm not going to do it."

It's not that Percy didn't believe his brother. Lance had defended him from bullies on more than one occasion. It was just that stepping on that field would be like kicking a hornet's nest, and even if Lance beat them up right then, they'd find Percy later. They picked on him enough, so why give them another reason?

The cold truth that Percy never wanted to admit was that he would likely be an outcast in his right peer group, too. He was smaller than the other kids his age and eccentric. His skin was fair and his hair dark, and he liked to wear sweater vests and sometimes glasses with fake lenses, and he'd walk around brandishing an unlit pipe. He was fascinated by smart people, and he wanted to mimic them. The pipe had come from a picture of J. Robert Oppenheimer he had seen. The man's gaze had made a grand impression on Percy's young mind. There was a certain smug something in the scientist's eyes that said he knew more than you and that he was very much aware of it. The glasses came from, among many other sources, a photo of C.S. Lewis working at his desk, focusing on the papers in front of him, lost in thought and possibly a world of great fantasy. The sweater with the long-sleeved, big-collar white shirt was because of Encyclopedia Brown, one of his favorite fictional characters. He knew that the Sherlock Holmes stories were more intelligently put together, but he liked the idea of a version of Holmes that he could be himself.

That was Encyclopedia Brown. Percy wanted to be the kid that figured it all out despite all the odds being against him. The cover of the old paperback he had of the first book in the series showed Encyclopedia in a sweater with full sleeves, but Percy adapted it. He thought the vest looked more professorial.

So, Percy was small and smart, and he dressed funny. In later years, he would learn to use this to his advantage, the way Tristan did with his big hair and his music, or even in the more confrontational way Lance did when he discovered mod and started to wear suits every day; in junior high, though, it got Percy into no end of trouble.

Except with girls. Girls saw Percy as a safe companion, as someone they could mother the way a bigger sister would treat her younger brother. This made some of the boys even angrier, oblivious to the fact that Percy wasn't really a threat to their standing with the female classmates. Most of the girls saw him *only* as a kid brother, and thus the opportunities for sticky romantic entanglements were few. They happened occasionally, though, and they were usually with girls who would for whatever reason decide that *they* wanted to cross that line with him; he was then far too bashful to make the move on his own. So, he would wander into some trumped up after-school study session where a lip-glossed, blossoming young woman would lead him to her window seat and nervously kiss him in the hazy glow of the sunshine. He would try to return their affection, but it usually would fail, and the girls would decide he just wasn't ready, he needed a different kind of feminine care, and things would go back to the way they were.

These encounters bothered Percy, though. It wasn't that he wasn't interested. Quite the contrary. The touch of soft adolescent lips stirred him, and he wanted to partake of them fully, but he was convinced he should resist. He had vague ideas in his brain about the meaning of purity, things that wouldn't fully come together until years later when he was writing about them. He was frightened that if he let himself succumb to a kiss, he would unleash something, and that something would spread over him like sores on a plague victim, and he would never be healed. He would be impure, and once he had stained his soul, there would be no cleaning it out.

Unfortunately, these weren't ideas he had come to on his own. Rather, they had the authority of concepts that had been planted in him by a source he believed implicitly.

Gwendolyn Mendelssohn had found her youngest son to be the most absorbent sponge for her favorite stories about the Round Table. Part of it stemmed from his many illnesses. He had a host of mysterious ailments as a very young boy, all of them somehow connected to fatigue and requiring him to lie in bed for days on end. The doctors could never quite figure it out, and Gwen furiously resisted the explanation that it might all be mental. Lancelot seized on the idea, though, when the boys were a little older. "You don't get it, dude," he said. "She *makes* you sick. You're a goddamn Baron Munchausen is what you are. There's nothing wrong with you that our loony mom doesn't *tell you* is wrong with you."

"Shut up, Lancelot, you don't know." Except Percy had started to suspect that he did.

During his bouts, his mother would sit by his side and read to him from *Le Morte D'Arthur*, giving particular attention to the parts with his namesake, Percival, also known as the virgin knight. "It was his purity and goodness that allowed him to see the quest through to the end," she told him, "and unlike Sir Galahad, he maintained his strength. Galahad asked God to transfer him into divinity before he could sin and ruin his goodness. Percival stayed behind and witnessed it. When Galahad was taken away to Heaven, he told Percival, 'Remember how ephemeral is this earth!' Do you know what that means?"

"Uh-huh. He wanted Percival to realize that the pleasures of this life were temporary, to keep that in mind always so that he wouldn't mess up."

"Exactly. That's why I named you after him, you know. It takes strength for a boy to stay true, and I could feel you had that in you. Sir Percival held on to his virtue all his life. After his quest, he entered into a monastic existence, dying a spiritual hermit at a ripe old age.

"Percival wasn't like the other knights. Like in his quest for Galahad, he was thwarted only because his sense of purpose was stronger than all the others. Their lack of faith dragged him down with them. You'll find that holds true in real life. You've got to be true to yourself, even when it seems hardest. If you set the way for yourself, others will follow. You're special. You have amazing gifts."

Gwendolyn cultivated what she saw as Percy's special talents. She encouraged him to read and to write stories of his own. She started him on piano lessons. Any stimulus he desired she tried to give to him. He took to the idea of his own specialness and wore it like the armor of his famous predecessor. "You realize you were barred from the quest for the Grail," Percy told his brother.

"*I* wasn't barred from anything," Lancelot scoffed, "because *I* was not born yet."

"They made Lancelot stay home because he had sinned. He had sex with King Arthur's wife, and he was tainted."

"You're such an ass. One day you'll realize it's better to be with a girl than hang out with a bunch of dumb guys. You know those jerks that really get excited about P.E., those dudes we can't stand? Those guys are like those stupid knights. When we get to high school, they're going to join the football team and smash each other around while wearing lame costumes. If you think it's better to be one of those guys, go right ahead."

Percy was convinced that Lancelot didn't understand.

Then when he was fourteen, Percy met Iris, and that's when he knew what Lance had tried to tell him was true.

*

Iris was a transfer student. She had attended an all-girls Catholic school all through the first eight grades, but in the middle of her freshman year, her parents divorced and she and her mother moved. Suddenly Iris found herself in the public school system. Gone was the structure, the order, that she had so enjoyed about the private school lifestyle. She hadn't so much been into the religion as she had the system. Sure, she liked the moral code, liked the process of struggle, failure, and redemption, but she wasn't quite so sure about all the damnation and self-immolation. They'd read about other places in history class or in novels, and the world seemed like such a fascinating place. Why would God build it for them if he didn't want his people to go out and enjoy it?

One carry-over from her previous schooling was Iris' wardrobe. While the Saint Ynez School for Girls didn't have a uniform, it did have a strict dress code. So all of Iris' outfits were comprised of knee-length skirts, single-color blouses, black shoes and white socks. Ironically, what made her part of the crowd at Saint Ynez caused her to stand apart at Santa Monica High. Sure, there were a lot of different cliques where people dressed in odd manners, but there was a formality to Iris' look, almost a throwback to the '50s, that made others notice her. She could sense that kids were looking at her and talking about what she was wearing, and she got a secret thrill out of being different for the first time in her life.

Of course, Percy knew none of these things when he saw her in the hallway for the first time. All he saw was a beautiful blonde girl whose sense of style seemed to match his own. He had taken to wearing dark, double-breasted suits by then. In some ways, it was to distinguish himself from his brothers: Tristan, who had graduated the year before, had a caramel pompadour and dressed like Morrissey in western shirts and pegged jeans; Lance, who was sixteen and a junior like Percy, had become a mod. That meant he wore suits, too, but of a flashier, '60s cut. He wore his hair long over his ears and short in front and back, and he usually had on a fedora. Percy was looking to an older era, to classic Hollywood stars and intellectuals. He had adopted Tyrone Power's hairstyle, his dark locks slicked back over his head. He wished life could be a sophisticated cocktail party where everyone told jokes like Dorothy Parker and talked about books the way Edmund Wilson talked about books.

It wasn't an outlook anyone else shared. Percy was fourteen at the time, still two grades ahead of other kids his age. Part of his chosen look, despite the obvious aesthetic attraction he had to it, was to embrace and emphasize the idea that he was different. He didn't want to hide from it, he wanted to show it off.

Percy would never forget the first time he saw Iris. He had heard about her, everyone had, but he hadn't really paid attention to the whispering. His mind was on other things, thoughts that have long since been lost. They were shoved away as soon as he lay eyes on her. Who knows what problems of the soul he had been solving when she first took over his.

They were in the school hallway, and she was at her locker. No one was talking to her. It was almost like everyone else was keeping an enforced perimeter around her, afraid to get too close. Iris hadn't seen him yet, and she would later tell Percy that she had only heard of him once, when some girl said, "You should hang out with that one kid, the one who wears the suits and things. You probably like the same weird stuff." That girl had thought his name was Chauncey.

That fateful day, Percy was walking the halls, minding his own business, lost somewhere in his own head, navigating through the crowd on autopilot, when the throngs suddenly parted and there she was.

Iris was standing by her locker, organizing her books in a black leather shoulder bag. All the other students had canvas backpacks with no personality. She had on a dark plaid skirt and a black button-up sweater over a white shirt. Her hair was pushed out of her eyes by a black headband. Her skin was luminous. It made Percy think of the coconut inside of a candy, the way the darker chocolate all around it made the sweet filling look all the more delectable.

As soon as he saw her, he knew he had to talk to her. He instantly recognized something about the way she carried herself as kindred to him. He would later write, "*As I approached her, I realized that something in me had been activated. A spark of electricity went off in my body, and I became like a theremin. The closer I got to her, there was music, and as she moved through my life, her comings and goings created new sounds, previously unheard melodies, from the high and hysterical tones that would aggravate my senses every time we would part, to the low hum of contentedness that occurred whenever her body was close to mine. I wasn't her instrument, she wasn't my conductor, there was nothing as self-based as that; rather, there was a symphony that required the two of us. In her presence, I became alive.*"

When Percy got near, he noticed that Iris clutched her bag closer to her chest. Did he scare her? Surely not. It was probably just nerves. He was nervous himself, and until he was right there, he didn't even consider that he had no opening gambit, no way to introduce himself. He started to search his brain, while also looking over her person, at things around them. It was the bag that she was throwing up as a buffer between them that gave him his answer. A single small, metallic badge was attached to the strap. He immediately recognized the design: a red rose on a black background.

"Hey, you like Depeche Mode," he said, pointing at the pin. It was 1990, and the *Violator* album was still pretty new.

She looked down at it, too. "Yes," she said.

"Me, too," Percy replied. He held out his hand to her. "I'm Percy."

She took the offer gingerly, her fingertips only barely meeting his, their hands more pushing against one another than either of them was gripping. "Iris," she told him.

"*Enchanté*," he said, and Iris giggled. She pulled her hand from his quickly and placed it against her lips, putting a stop to her laugh. "What's so funny?" Percy asked.

"Nothing," she said. "You spoke French. It's sweet, really."

"But kind of corny?"

"Yes. Kind of corny."

They were fourteen, an age where sharing the same favorite band was the most important fact in the world. Percy wondered if any of the scholars and mental giants he so admired had any theories about pop music, or if they ever looked at entertainment in general and how it binds people together. This was the springboard into his and Iris' relationship, but it would be a lasting theme. With her Catholic background, Iris was particularly taken with Depeche Mode's religious imagery, a topic she and Percy would discuss at length and eventually inspired one of Percy's most important papers: "That is Walking on Hallowed Ground—Depeche Mode's Pop Music Soul." The essay was one of the reasons he eventually worked his way into popular consciousness. People saw that he liked the same things they liked; he wasn't just some guy who sat in a big house thinking big thoughts. "*In Martin Gore's lyrics*," he wrote, "*the author manages to merge the sacred and the profane in ways that so few artists have been capable of, finding the connections between religion and love, between God and life on His Earth. It's not that these aren't easy connections to make, but Gore has neither the fear of the overly pious nor the predictable blasphemy of the typical religious refugee. In fact, in his most concentrated meditation on spiritual beliefs, the 1993* Songs of Faith and Devotion *album, he reveals himself as a writer with a vocation. In songs like 'Condemnation' and 'Judas,' he refuses to apologize for walking the walk while lambasting others for not doing the same. Even in a straightforward, skuzzy sexual romp like 'I Feel You,' the opening track and lead single, he calls his lover's bed 'my kingdom come.'"*

Those and many conversations were to come, but on that first meeting, as Percy walked Iris to her class, neither had very much to say. "The new album is great."

"I like the acoustic 'Personal Jesus.'"

"And the harmonium version of 'Enjoy the Silence.'"

"Uh-huh."

He wanted to hold her hand, but he felt hot and sweaty, so even if it wasn't too forward and emotionally awkward, he couldn't have brought himself to do it for fear of grossing her out. When they finally arrived at the door for her class, Iris said, "Well, this is it."

"What do you have this period?"

"Health."

"Oh, yeah, I remember that. In 11th grade, it's Psychology instead."

"That sounds better. I don't need to be told not to smoke. Like I'd have missed that it's bad for me."

Percy smiled.

"Where are you going?" Iris asked him.

He didn't want to tell her that he needed to be all the way on the other side of the building. "I have English," he said. "We're reading *Hamlet*."

"You'd better go, then. You know that hesitation is his fatal flaw, right?"

Percy was liking her more and more.

"I heard that," he said. "Maybe that's why I can't identify with him."

It was an ironically brave thing to say, since he chickened out before saying anything more. They both looked at each other a moment, and then Iris waved shyly as she turned and disappeared into the classroom.

Percy ran all the way to his own class and was out of breath and even more sweaty when he got there. As the teacher worked them through the tragedy in Denmark, Percy's mind wandered far away from the poetry on the page. All he could think of was Iris. Why had he not said more?

It was a mistake he would have to fix, so as soon as the bell rang, he ran all the way back to where he had left her. His suit was damp by the time he reached her, and his bangs were falling in his face, but when she saw him she smiled.

"You're back," Iris said.

"I am."

"You seem rushed?"

"No. I just wanted to know, do you want to maybe meet up during lunch tomorrow? Maybe we can hang out?"

"Okay."

He laughed. "Okay. Good."

"Meet me at my locker, Percy."

"I will, Iris."

It was the first time he had said her name, and nothing sounded more natural to him in the world. It felt like his mouth had been formed in just the right shape to release the sound. *Iris.*

*

When they met the next day, things between Percy and Iris went more smoothly. They talked for the entire lunch period. It didn't matter what subject one of them came up with, if the other person wasn't already interested in it when the topic began, he or she would be by the time it was concluded. They agreed to meet again the next day for lunch, and by the end of the week, they were not only meeting for all of their lunches but seeing each other between classes, as well.

On Friday, Percy didn't want the week to end, he didn't want to face the long pause without her. Neither of them had yet approached the other's life beyond the school grounds. Sure, they had talked about their family and home life and other things, but neither had attempted to place him or herself in the other's existence. It was a big step. It would start defining something that maybe Percy didn't want defined. What if he was wrong? What if Iris thought he was fun to hang out with, but to do this, it would reveal they weren't thinking in the same way? Some girls liked to have boys they talked to at school, but when it came to real life, they weren't welcome. He'd seen it happen to his brother. Lance had thought this girl Becky was really someone he liked and that she liked him, but then when he phoned her up once, she asked, "Why are you calling me?" She had given him the number!

Even with that as his risk, though, Percy had to go through with it. He couldn't imagine a life where he and Iris were just friends and nothing more. He wasn't interested. He felt too strongly. It was all or nothing.

"Iris?"

"Uh-huh."

"Do you mind if I call you this weekend?" He used all his breath to ask the question, and he wasn't going to take another unless he got a positive answer.

"You'd better call me this weekend. If I can't talk to you, I'll go through withdrawals."

Percy inhaled again. *Thank you, Lord.* It was even better than he could have hoped.

Iris took a spiral-bound notebook out of her bag, and, using a purple pen, she wrote her name in big, curly letters. She wrote her number underneath. Then, she ripped it out of the notebook and folded it up. Percy was elated when she held the paper out to him. It looked like an amazing treasure, the key to all life in grape-colored ink. Only as he reached for it, she snatched it away, pulling it out of his grasp.

What was going on? Had it been a cruel joke? Percy felt as if he would collapse, like a wilting Southern belle in a Tennessee Williams play. In one gesture, Iris had smashed his glass menagerie.

But then, she placed the paper to her mouth and she pressed one edge of it between her lips, like she was biting it without using her teeth, sealing it with her spit. She held it out to him once more, and this time he took it. The wet imprint of her kiss was still visible.

Things couldn't have been more rosy. There was no harsh comedown from this romantic beginning. The first tentative phone call, a scant few hours from when the couple had parted, went swimmingly. In fact, Percival realized once it was done that they had actually gotten *more* personal once they were no longer face to face. Iris opened up about how she thought her mother secretly hated her and how it came out in side comments about the way she did her make-up or the way she was growing up. "If I hear the term 'awkward phase' one more time, I may actually kill myself," she said.

For his part, Percy told her that sometimes he wished he didn't have to go to school, that the other boys drove him crazy and that he'd rather study at home. How he was sick of practicing the piano, it was tedious and no longer something joyful, but stopping would break his mother's heart. How his brother Lance was always giving him a hard time. "Sometimes I wish I had no brothers. Lance is a jerk, and Tristan is just too good at everything."

"Oh, come on. Look who's talking about 'too good at everything'!"

"Quiet! I'm in an awkward phase. I need space."

"I dare you to make that joke to my face next time you see me."

"You're on. How about we go to a movie or something tomorrow?"

"Okay."

Percy couldn't believe how easy it was. Lance was full of stories about how hard it was to ask girls out, but Percy hadn't really tried it before. There was really no trick to it: he merely suggested it, and she agreed.

The date was to take place at the mall, that way they could meet and their families would be none the wiser. There was an agreement between them that they didn't want to share what was happening yet. Iris didn't want her mother snooping, and Percy didn't want to endure Lance's endless, niggling questions. They didn't make it to any film, but instead walked around and around, talking and holding hands. For Percy, that was the best thing he could imagine, having someone he could talk to like that, someone whose voice he never tired of, who never said anything he didn't want to hear. With other girls—with other *people*—he always reached a point where he didn't know where to take the conversation. Usually, their interests ran out. These friends wanted to talk about modern things, stuff that was popular. He could talk about those things, too, because he liked a lot of them, but he wanted to go beyond what was new and flashy, because that was everywhere. It bothered him that these other people didn't care about the fact that Percy had watched *Bringing Up Baby* on cable the night before or had just finished reading Kobo Abe's *The Face of Another* and had found it thick and syrupy and was thinking of reading it again because he hadn't quite gotten it all. Iris didn't already care about or know all of those things either, but he could talk to her about them, describe them to her, and she would listen and she would get it and be able to engage in the *ideas* even if she didn't know the things themselves.

Percy loved the way her hand felt in his. He could feel the ligaments, bones, and veins on the back of it, rolling his fingertips across the ridges. It made him feel connected. The way it went to his head, it was like gravity had let go of him and he would float away from the Earth, except for Iris anchoring him there. He saw a child's balloon that had accidentally been released and was now bumping against the skylight way up at the top of the mall, and he wanted to point at it and whisper to her, "Don't let go, or that will be me." He knew she'd call him corny again, and he figured that though neither of them would really mind, it was best to save it for later. Things were going just fine without any extra effort.

As they walked and as they talked, Percy splintered from himself. It was a talent he had always had, being both an observer and a participant in his own life. The Percival in the mall was quite present, engaged in the conversation, listening and responding with absolute attention. But there was a Percival elsewhere, hovering above the couple like a mental ghost. This Percy was like a soothsayer, and his role was to unlock the future, to crack open the possibilities, and divine where his corporeal counterpart was going.

In this instance, speculative Percival was peering into his future with Iris. Since time could bend to his will, he could view a large number of events in a short span. He saw them go to prom together, he saw tearful conversations as they tried to decide how they would handle his going to college before her, a summer vacation in Paris, a wedding by the sea, Iris by his side through literary success and fame, children. There was something hazy off in the distance, a fog of tragedy that he dared not enter. If he was to be left alone, Percy did not want to imagine it, not even if he could see the warnings in some hope that he could stop it. It would be a vain desire and all the more crushing when it all fell to pieces in his hands.

There was also one other event he refused to look at, because it was one he was going to make happen then and there in actual life. He wanted to be surprised.

When it happened, they were outside. They had stepped out to get some air, to feel the sun. There wasn't much traffic where they were, near a back parking lot. Iris was leaning against the wall, staring off into the horizon at a couple of marshmallow clouds ambling by. Percy liked the way her skin looked in the sun, how the light ran smooth over her cheeks like paint. Her lips were two slices of pink grapefruit, curved slivers full of juice, and he did not want to even consider resisting them.

"Hey...." he whispered.

Iris turned to look at him, her eyes blue and sparkly, her hair so yellow. "Yes?" she asked.

In reply, Percy leaned in and kissed her. Her lips were indeed juicy, and they burst against his, but they weren't tart like pink grapefruit, they were sweet like jelly candy. He felt them part, and the two of them joined, trading their tastes with one another until it was one sugary brew.

In that moment, Percy didn't think of anything *but* the moment. It had to be something that he was aware of as it was happening, since to go beyond it—to imagine the future, to analyze any part of it—would have invalidated the feeling. It was something he realized that night, back home, when he pondered the wondrousness of it all. Soothsayer Percival was nowhere to be found. Rather, the boy was completely there, a whole self, possibly for the first time in his life. He kissed Iris and was kissing her only, and he wasn't being the troubled thinker, wondering what it all meant. To his young mind, it was because it had meant everything. There was Oneness. Life in a single occurrence.

Percival Mendelssohn, age fourteen, had found the answer.

*

The relationship between Iris and Percival bloomed as only young love is allowed, but it wasn't always easy. Right after that first date, Lance sussed out that something was going on. "You seem perky," he said. "You're not your usual pale self."

"I drank a big soda at the movies. It's probably all the caffeine."

"Oh, yeah? What did you see?"

Percy paused.

"Dude, if you're going to lie to me, at least be prepared for the most obvious question."

"Well, it wasn't very good."

"Right. So bad it made you forget the name."

"Something like that."

Lance gave him a hard pinch on his shoulder. "All right, man, spill. What were you really doing?"

"Nothing."

"'Nothing'? 'Nothing' means it's a girl."

"She's not a girl."

"'She'? What's her name?"

"I was saying there wasn't a girl."

"Nuh-uh. You wouldn't have changed the pronoun like that."

"You're not as smart as you think."

"That's okay. I have a rather high opinion of myself, so being short of the mark still puts me ahead of the pack. If she's not a 'girl,'" Lance teased, "what is she? A princess? Don't tell me she's a woman. Oh, gross! It would be just like you to date a teacher!"

Percy threw up his hands, shook his tiny fists in disgust. "You see how you are?" he groaned. "Where do you come up with this ridiculous stuff?"

Lance slapped him with the back of his hand on the same spot he had just pinched him. He laughed. "For such a smarty, you're dumb as fuck," he said. "Like I don't see you with that new chick every day at lunch? Dude, good for you. Girls will destroy your soul and empty your wallet, but they're so much fun."

"Do you know what the word 'misogyny' means?"

The older boy pointed at his own chin. "You see this?" he said, smirking. "This is the face of me not caring."

At school, too, it added a new vigor to the teasing by the other boys. Percy and Iris liked each other too much not to be open about it, and so pretty soon word got around that the weird brainy kid and the Catholic schoolgirl were an item.

"Do you guys pray together?" one boy asked him. He was in a group of three, and they descended on Percy together.

"No way," another boy said. "They talk about clothes and things. He tries on her plaid skirts."

"Come on, Percy, give us the details," the third mocked. "Has she shown you her rosary?"

Percy glared at him. "That's surprisingly creative for someone like you," he said. "It's almost clever."

Normally, Percy didn't fight back because he didn't really care about himself. This time, it was Iris they were messing with, and it raised the hackles of the sense of chivalry all his mother's talk of knights had instilled in him.

The boys didn't like this side of him. They preferred it when their taunts went unchallenged. The third goon moved in close, his nose nearly touching Percy's nose. He spoke through his teeth. "Are you calling me stupid? Huh? Are you, braniac?"

The second of the thugs came up on Percy's side, boxing him in, his back to the lockers. The last of the boys—the first to speak—stayed back, but he kept taunting. "I bet he wishes he had her Bible now," he said.

"That doesn't even make sense," Percy muttered.

"What did you say?" the third boy asked.

"Is it true about Catholic schoolgirls," the second boy snarled, his breath hot on Percy's cheek, "that they're all repressed and shit, so they get real wild in the sack."

"I bet she cries like Virgin Mary every time he sticks it to her." The third boy was getting more menacing with each comment. His arm was up, and he reached past Percy's left shoulder, placing his hand flat on the lockers. It rested between Percy and the other bully. "Does she call out to God the harder you ram it?"

Feeling trapped and angry, Percy knocked the boy's arm away, accidentally knocking it so that the bully's elbow smashed into the nose of the second bully. He stumbled backwards, clutching his face. "Son of a bitch!" he shouted. "That hurt!"

The first boy dutifully rushed to him. "Are you bleeding?" he asked.

"I don't think so. Kick that little fucker's ass."

It was clear to Percy that he was going to get punched, maybe more. It was rare that he was actually faced with violence. Just accepting the insults usually worked in his favor. The bullies got bored with his kowtowing and it was over much faster than if he encouraged them.

But this time some other kind of honor was at stake. He had never felt that before. Anything said about him didn't bother him because he knew the truth, and that defined him, not the jokes of sub-literate bullies. Letting them talk bad about Iris, though, was another matter. It seemed to him this was a point where he should stand up. It was all that existentialism he had read put into practice. Doomed is the man who does nothing!

Percy pushed the third boy away from him. He used both hands. If nothing else, he would get away from the lockers. The thug took a couple of steps back. He looked at his prey with surprise. He laughed. "It's about time you grew a spine," he said. "Maybe fucking the church girl *has* done you some good!"

"You shut up!" Percy said. He was waving his arm wildly, pointing with his finger. "Don't you talk about her!"

"We finally found this kid's hot button."

"I don't care," the one with the injured nose said, still holding his face. "Just kill the little dick."

The third boy lunged at Percy, his arm drawn back to punch him, but Percy lunged as well, and their bodies crashed together. The bully's punch landed stillborn on Percy's back. In return, Percy slapped at his shoulders. "You shut up!" he shouted. "You shut up!"

Suddenly, he felt a tug on the back of his jacket. The first boy had grabbed him and yanked him off of his friend. "You call that fighting?" He was laughing, mocking him. "You're like a kindergarten girl."

Percy struggled to get out of his grip, which was a bad idea because it took his eyes off his other attacker. The boy was on him before he knew it, landing a punch at the top of Percy's left cheek, the side of his fist smashing into Percy's eye. Using the boy holding him as leverage, Percy lifted himself off the ground and kicked both of his legs like he was trying to shake off his bed sheets. He felt a couple connect, and he was surprised by how it felt. It wasn't like kicking something hard and solid, but like plunging his feet into pillows.

Everything seemed to be speeding up, and just as Percy engaged in one action, he was suddenly thrust into another. The boy holding him spun around and tossed his body against the lockers. It rattled him. It reminded him of playing baseball in P.E., the few times he actually hit the ball, the way the crack of the bat shot through his body. Kind of like hitting your funny bone. He didn't linger, however, but rebounded off the metal doors and ran into the group of boys, swinging his arms in any direction they would go. He thought his fists had hit one or two of them once or twice, he didn't know. He couldn't really make out details, just shapes, moving blurs. Then he slammed into someone, and he just kept pushing at the body, kept pounding his fists against the boy's chest. The person was shouting something at him, but the words were indistinct. Percy realized he was yelling over the top of them. More like screaming, really. Suddenly the boy's hands were around Percy's wrists and he couldn't swing anymore. He struggled, but the boy had him, and Percy dropped to his knees. He stopped screaming, and it turned to crying. His anger was hot, it was spilling from his eyes. Had he been crying all along?

Percy could hear the voice now. Whoever it was kept calling his name. "Percy! Percy! Percy!"

He recognized the voice. He looked up, his vision finally focusing, even though it was still clouded by tears. It was his brother. Lance was the one holding him by his wrists.

"Percy, calm down!" he said. "It's okay, dude, they're gone."

He didn't understand. "Lance? What are you doing here?"

"You're lucky. Someone saw you and came and got me. If they hadn't, those guys were going to kill you."

Percy looked around. The goons were nowhere to be seen.

"What happened? Where did they go?"

Lance pulled his brother to his feet. He cupped his hand under Percy's chin, trained the younger boy's eyes on his. "Look at me," he said. "Look! Are you all right?"

"Yes. I don't know. Where did they go?"

His older brother held Percy by his shoulders, straightening him up.

"They're gone. Once I got here, I just started punching and they took off pretty quick."

"You did it?"

Lance laughed. "You helped a little, too. Though, I think you hit me more than you hit them. You actually have a pretty decent punch. I think you bruised a rib."

"You did it? How could you?"

"Man, it was three against one. They were going to slaughter you."

Percy looked around. He was crying again. None of this made sense. *What had happened?*

"Why did you do that, Lance? Why did you?"

The elder boy looked angry. He pushed Percy away from him. "Is that 'thank you' in Percy-speak? You know I don't let anyone mess with my brothers."

"But I was supposed to do it," Percy cried. His voice had gone high, he sounded hysterical. "I was fighting them."

Lance shook his head. "Yeah, you were. So what? What's it matter if I helped?"

Percy pounded his chest. The tears were coming fast, and they seemed large, giant drops of water the size of marbles. "*I* wanted to do it. *I* wanted to."

"You're cracked," Lance said, and he stormed away, blowing his sibling off with a wave of his hand.

After that, the teasing didn't stop, but it remained more covert. Comments were made under the breath, followed only by stares. It bugged Percy, but if Iris noticed, she never made mention of it. When they were together, it didn't matter what anyone else thought, anyway. They were falling in love, and the rest of the world wasn't a part of it. There was only room for two.

5.

Passivity was no longer an option.

Everything Julia had gained at Percy's house was a result of her pushing for it. If her encounter with Percy in the garden was anything, it was proof of that. She had to create more opportunities to see him.

Val left the house every few days to get supplies. He did this during the day, when Percy was still sleeping. Julia was never told he was leaving, he would just be gone. She assumed this was so she would not dare to try anything funny. If she didn't know when Val had departed, she could not gauge when he would return. Julia had tried to get Val to take her along when he shopped, hoping that maybe the excursion would bring them closer together, force him to bond with her, but he would have none of it. She also tried giving him a shopping list. He looked it over, screwing up his face like the paper offended him. "Pomegranate juice? Sesame rolls? Milk candy?"

"Yes. Not everything we eat needs to be so regular, you know."

"I make what the person who is paying likes. Do you have money for this?"

"Some. Take me with you, I'll stop at an ATM."

"I've got a better idea. How about you eat with us and not whine about it?"

There was a finality to his tone. It was a slamming-door of a statement, not a question.

If she wasn't going to be allowed to go with him, then she would have to turn that unguarded time to her advantage.

There weren't a lot of places to hide around the siheyuan. It was too small. Just about every space was already filled, and any spot that remained open wouldn't particularly shield a whole person. However, the room that Val had given to Julia was close enough to the front door that, if she remained quiet, she could hear any comings or goings. It would take patience. Her new routine was getting up in the morning, making an appearance, watering her plants, and then demonstratively grabbing a new book from the library and making sure Val knew she was going to retire to her closet and read it. She would maintain an air of *ennui*, as if the days of him ignoring her and being confined to the quadrangle were becoming too much. A yawn, a stretch, and a mumbled *adieu*.

Then she would sit there on her bed, attentive, listening, waiting.

The first time Julia tried it, Val left within the hour. She couldn't believe how easy it was, but then that made her think she was too lucky and she was scared to try anything. Two hours later, when Val came back in with a box full of cleaning supplies, she felt dumb for being so wishy-washy.

The second time, Val didn't leave at all, and the third, it took much longer for the man to go out on his errands than it had that first day. This time Julia was determined not to let the moment pass without trying *something*. As soon as she heard the front door close, she tiptoed out of her room and went to it, pressing her ear against the wood to listen for any signs that Val might be coming back. When she heard nothing, she moved to the small window on the side of the door, looked out. The alleyway was empty.

Still on tiptoes, walking as though she might trip some sophisticated, invisible alarm, Julia made her way to the back of the house. She followed Val's usual path through the kitchen. Best to enter Percy's room through the door he was used to Val coming through. It might be less startling that way. For some reason, Percy's door felt heavier than all the others in the house. When Julia pushed on it, it didn't give easily, she had to put her muscles into it. Once it was breached, she caught a whiff of ginger coming through the crack. The rest of the house smelled so stale and old. How was it that this room was different, this tomb? She thought of samurai and how they wore flowers under their helmets so that if they were beheaded, their skulls would remain fragrant.

Percy was still asleep. He was tucked into himself, his arms crossed underneath him, his head sideways on the pillow. Blankets were tangled around his legs, his knees pressed up to his stomach. His breathing was heavy, like a child's. His skin was so pale, that when combined with his black hair streaked with gray, it had the effect of making him appear to be in black-and-white. A classic movie star whose light was fading.

He didn't look peaceful, exactly. There was nothing serene about him lying there, sweating, his eyes pinched closed. He more looked like he was far away, deep into his sleep, like it was a weight that was strapped to him, dragging him down, pulling him into the mattress. Julia didn't want to disturb him. Not yet. She knew now that she could get into his room, and that would be enough for today. Small steps.

When Val returned that day, Julia was waiting in the kitchen. He asked her what she had done with her morning, and she said, "Nothing much." He looked at her like he didn't believe her. Did he know? No, there was no way he could. She was just being paranoid. Val was not all-powerful. One could be pulled over on him.

Just in case, Julia gave Val another request for food, thinking that if she remained a pest, he'd not be suspicious. "Kiwi," she said. "I'd love it if you'd pick up some kiwi."

Val grunted at her. Mission accomplished.

The very next day, Val went out again. It was early, Julia had barely even gotten awake. She wasn't dressed, hadn't showered. She wondered what it was he was going out to get. There wasn't that much they needed, there were only three of them. Yet, he went out all the time. Could it be a trick? Had he been trying to trap her all along?

Julia got up and went to the bathroom, quickly washing her face, pulling her hair back and tying it with a small rubber band. She wished she had her make-up with her, or anything beyond the usual that Percy kept seeing her in, but there was nothing to be done about it. She got dressed and headed back to Percy's room.

This time, Percy was not asleep, but was sitting up in bed, reading, turned away from the door. His back was bare, the skin paler than even his face. He had freckles on his shoulders, and a few moles along his spine. There was some music playing quietly in the background, a soft female voice singing plaintively in Chinese. Julia quickly translated a couple of lines in her head. "*Look, the moon at that moment, it used to represent someone's heart, in the end it's still the same....*"

Julia watched him sitting there. Once again she wished she had the power to read his thoughts. This man's books had been so inspirational to her, and how amazing would it be to understand how his mind worked. A quiet moment like this would surely be the most telling. No guard, no pretensions, just alone with himself.

Only he wasn't alone, and he knew it.

"Can I help you?" Percy asked her. He didn't turn around, but he did reach for his familiar bed sheet and pulled it over himself, once again hiding under it like it was a protective tarpaulin designed to withstand the attack of wind and rain.

She was startled by his voice. She had underestimated how alert he was. It was Val's fault. He tried to make her think that Percy was some kind of empty shell. "The man you're looking for is gone," he told her. "And you can't possibly understand where. The man you've seen is a spook haunting his own house."

Though she was wrong, of course, she imagined then that maybe Percy was the one with the paranormal powers, the one who could read minds. If you entered his hermit's cave, you were under his spell.

"Can't you see I'm busy?" he asked her, more testily now, his anger riled in the pause left open by Julia's lack of a reply.

Putting a hand on the doorknob, Julia began to step out of the room, closing the door with her. "Sorry," she said. "I...I didn't mean...."

Percy twisted his torso around, held up a hand. "Wait!" he exclaimed. It boomed in the empty house. Without moving her head, Julia did a quick look around to make sure the walls weren't coming down.

"Stop," Percy said, more gently. "No, I'm the one who is sorry."

What?

Julia stepped back in. She didn't know what was happening, but she was going to seize it.

"I should have knocked," she said. "Really."

"Forget it," Percy said. He had turned all the way around now. He was cross-legged on the bed. The sheet was pulled over his bare chest and back, and he looked like he was waiting to get a haircut. He extended both hands from a crack in the middle of his covering and waved them at her, back and forth, crossing over one another like he was trying to shake something off them—or as if he had said "Abracadabra" to make her disappear. "Let's talk no more of that."

"All right." Julia took another step forward, then paused, the way a girl does when she is walking out on a cliff that she knows is unstable and isn't sure where the breaking point is, each moment a test of danger. She could smell the ginger again, tangy. It was in her nose and in the back of her throat, sort of like she had swallowed strong ginger ale the wrong way.

"You're my guest after all."

That was the last thing Julia had expected to hear.

"Julia."

Okay, make that second to last.

"It is Julia, isn't it?"

"Uh-huh."

As she moved closer, the ginger smell gave way to something else, something similar to what she had smelled on the first day she had walked through the house. Like something decaying. Like water at the bottom of a vase when Valentine's flowers have been kept for too long.

Percival grabbed some pillows from off his bed—big square ones, with paisley patterns and bright colors, tassels on the edges—and dropped them on the floor. He gestured over them. "Sit down," he said.

The cushions were soft under her. Julia folded her legs to sit cross-legged like Percy was, adopting his posture. She had come into the room expecting to take control of the situation, but the fact that he had instead was even better.

"I apologize that this has taken so long," he said. "I shouldn't have invited you into my home without a proper welcome."

"It's okay," Julia said. "I understand."

"I'm out of practice when it comes to social mores."

"Yeah, I guess it's been a while."

Percy smiled wryly. "You might say that."

He was running his fingers along the edge of his sheet, feeling the threads. He looked at Julia and she thought there was something in his eyes, something inquisitive. "Do you want to ask me something?"

"Can we get one question out of the way? Before we go on?"

"Sure."

"I've asked you this before, kind of, and you only kind of answered. Why did you come here?"

The way he said it, Percy made it sound like it was very matter-of-fact, but at the same time there was no question more important than that one. Julia had to think about it. She had tried to tell him in the garden what she was feeling, but it came out all wrong, and she didn't want to mess it up again. How could she describe how important this contact with him was?

Julia was thirteen when Percival Mendelssohn had disappeared. She hadn't heard of him before, hadn't yet read a word of his writing. Yet, something about his story fascinated her. On the one hand, it was sad. He had lost his wife to suicide and rather than confront the void her death had created, he had left. On the other hand, how exciting to be gone and no one knew where. Even at that young an age, she realized how amazing such a thing could be, a complete rejection of other people's rules.

All the news reports either in print or on television seemed to use the same photo. He was in a tuxedo, bent slightly at the waist, his back against a wall, smiling. He seemed so happy in the picture, so far removed from the darkness that now surrounded him. What had happened? How did this man with the slicked-back hair, almost immaculate except for the little tuft near his bangs that looked like it would spring up if given the slightest provocation—how did this tragedy happen to *him*? He looked like the boy with everything, so how could he lose it all?

It was partly what made her choose his book for her report that year in English. Maybe it would give her some idea. She didn't just approach him as a teller of stories, but almost like a secret messenger smuggling her coded explanations of his life. There was something beyond his fictions. It wasn't like Jane Austen, who was long gone and no longer accessible. Percival Mendelssohn was still here, still on Earth. When it came down to it, they could be friends.

Of course, she had no idea at the time that she would travel thousands of miles around the world to try to make it happen. She also had no idea what kind of state she would find the man in. He wasn't the glittering image from that photograph. More like someone had taken the photograph, crumpled it, kept it in her pants pocket and run it through the washer, and the devastation of the washing was visited upon Percy's physical body as if by voodoo.

Again Percy moved to fill the gap in the conversation.

"You said in the garden that you didn't want to jinx yourself by thinking about what might happen, but surely there was something you *wanted* to happen. Why did you come here? You didn't just want to find me for the sake of finding me. There's got to be more to it."

---

f.

When Julia first learned that her college had a Percival Mendelssohn society on campus, she was ecstatic. Finally, she could get together with people who shared her passion for his writing and talk about it and all the important issues that related to it. "It's what college is supposed to be about," she told her roommate. "The free exchange of ideas!"

Her parents had never understood her obsession with Percival's books. They were too ignorant of what the books were actually about. They had never read any of them, instead relying on the Church's propaganda and smear campaign. "He doesn't believe that God is better than man," her mother said. "How can you give so much time to a man like that? It only encourages him when people buy his books."

"He's not really saying that, Mama," Julia argued. "It's not about one being better than the other. It's about living a modern life and balancing all the things modern society teaches us with our personal faith. It's like he's trying to give us a map to get through it."

"It's all just so morbid, Julia. What is that book? The *Someone Dead* book? Why is he talking about death? I thought it was supposed to be about life."

"It is about life. The thing about being dead, it's a metaphor. You know, people who wander through life without really living."

"And all that stuff about suicide," Papa said. "What is that? Our love of Christ is not about kicking the bucket."

"Oh, *please*!" That one really got Julia riled up. "The Catholic Church is entirely about death. All organized religion is. Look at the artwork. Paintings and statues of Jesus on the cross, bleeding to death, outnumber ones of him peacefully praying something like five to one. The entire focus of modern Christianity is how we're all going to die and how to avoid getting punished on top of that. It's all wrapped up in living a certain way because you fear the consequences of pursuing the alternative, rather than seeking some kind of understanding about why living a good life is just the right thing to do."

Her mother clucked her tongue, the usual signal that any discussion had gone as far as she was going to allow it to go. "I don't like having that man's books in my house," she said. "It's like you're inviting a vampire through our front door. He can't come in unless you ask!"

Julia folded her arms. "Well, you're going to have to accept it somehow. Either that or you might as well brand me as a devil and find some stake for me to be burnt on, because I am those books. Percival Mendelssohn speaks for me. He takes my thoughts and puts them together for me in ways I can understand."

"Don't say such things, my little daughter." Julia's father looked horrified. "You break my heart."

"Then let's just stop talking about it."

And they did. The name Percival Mendelssohn never came up again.

Finally, the moratorium would be lifted. She was at Lewis & Clark in Portland, Oregon, one of the most famously liberal cities in America. Here there would be open thinking, and she could talk about Percy's books, and people would listen and understand. How important those two things were. Listening. Understanding.

The Percival Mendelssohn Society met every Thursday at 4 p.m. When that first Thursday rolled around for Julia, she woke up excited, ready to dig into some deep philosophical ideas. As the day wore on, however, her confidence began to wane. She started to feel nervous. What if all the other students were older than she, had been there longer and understood Percival better? She imagined stepping up to a podium and introducing herself. "Hello, I'm Julia Marie Jiménez, and I'm a Percival

Mendelssohn fan."

"Hello, Julia," the crowd would parrot back.

"I read my first Percival short story when I was in my freshman year of high school. It was an assignment in my English class. We had to go to the library and pick an author and read a short story and do a report on it. I picked *The Ballad of Strangelove*, and I can't exactly say why. Part of it was probably because I had heard of Percival and knew he was slightly scandalous. It also helped that it's kind of a slim volume."

A few people would chuckle, but it didn't sound like they were laughing with her. One girl would even snort derisively, "That's a pretty shallow start."

"I know, I know," Julia would say in her own defense. "Ironically, too, the story I read was 'Deep End.' And, of course, it had a profound effect on me."

"How could it?" a ponytailed grad student would shout, so contemptuous of her that he wouldn't even lift his hand to point, instead gesturing with his Birkenstocked foot, not even uncrossing his legs. "You were a superficial child. You couldn't have possibly understood it."

"Not all of it." Julia could feel herself withering under the scorn. "No, of course not. A lot of the subtleties would take me years to digest. But the *emotion*—"

"Even if we accepted the less ridiculous reasoning that you read *Strangelove* as a sort of act of rebellion, that story isn't about rebellion. You were trying to show off, thinking how cool the book would make you look. 'Deep End' is about personal emotion and ignoring the judgment of the outside world."

"I know that, of course, but I—"

"Do you really know anything about this work?"

"I was a kid, I hadn't—"

"It sounds to me like you still are. Quit wasting everyone's time and go somewhere and grow up."

The fantasy meeting continued this way until Julia was reduced to tears and ran out of the room. The scenario gave her serious pause. Yes, she knew it was a ridiculous concern, and the arguments that she came up with for these bratty college students didn't even make sense—but that didn't make the anxiety any less real. What if she was a shallow thinker? What if they laughed at her? She had only just started school; they might all be far more sophisticated at analysis. She wasn't going to talk herself out of going, but maybe she should sit back and listen before she engaged.

The gathering was held in a small classroom and was attended by about ten people. Before they came to order, they milled about the room chatting, and it was clear that they all knew one another. Julia had the horrible feeling that she had been asked to tag along to a party thrown by someone she had never met, and the only person she would have known—the girl who had invited her—had not shown up. She was the awkward Filipino girl hiding out by the punchbowl. Even worse, everyone else in the room was Caucasian. It was easy to forget when living in Northern California that there were still places that were mostly white. It wasn't the first or last time she'd felt like an oddity in Oregon.

Across the room, there was another girl standing alone. She looked young, too, and she wore a tight pink T-shirt, a plaid miniskirt, and she had studded leather collars around her neck and wrists. Her hair was burgundy and cut in a sort of pageboy shag. Julia was giving her the once-over when the girl looked back at her. Eye contact was accidentally made, and the girl pushed herself off the wall she had been leaning on and came over. "Hey, this your first time, too?"

Julia laughed a nervous laugh of relief. "Yes! How did you know?"

"I noticed that look of fear on your face and thought, 'Man, that girl looks like how I feel.' I'm Julie, by the way."

"No way. I'm Juli*a*."

"Bizarre."

The coincidences didn't end there. They were both from California, though Julie was from San Diego. They had both left home for the first time to come to school here, were living in the dorms, and though Julie's haircut had been the same for a while, she had been forbidden to dye it while she had been at home. Her parents attended a Pentecostal church called the Assembly of God, and they had actually once accused Percival Mendelssohn of being possessed.

"That's nuts," Julia giggled. "So, like, is that the church where they speak in tongues and heal people with snakes and stuff?"

"Well, most congregations have left the snake-handling behind, but yeah, the tongues thing is still happening."

"Have you ever done it?"

Julie made a guilty face, like she'd been found out for something she really didn't want to admit. It involved clenched teeth and stretching out her mouth to one side, like it was a long gash. "Yeah, when I was young, they shipped me off to this camp where I got kind of caught up in it, and they were doing this big group thing where we were all praying and reaching for the sky and asking God to bless us with the ability."

"What was it like?"

"I got kind of tingly, actually. Like, my lips were on fire. They get you all chanting and counselors were walking around encouraging us to let go, to just start letting sounds come out of our mouth, to try not to say words. I just kind of descended into this moaning gibberish. A couple of years later, I had this rich friend who had hired a hypnotist for her sweet sixteen, and I was one of his volunteers. The sensation was exactly the same, and I realized that the whole camp thing had just been mass hypnosis. Speaking in tongues is going into some kind of trance, and it's no holier than lip-synching to EMF, sadly enough."

"Wow. Here I thought the Catholics were weird for eating magical crackers and stuff."

The girls had to stop the exploration of the Twilight Zone of their twin existence because the meeting was being called to order. Everyone was arranging the chairs in a circle in the center of the room, and a rockabilly looking guy with a slicked-back pompadour and dark sunglasses was at the head of it. He sat with his chair turned around backwards, straddling it. He had on very blue blue jeans and heavy motorcycle boots.

"All right, everyone, let's get started," he said. His voice was deep and gruff, but he had a perpetual smile. The impression was that he was a tough guy, but really a sweetheart behind it all. He introduced himself as "Teddy, short for Theodore, and some folks call me Teddy Boy, but you really have to know me for a long time to do that...and also know how to take a punch to the gut." His smile got bigger, lest anyone not realize he was kidding.

The meeting began with an open call to see if anyone had anything they wanted to discuss, any news about Percival or new credible rumors regarding his whereabouts. From there, they had a more focused discussion about the essay "The Blind Leading the Faith," which had been the agreed-upon reading for this session. Teddy called it "a celebration of adventurous religiosity." For over twenty minutes, the attendees shared their impressions of the piece, and there was very little dissension in the ranks. Everyone pretty much agreed on the author's intent, and so the conversation ran its course.

Teddy stood up and turned his chair around the right way. "Before we go, we do have an important item of business," he said, propping himself up on the chair with his right arm. "I'm sure everyone has noticed that we have two newcomers this week." He gestured back to Julie and Julia. Julia felt herself blushing, but when she cast a glance at Julie, she saw that the other girl was rolling her eyes, seemingly unafraid of public attention. "Forgive us for not formally welcoming you earlier," Teddy continued, "but we prefer to let you come in on your own terms, listen, and see if it's right for you. If you like what you heard, come back next week, and be prepared to introduce yourself proper."

He then gave next week's assignment: to read the first three chapters of *The Other Side of the Street*. There was enough time in the rest of the semester for the group to read Percival's entire magnum opus together.

Both girls did return the next week, and the introductions they gave of themselves bore no resemblance to the Alcoholics Anonymous-style testimony Julia had imagined. It was short and simple and no one challenged anything she said.

In the seven days between gatherings, the two girls started hanging out together, meeting in the dining hall, studying in each other's rooms, and they even had gone off to see a Cameron Diaz movie on the weekend. They joked that they were Lindsay Lohan in *The Parent Trap*, but the mixed-race version. One twin was white, the other brown. The only glitch was that if they were going to trick their parents into getting back together, both of them only really wanted to keep their fathers, which probably wouldn't work. Julie's mother was a secret drunk and her constant badgering had driven her daughter to a bout with bulimia that, thankfully, her father had spotted early and so Julie had managed to beat it. "They sent me off to camp again, but this time it was like I was in *Girl, Interrupted*." What everyone had failed to notice, though, was that in addition to binging and purging, Julie was also cutting. "I only tell you this because I want you to know," she said. "I don't usually tell anyone, but you might have noticed that all of my shirts have long sleeves."

The day of her confession, Julie was wearing a baby-doll tee that had the logo for the band Garbage written across the chest in rhinestones. She was wearing a sheer black shirt underneath it, and the ebony sleeves picked up the coverage where the tiny white sleeves of the band shirt left off. Julie pulled back the right one, revealing several dull, horizontal scars on her forearm. "I haven't done it in a while, so most of these are healed. Some of them are permanent."

Julia didn't know what to say, so she opted to tell her new friend exactly that.

"Then don't say anything," Julie said. "As long as you don't judge me for it, it's cool."

Julia didn't judge her for it. In fact, she kind of envied Julie. She'd never have the guts.

Not only had the girls been required to stand up and explain who they were at their second Percival Mendelssohn Society meeting, but after it was all done, Teddy came over and made a point of meeting them face-to-face. "I'm so glad we have some new blood in here," he said. "To be honest, I'm getting a little sick of the same old opinions from the same old co-eds."

He laughed, flashing that big smile again. Julie would later make fun of it, noting that it was fake. "He's like that snake in *The Jungle Book*," she said, and then sang, "'*Trust in meeeee, just in meee.*'"

That didn't stop either of them from accepting Teddy's invitation for coffee that night, however, where he insisted they could all three get to know each other more personally, away from the "bullshit setting of a classroom." Still smiling, he said, "I'm no teacher! I'm one of you guys. I'm only twenty-two!"

They went to a café on campus where the baristas were playing the same Radiohead record over and over. ("At least it's the second one," Julie said, "so it's good.") They stayed there about two hours, watching people come and go, and when it seemed like the café was the most crowded, Teddy asked them, "Hey, do you want to see something?"

The way he gestured at his own body seemed kind of lurid. Julie and Julia traded a suspicious look with each other, which made them both giggle. "I guess," Julie said, "as long as it's nothing illegal."

Teddy took off his leather jacket and draped it over the back of his chair. The action released a sort of musky smell, possibly a result of the wet splotches visible in his underarms. Julia liked it, though. She always thought boys should smell like boys.

Once the jacket was off, Teddy grabbed the bottom of his shirt and pulled the front over his head. His sleeves were still on, but the rest of the shirt was stretched across the back of his neck, exposing his muscular chest. Teddy pointed to a lone tattoo on his left breast. "I got the idea for this from reading Percy's books," he said. "See, it's a heart, tattooed over my real heart, except there is a metal cuff around it, and a ball and chain is attached. You see?"

The girls nodded in unison. "Mmm-hmmm."

"It's like how we're all shackled to our hearts, to our emotions, you know? That's life, right? And depending on your point of view, it can either be good or bad."

Neither Julie nor Julia really said anything about it there, but later, they would compare notes. They both thought it was a little over-the-top and pathetic but yet couldn't dismiss it outright. There was something kind of cool about him taking that kind of metaphorical action. "Like he's trying to make a philosophical concept into flesh," Julia said.

"Yeah, and forcing himself to live it."

"Yeah."

Then Julie tumbled into an uncontrollable giggle fit. "Oh, my God! He's such a poseur! You know what it is? It's like Mormon secret underwear!"

"What?"

"You never heard about that? Mormons wear this special underwear with symbolic iron-ons or something of sins they have to remember not to commit. Like, if you're a horndog, you get a 'no sex' symbol or something, and every time you pull down your pants, you see it and think, 'Oh, yeah, I gotta not be a horndog.'"

"They do not!"

"They do! They told me at my church. And that's what Teddy Bear is doing. He's reminding himself to feel every time he goes to the gym to work out his pecs." Julie lowered her voice in a gravelly impression of Teddy's. "'Don't be macho, life is pain. Grrrrrrr.' What a douche!"

Julie didn't seem to think that highly of Teddy, but Julia still liked him. Yeah, he was a little earnest, but since so many people felt nothing, she was ready to cut him some slack. And though the pair weren't prepared to let Teddy in enough to make their union an official trio, he did start to hang out with them pretty regularly. He shared an off-campus apartment where there was a TV and VCR, so the girls often went over to watch movies, sometimes doing two or three in a night. Teddy usually picked up the tapes, and he seemed to have a penchant for either disjointed black-and-white films where everyone spoke in French or grainy indie movies where attractive young boys broke away from either bourgeois fathers or poverty-stricken, abusive mothers by being hustlers. Sometimes both types were in the same picture! Julia wondered how much Teddy actually liked the movies. When they were finished, he'd talk animatedly about how they were innovative and edgy, pushing the boundaries of storytelling without some fake structure being imposed on them, but to Julia he sounded like he was reciting the words, almost like he'd thought of them—or worse, *read them*—beforehand. Still, there was a sort of naïve passion to his speeches that was endearing. He was trying *so* hard to be a deep thinker that it was kind of sweet how he was obliviously splashing around in the kiddie pool.

Julie, on the other hand, got fed up with the programming. "I swear to God—or Godard—whoever you hold more faith in, that if we don't watch something funny next time, I'm not coming anymore."

In deference to her request, Teddy got *Some Like It Hot* for their next night over, but Julie soon found another reason to not hang around as much.

When the girls met, Julie was in what she called "a self-imposed dry spell." Her last boyfriend, whom she had been with for two years, had turned out to be a real jerk. Julie was annoyed with herself for having taken so long to figure that out. "We had our first fight six weeks into dating, and he almost hit me. He hauled back his fist to do it, but he caught himself and punched the wall instead, and I acted like *that* was some kind of indication that he was actually sweet because he restrained himself. I thought that meant he'd be willing to change. Not bloody likely!" She affected a thick Cockney accent for the last line, and then laughed so hard at her own mimicry skills, she snorted.

Eventually, though, that dry spell was to meet its natural rainy season. Boys noticed Julie wherever the girls went. Julia would see them staring at her friend, elbowing their buddies and giving the head-nod in Julie's direction. She thought Julie was oblivious to it, but it turns out the girl knew it was going on the whole time. "If you let them know you noticed, they'll think you're interested," she said. "And if you are interested, you *really* don't let them know you've noticed. They need to find their own way over here, you know what I mean?"

Her first hook-up was at a Halloween party. The boy was in a tiger outfit. It was a big furry jumpsuit with a big zipper down the front. Julie asked him, "If I pulled the zipper down, what would I find underneath?"

"Spots," the boy said. "I'm really a leopard."

Julie laughed. The boy was in.

Only, he wasn't to last. "At least this one admitted he's a leopard," she said, "and we all know what leopards *can't* do."

The chains were off, however, and there was no stopping her. Most boys only got one date, two at the most. Julie wasn't going to settle until she found the very right one. While she was looking, Julia was back to the library by herself, or maybe coffee with Teddy. And now that Julie was missing movie nights, there was no filter on Teddy's choices. "The guys down at the video store had almost started to think I'd forgotten where the Nouvelle Vague section was," he joked.

He held up the box for Godard's *Two or Three Things I Know About Her*, and after they were done watching it, Julia said, "You know, I didn't realize, but all of these French ones from the '60s are about female prostitutes, and all the American ones from the '90s are about boy prostitutes. What caused the shift?"

Teddy laughed. "I don't know, but that's a good point. You know, once when I was a kid, my parents took me to see this Easter pageant at an outdoor amphitheatre. It wasn't a big production, it was at a campground or something. Anyway, there was a scene with Mary Magdalene and how people were shocked Jesus was with a lady of the evening, so it's an old theme."

"I guess."

"The funny thing was, I didn't know what the word meant, so I asked my parents, very loudly so that the whole audience could hear, 'Mom, Dad...what's a *prop*-itute?'"

Again, like all of Teddy's stories, it revealed a certain misguided inquisitiveness. How funny that it had started at such a young age!

They sat close that night, facing each other, their feet up on the couch. They were used to having a third, more sarcastic voice in the room, and the discussion would often have to bend to cater to it, but not anymore. They could exchange ideas without any interruption. Teddy's story led them to talking about their families and their childhoods. Julia liked the way Teddy talked about being a child who felt strange in comparison to the rest of his family, like he never really fit. He said it was like on holidays when there was a kids' table and an adult table, and the one for the kids was always smaller, lower, and less stable. He was convinced that this was to keep him from seeing the top of the adult table, which had to be wider and sturdier to hold all the food. If he could see what was on the adult table, he'd know that there were more things available than what he was being allowed to have. "That was the sense I had all my life," he said. "That there was something beyond me that I couldn't know, or that they weren't telling me about."

Teddy did most of the talking, but when Julia chimed in, he seemed to listen, and that counted for something. In fact, when she was explaining to him how she thought Osamu Dazai's 1947 novel *The Setting Sun* anticipated the work of Percival Mendelssohn by half a century, he was looking at her intently, his eyes connected to her eyes, and as she heard herself talk, she began to realize that she really, *really* liked Teddy. Yeah, she and Julie teased him and made jokes about him behind his back, but that was just them being girls. There was nothing serious about it. Really, if there was one thing pointing to how she had felt about him this whole time, it was how pleased she was that he was so goofy, that there were these quirks and pretensions to make fun of. At least they were genuine.

The way they were sitting, it would have been so easy to lean forward and put her lips on his, to kiss him, to taste his mouth. She closed her eyes for a second, still talking, letting her voice operate separately from her, and in that instant, she saw the kiss clearly, felt the sensation of it, the slight flavor of beer on his tongue, the warmth of his breath.

Opening her eyes, she saw Teddy was still listening, still focused on her, but he hadn't noticed her momentary self-indulgence. If he had, then maybe what she had fantasized about would have happened, but since he hadn't, she had to let the moment pass. It wouldn't be fair to Julie if she made a move on Teddy. It would disrupt the whole dynamic of their group, and they couldn't all be friends in the same way again. Besides, it was presumptuous enough to imagine that he'd *want* Julia to kiss him. If she was wrong, if Teddy rejected her, the result would be even worse.

Letting a desire slip by without acting on it was not the same as quelling it, however, and the feelings began to fester. Pretty soon, it was a full-blown crush, and Julia couldn't stand it anymore. She decided to tell Julie. If she could get it out there, maybe it would be easier to deal with.

Not surprisingly, Julie already knew. "I mean, *duh*," she said. "You're always sticking up for him when I give him a hard time, and the way you tell me everything he said when I wasn't around, it was pretty obvious."

"How long have you known?"

"Practically from the first time he took us out to coffee. I suspected."

"How was it *I* didn't know?"

"I don't know. Love is blind, so I guess that means it can't see itself in the mirror."

When she heard why Julia hadn't made a move on Teddy, Julie laughed. "That's dumb, dude. You should've totally gone for it."

"You don't mind?"

"Of course not."

"But how do I even know he likes me?"

"He's a *guy*. You're totally cute. He *likes* you!"

"I don't know. If he doesn't, it would screw everything up."

Julie shook her head. "You're hopeless. Look, he and I are both sticking around over break. While you're gone, I'll find a way to ask him. By the time the next semester starts, you'll know. And I guarantee you'll have a boyfriend."

Returning home, Julia thought of this plan between herself and her best friend as an extra-secret Christmas present, one she would save to open. Like when she was a little girl and she would hide candy in her room and not think about it until she forgot where she had hidden it, to be found at some later date, a sweet and pleasant surprise. So, too, was the answer to the riddle of her and Teddy. She wrapped it up and tucked it away. She didn't think about it on the train, and she didn't dare mention that she had made a male friend to her parents—making the time with Arturo all the more unbearable—this was something she wasn't going to share.

On the train ride back, she took the gift out of its hiding spot and held it in her lap, feeling it in her hands, tossing it from one palm to another, anxious to get back to the dorms and open it up.

When she got back and went to Julie's room, Julie wasn't there, only Julie's roommate. Julia had woken the girl up, and she stood naked behind the door, only peeking her head out a crack. Her hair was tied back with a waistband that had been cut off of sweatpants, and the air coming out of the room was stale and smelled like sweat and hummus. Julia was pretty sure that the blurry shape in the back shadows of the room was a man. "I'll let her know you came by," the roommate said before closing the door.

That was odd. She had e-mailed Julie the train times, so she knew when she'd be getting back. Why wasn't she there?

Back in her own room, Julia's own roommate was back. She was listening to Jars of Clay and singing along while unpacking her clothes. She took each article of clothing out of her suitcase, unfolded it, and then folded it again before putting it in the drawer. Julia watched her for about ten minutes, a slow process of removing, undoing, and redoing. She even did it with her socks. They had been balled together, one sock shoved into the other sock, and when she took them out, she pulled them apart and made a second ball for the closet.

It was maddening. Julia couldn't watch it anymore. The annoyance was only exacerbated, too, by her need to know the answer to the riddle. She knew she was jumping the gun a little, but she decided to call Teddy's house.

The phone rang three times before it was answered, and it was actually Julie on the other end. "Oh, there you are," Julia said. "I've been looking for you. Did you forget I was coming?"

There was a pause. "Um...no?"

"Don't tell me you waited until the last day to complete your mission, Julie! You're a bad secret agent!"

Another pause. "Listen, now isn't a good time to talk about this."

Julia laughed. "Oh, okay. I get you."

But Julie didn't laugh back. She was playing it serious.

"How about I grab some snacks or something and come over?" Julia offered.

"Umm, no. I don't think that would be a good idea either."

This evasiveness was starting to worry Julia. "What's going on, Julie? Is everything okay?"

"Yeah, I'll just talk to you later. Okay?" Julie said before hanging up the phone.

Julia shrugged. It was odd, for sure, but she hadn't really considered there was anything to it. Not until she sat down on her bed and once again listened to her roommate singing under her breath did she even start to ponder the alternative explanations.

*

The window of Teddy's apartment could be seen from the street. Julia stood across from it and looked up. The lights weren't on, but the flickering glow of the television was visible. Were they watching a movie up there? Was it even them? It could be one of Teddy's roommates. She tried to concoct an excuse for her being there. When you show up at someone's place even though you've been told not to, it requires a certain kind of obliviousness. She could walk in and pretend she hadn't heard a thing Julie had said, or have some reason why she'd ignored it.

Then she saw Julie pass by the glass. She was wearing only a T-shirt, no pants—or at least that was how it looked from the ground. It was hard to tell.

Julia would have to step up her excuse-making.

Boredom was good. She would say she was bored, happy to be back from her trip, ready to re-establish some contact with real humans. It wasn't enough, though, so she walked back up the block and bought some microwave popcorn and soda from a convenience store before heading back.

Teddy lived in a secured building, but someone was always leaving the door propped open, stuffing paper in the lock so the latch couldn't catch, so Julia didn't have to ring up to be let in. If her suspicions were true, surprise was on her side.

She wouldn't have to knock. The apartment door was broken, the knob loose, and if you knew how to shake it right, it would actually open the door. It would be perfect if Julia had wanted to be a cat burglar. She'd go in right after she knocked, but she decided to give advance warning so that if they actually were in the *middle* of something, they could get out of it before Julia would have to see it.

Knock knock.

Julia opened the door in time to see a body dash out of the room, clutching its naked chest. She knew it was Julie, even if she hadn't seen the body's face. She could tell by the way Teddy was looking at her, the cartoon horror of his open mouth and wide eyes, as he got off the couch and grabbed a cushion to cover his exposed areas.

"I'm sorry," Teddy said, after a moment where they both stood frozen, afraid to move.

Why was he apologizing? He hadn't done anything, really. He didn't know.

"I mean," he stumbled, "Julie told me, and—well, one thing then another—"

Except he did know. He did.

Julia closed the door and left.

In the long run, what had surprised her more than the betrayal was how no one seemed interested in doing anything to fix it. Not even fix it, but to *explain* it. Julia didn't call either of them and immediately stopped attending the meetings of the Percival Mendelssohn Society, and it was like she had never been a part of any of it in the first place. Neither Teddy nor Julie ever picked up the phone or came to her dorm or did anything to find her. She had severely misjudged them. This whole thing was a clear indicator of how *they* viewed the friendship.

Julia saw both of them once or twice, randomly, spied across campus grounds. She'd be heading in one direction, to or away from class, and Julie or Teddy would be heading in the other. Funny, she never saw them together. They were always alone or with some new person she didn't know. Just like that, the trio was dissolved, and, more importantly, even though it was supposed to have been more solid, there was no bond between Julia and this other her, her Bizarro doppelganger. Lady Julie of the Funhouse Mirror was no longer her friend.

When Julia really stopped to think about it, it all made her feel uncommonly sad.

6.

That wasn't the story Julia had intended to tell Percy. It also wasn't as detailed when it came out of her mouth. He got more of the synopsis than the full rundown. Really, it was more of the beginning of what had led her here, and in the end, maybe it wasn't as important as the other things that were more directly related to her decision to find him. Still, she had to start somewhere if she was going to make him understand, and the story of her mishaps as part of his academic fan club seemed like an okay place to get the ball rolling.

Percy listened intently, and some of it, particularly the parts where opinions were given of his writing and Teddy's tattoo, even made him chuckle. "He did not," Percy laughed. "Did he?"

"He did."

"You have to imagine he got the ink where he did so he could show it off. You wonder how many times a day he unveils it and acts like the person he's showing is the 'special one.'"

Julia liked that Percy was letting the air out of Teddy's tires a little. It actually reminded her a bit of when Julie would do it, and it made her sad to think of the lost friend, but it also made her smile to think who it was that was taking her place. Even if only for a brief moment. Her chest swelled with an unparalleled excitement at engaging in a discussion with her hero. It was as if her torso were a helium balloon and his voice controlled the nozzle that filled her.

"Did no one ever mention that they found it ironic to be in a society for an author who advocated standing on one's own?" Percy asked.

"No."

"It's amazing how the flocking instinct takes over. I imagine that right now, somewhere in the world, people who are afraid of human contact are sitting in a dingy room drinking coffee and chain-smoking cigarettes, discussing exactly why they are afraid of each other."

Julia laughed. "Like political parties for anarchists."

"Then there are those who seek that which should not be sought."

This froze Julia. She knew what he meant, knew that he meant her. But then she also thought that was rather presumptuous of her. Sure, he had taken the time to speak with her, to listen to her idiotic story, but how much was he really there? Sometimes when he laughed, the way his eyes wandered off to a different point in the room, it almost looked like he wasn't really laughing at something funny in her tale, but was enjoying a private joke instead.

"You can respect that, though, can't you?" she asked. "Your books are all about searching, about accepting the consequences of the quest."

"True, true."

"Even your writing, the act of chasing down the things you did with words, many people didn't want you going after them, but you did, and you took your lumps."

If he had looked distant before, Percy seemed immediate now. His eyes narrowed, and there was no denying *whom* he was looking at.

"Is that what you'd call it? My 'lumps'?"

Julia swallowed hard. "I didn't mean—"

"No one ever means anything. We spend eternity trying to deny all meaning, only to find that it's inevitable."

"What is? Meaning? Or eternity?"

Without answering, Percy raised himself up, straightening his back and extending his neck like he was sniffing the air. He turned his head to look toward the front of the house. "He's home."

"What?"

"Val is here."

"I didn't hear anythi—"

"You'd better go. He shouldn't see you here."

"What? But this is your house?"

Percy was on his feet now. He grabbed her by the shoulders. She was surprised by his strength. He looked so frail, like his limbs could break if you snapped them with something as light as a rubber band, and yet he had her standing and was rushing her out the door.

"Quickly. Go through the library. He's going to head straight to the kitchen. We'll be in the clear."

His voice was panicked, so Julia didn't argue. A glance through the window of the library confirmed that Val really was home, he was over in the kitchen. How had Percy known? They couldn't hear the door from the back of the house. It was like he was attuned to the vibrations of the building, could sense how everyone moved within it. He had also known when she had entered his room, even though his back was turned.

Then again, she had also surprised him in the garden that previous night. Perhaps his perceptions were like she had suspected his attentions had been in the conversation: they came and went.

Returning to her room, Julia lay down on her little bed. Resting on her side, she hugged her knees to her chest. She felt the sheet on her cheek. It was flannel, but old, washed too many times. She could feel the little fabric pills that dotted its surface. When she saw cloth in a state like that, it always looked to her like the material was sweating. The flannel was still soft, but the bumps made it rough. It was both smooth and coarse at the same time—which was only fitting in this house. She had felt she was of two minds ever since she had walked through the door. The constant question of "Should I stay or should I go?" was not helping. The two men, so hard to read, alternately seemed okay with her being there, and then not—and with Val, it was really more like resignation.

This encounter with Percy today had been the same: she was elated that she had conversed with the man but scared she had screwed it up; impressed that he spoke in heavy sentences like the kind he wrote, but then not convinced he was any more clear on what he meant than she was; she had thought he had liked her, but then thought he found her rude and offensive.

Oh, who was she kidding? If a weird girl showed up on her doorstep and refused to go home, and then told her about some silly college soap opera, she'd think that girl was a complete whack-job. The best she could hope for was that Percy saw her as some naïve teenager who meant well. A pat on the head, a conciliatory smile, and ta ta, little girl, go back home to mommy and hope that your hair has finally returned to the length she thinks it should be. How stupid! This was like crushing on a professor or something! How many other girls would fall for Prof. Mendelssohn this semester? Like she could even hope to be unique. "Oh, Julia, your questions are so much more interesting than all the other young co-eds who hurl themselves at me!"

Yeah, right.

But dear God, that's what it was, wasn't it? Admit it, Julia. You have a crush on Percival Mendelssohn. Sure, there was always that dreamy element of how he posed in his photographs. Julie had said it. "He has flirty eyes," she said. "You know that half the time he doesn't mean it, too. You just have to figure out which half he does."

Now that she had seen him in person, though, it wasn't just swooning over a face on a dust jacket. Sure, he was more pale, skinnier, older than the last picture that had been taken of him, but when his eyes weren't looking away, there was still a pick-up line floating in there just waiting to be said. And when he did speak! Swoon! That voice of his was like sweet tea with just a hint of gravel, just a little rasp like the sugar was scraping against the bottom of the cup to add a manly flavor. He could say *anything*, it didn't have to be important.

Yet, it was important. Here she was, with the man she admired, whose mind she admired, and he was sharing with her. Why had she done so much gabbing herself? Meeting Percival Mendelssohn and monopolizing the conversation with stories about dorm life was like meeting Pavarotti and singing endless rounds of "I'm Henry the VIII, I Am." By the time she had shut up so that Percy could get down to the nitty-gritty of it, her time was up. He and Val were probably hatching a plan right then to get her out.

These thoughts—and others of the exact same stripe—did laps in Julia's head until she finally drifted off to sleep.

*

The encounter with her hero must have drained Julia more than she realized, as she slept all through the rest of the day and on into the wee hours of the next morning. She only awoke when she heard the sound of distant scratching, faint at first, but it invaded her dreams and became a part of them, an image that could be related were it not for the fact that Julia's memory of it dissipated the moment she rose. It was there when she first opened her eyes, but it was gone before she got to the door. That's where the scratching was coming from, and when she opened it, the aggressor whose claws were attacking the wood strolled in. Julia crouched down and pet little Lancelot, returning his scratching with some forceful scrapes under his chin. Lancelot closed his eye and reveled in her affection, purring in praise of her skills.

Julia reached to close the door as she was feeling like crawling back to her bed and curling up with the cat. Lancelot often came in, and he liked to slumber on the mattress next to her head. Julia was a restless sleeper who had always tossed and turned through most nights, but the positioning of her feline friend had a strange stilling effect. She managed to sleep each night while giving Lancelot his space.

That was not to be in this particular instance, however, for as she shut the door, she saw there was something else waiting for her just outside it. A book. It had a blue cover with the silhouette of a woman wearing a bowler hat. Julia slid it across the floor. She rubbed her hands over the dust jacket, felt the slickness of the paper, the embossed figure of the woman being shinier and smoother than the rest. How had it got there?

Crawling on her hands and knees, Julia poked her head out the door. Up the hall, the library was closed. The other direction faded into darkness. She could see some light through the window, out into the courtyard, but it wasn't from anywhere else in the house, it was only the night sky, what the stars and the sliver of moon could give to them.

She lifted the book and clutched it to her chest, almost as if it were some illicit contraband and someone (Val, probably) could come along and snatch it from her. It felt like a secret. Closing the door meant it would be hers.

Sitting on the bed, she looked at the cover again. Milan Kundera's *The Unbearable Lightness of Being*. Lancelot was sitting on the floor cleaning himself, and Julia lifted the book so he could see. He was already in on the secret after all, but he didn't seem to care. "Did you bring this?" she asked, but he did not answer.

Cracking the cover, she found a postcard inside. Audrey Hepburn standing on a street corner. She wore sensible pumps and a black dress that went down just past her knees. Her hair was short, done up in small buns on the side, a slight part to her bangs. She was standing in profile, sort of hugging herself, her hands crossed just under her breasts. Audrey had a sweet smile on her face. Julia turned the card over, and there was writing on the other side. "*You were standing like this when I first saw you*," it said. "*Read this book. It's full of wonderful ideas.*"

The card wasn't signed, but she recognized the handwriting. In all of Percy's books, the dedication pages were written in his scrawl, so most of his fans could recognize something done by his own hand. Her favorite dedication was in *One*. She didn't care if it was a little obvious. "*For Iris, the only.*" It was so romantic. If Julia ever wrote a book herself, it would only be so she could compose a similar epigram for someone she loved.

Percy wanted her to read *The Unbearable Lightness of Being*. She had seen the movie and liked it, but it probably wasn't the same, it never was. Not that it mattered, she would never have dreamed of trying to fake it and talk to him about the story having only seen the film. Percy wanted *her* to read it. That was huge! He had picked it for her.

Julia propped her pillow against the wall, leaned back against it, and started to read....

*

The beginning of the novel threw Julia off. It started with profound thoughts about the novel's central question regarding how its characters would live—is it better to be heavy or light? Should we accept the encumbrance of mortality, and by accepting, rise above our station, or should we seek to deny all bonds? And how would such a decision affect our connection to the people around us?

A little of the way in, though, the book shifted fully into the story, and it became evident that the first couple of chapters were just the authorial voice—which was in itself a character, almost a participant in the narrative—setting the scene for its drama, creating the backdrop for the unfolding events to lean against. Once Julia hit that spot, she was immediately sucked into the story of Tomas and Tereza and she remembered the woman in the bowler hat, the one on the cover. She was in the movie: Sabina, Tomas' lover, the one who lives light, who teases the weight away from the others. (It should be noted that as soon as Julia made this judgment, she immediately wondered if it was correct. Was it so simple to cast Sabina as the transcendent figure and confine Tereza to the earthbound struggle, with Tomas torn between them? Given Tereza's serene sweetness and Sabina's sensible cynicism, it could also be argued the other way.)

The romance of the novel was the main draw. Tereza's unflagging love for one man, despite how he had a knack for destroying the ones who loved him—it was so tragic, so beautiful, and so true to what Julia understood of the heart. Tereza was almost like one of her beloved Jane Austen heroines transplanted to the 20th century and forced to contend with modern man.

On page forty-seven of the version Percy had given her, it became obvious to Julia why he had chosen the book. When Tomas and Tereza met for the first time, she gravitated to him because he sat and read a book in the bar where she worked. She saw books as an "emblem of the secret brotherhood." No one had ever read in her bar before, and it distinguished Tomas as someone who read rather than one of the many who did not. Tereza herself was reading Tolstoy, and so, too, had Julia when she first arrived!

Julia had come to Percy via books. Books were important.

Then there was also Tereza's brave decision to follow Tomas to Prague. He hadn't really made an invitation, he had just been friendly, but she took that leap and she went, all because she believed that she should.

Just as Julia had come to Beijing.

Julia's favorite line, by far, was in that same section. "*The crew of her soul rushed up to the deck of her body.*" What a great way to describe the sensation! She had felt the same way, first outside the door when she had initially confronted Percy, and then last night, when they had actually talked. How splendid to find them both now mirrored in fictional counterparts!

She fantasized that she was Tereza and Percy was Tomas, but then who did that make their Sabina?

*

The act of delivering the book to Julia had been a big step for Percy. Their talk in his bedroom had been tough for him. It wasn't that he didn't want to speak to her; on the contrary, it had made him realize how much he had missed conversing with people. As with all of his conflicting feelings since she had arrived, it was shocking to him to discover that regardless of how actively he had denied himself the pleasures of the outside world, it was extremely easy to slip back into the habit of enjoying them.

Toughest of all, though, was the act itself, was remembering what it was like to speak and to communicate. It was the basics, things like sentence structure, and the speed with which he processed what she said and then formulated a response. How he must have sounded to her! She was looking for him to be articulate, and here he was stuttering and stumbling like a victim of a massive head trauma.

Of course, some of the things she said made him bristle, too. He felt like a snail being poked with a stick, and he just wanted to retreat back into his shell. He supposed it was inevitable that some subjects would come up. The why of the situation would be what any normal person would want to know first.

And, of course, that was the problem. He wasn't normal. *This* wasn't normal. It had been hard enough to live up to his own image of who he should be. He was good at it from the start, but probably too good; he'd set the standard high. It had been seven years since anyone had last seen him, too, so the pressure was even higher. How could he be a man he no longer was?

What it boiled down to, though, was that he wanted to understand why she had come and have his own motivations understood by her in return. Otherwise they were at an impasse. He thought the Kundera book was a way to do that, to show her he got it and give her the tools to get it, too. Plus, he knew books. *Books* he could talk about.

So, Percy went to the library and found the book and tiptoed over to her door. He left it there for her, and then retreated. He saw his cat Lancelot watching, but he paid the tom no mind.

After his mission, once he was back in his room, Percy realized there was no going back now. The postcard in particular, that had sealed the deal. It had been harder to find than the book. He had boxes and boxes of them. Val always came home with more, postcards of all varieties—famous people of every kind, art, architecture, you name it. Percy had tried to keep them organized, but it had become a nearly impossible chore. He loved looking at them, though, loved each new acquisition. It was his version of mail, messages from the outside world, life captured on a sturdier stock.

The choice of Audrey Hepburn, it was terribly romantic, and it made Percy nervous. He was sending Julia a message, and he didn't know if it would come through—if any of it would. Why would she think this ridiculous man was flirting with her? It was an absurd notion. He even found it so. It couldn't be flattering. She was the first woman he had seen since 1999, so it wasn't like she had any competition.

Oh, God, the doubt...he had been with Iris so long, he had always been dismissive of these anxieties when he saw them in other people. And what of Iris? He could not forget about Iris. He had no right to expect anything like romance from this girl. That was not something he could indulge in. Such ideas were banished.

No, he would be polite to her while she was there, help her fulfill whatever quest she was on—again, it was absurd to assume she wanted anything from him but what she said, such a frightful old man!—and then have her go home.

When Percy emerged from his room again, he was now completely dressed. He wore khaki pants and a light blue Polo shirt, under which he wore a dark, long-sleeved T-shirt. Val did a double take when he stepped into the kitchen. "Percy, what's going on?"

Percy held out his arms in front of him and looked at his sleeves. He looked at the front of his shirt and the legs of his pants, as if he had to remind himself of what was happening because the sight of him in this outfit was so bizarre. "I have to be presentable," he answered truthfully. "We have a guest now, and it won't do for me to be wandering around here half naked."

For the time being, he was keeping it to himself that the signal had been sent that he was willing to engage in further interactions with her. The answer was accurate enough without that added tidbit.

"I suppose," Val said, "but I still say the more pleasant we make it for her, the harder it will be to get rid of her. I'm already formulating a plan for pulling up stakes as soon as we get her out the door."

Percy clucked his tongue. "But where will we go, Val? Do you realize I've lived here longer than any place other than the house I grew up in?"

"We knew it would happen sometime, Percival. Just because it took longer than we expected, we shouldn't let ourselves get complacent."

"I guess not," Percy said, looking down at his feet. His cheeks were flushed. He felt the heat in his face like a boy who had just been scolded.

"Have you thought about what it will be like if you are found? The explanations people will demand. You'll never get a moment's rest."

"I don't think Julia would do that to us."

"Don't be so sure. You can't forget what people are like. You haven't had any contact with another person in so long, I worry you'll be too easily charmed."

"I'm not."

"Good. I don't trust this girl, sir, and neither should you."

Percy nodded as if he agreed. Keeping the messages that were now starting to pass between himself and Julia a secret had definitely been the right way to go.

*

Julia found Percy out in the garden. He was filling bowls with food for the cats. The dishes were in various corners of the courtyard, and different cats went to each one. "Val usually does this," Percy said when he saw her. (He never really went in for traditional greetings, it seemed.) "It's quite clever, really. All the different bowls scattered around, it keeps them from fighting."

She immediately noticed that he was dressed. A full outfit and doing household chores? This wasn't the specter she had been confronted with over the preceding weeks. She thought better of acknowledging the change, though. Calling attention to it might cause Percy to retreat. Instead, she said, "I got the book."

"Good. I was a little worried Val might see it first and reshelve it."

Julia looked around. "Speaking of Val...?"

Percy now looked around, too, but more up at the open sky like he was scanning for a plane or a UFO. "Don't worry. I think he's doing laundry or something. We have a little time."

"Oh."

Sitting down on the rim of the empty fountain, Percy picked a stray weed and twisted the stalk around his finger. Its green fiber splintered, and he considered the new fronds it created. "Did you get much of it read?" he asked.

"Much? Are you kidding? I read the whole thing! Once I started, I couldn't stop."

Percy nodded, but didn't say anything, just kept pondering the grass. Taking a chance, Julia crossed to him and took a seat next to him. Being so close, her body began to tingle a little. She felt her breathing slow down. She was nervous.

"You know, there was that part early on, where Tomas and Tereza meet, and there are little coincidences that draw her to him, and the author tries to set the reader straight, that these aren't writerly tricks but the way life is structured—it reminded me of the introduction to *I Was Someone Dead*."

Percy smiled. "Really?"

"Later, too, the narrator—be it Kundera or someone else entirely, someone he invented—talks about them as characters in a novel. It was like how you wrote about there being no real importance to questioning fictional truth versus the truth of reality. You know, that there is no one perception of any given event."

"That's funny, because I was writing *I Was Someone Dead* in a sort of pocket. It had been sitting in my drawer for a while, and I picked it up again while I was taking a break from *The Other Side of the Street.* Coincidentally, I read *The Unbearable Lightness of Being* right after, and it just killed me."

"Really?"

"I felt like Kundera was doing everything I was endeavoring to do, only he did it first and he did it better. It was devastating. How could I compete?"

"I don't know. I doubt it would surprise you if I said I think you did all right."

Percy laughed. "Oh, I'm satisfied with it. It's all one fine thread, really. All of these things, they're connected. My editor, Zoë, and I talked about the book, and she remembered a story about F. Scott Fitzgerald and Gerald Murphy that reminded her of Franz in the novel, when he's trying to discern the difference between his life in books and his life in the real world, and the narrator says he has it kind of backwards. The life events he's been imagining have lost their pageantry in Franz's perception. He's given them more weight than what he does from day to day. Do you know who Gerald Murphy was?"

"No."

"Well, the most important fact about him was that he and his wife were kind of the inspiration for the Divers in *Tender is the Night.* So, history has supplanted his actual life with the one Fitzgerald created for him. In an ironic way, though, despite the rift Fitzgerald's novel caused between him and the Murphys, this kind of fame fit with how Gerald Murphy looked at the world. He told Fitzgerald that the world of invention, the elements he could make up and thus, alter, was more important to him than the events of life that actually happened, events that were inevitable and unchangeable. Fitzgerald was baffled by this because to him it sounded like some kind of dodge. Rather than deal with the harsh stuff, you duck down and let it fly over."

"That makes sense."

"Not to Murphy, and it's surprising that a writer, whose stock and trade is imagination, missed his point. The things that happen to us, how our lives play out, to Murphy these were static events. He accepted them, but in an almost medieval way. Fate was at work; it dictated how existence played out, and as a human, he was powerless to change it. Thus, all action was meaningless on its surface; only by imagining something beyond what was in front of his face could he divine meaning from it."

Julia thought about that for a moment. "Does that mean he was doing what you were talking about yesterday, that he was running from meaning?"

"In one way, sure. In another way, he was running to it, trying to jettison the meaningless so he could get to its opposite. It all depends on point of view, what a person chooses."

"To be heavy or light."

"Precisely."

"That's an amazing connection."

"You see what I mean by the thread? Three different writers at three different times all trying to break down the barrier of story. Not that I flatter myself into thinking I'm any more than the loosest knot in the line. I'm nothing if not an exercise in diminishing returns."

It was clear that he was kidding, at least insofar as she knew he was being wryly self-deprecating rather than dramatically so. Surprisingly, he was even smirking, so Julia let it slide.

"Isn't that religion, too, then? Stories recorded and passed from one generation to the next to explain why things happen the way they do."

"Perhaps. Or they are stories to get beyond what is mundane. What is Heaven but a place we've carved out for ourselves where we can live happily? Mortality doesn't seem so bad if there's an escape clause. You can always get out, always forget the pain and the regret and the mistakes that make life unbearable."

The next natural question for Julia to ask was, "Is that what this is, then? You've created your own Heaven on Earth to get away from the bad things that happened to you?" Not only did it seem like an inappropriate thing to ask, but it also seemed to be a question that answered itself. After all, she was here for the same reasons. She had come looking for him as her own means of escape. It made her think of how in the book Tereza's reasons for leaving her home and pursuing Tomas to Prague were boring ones because where she was coming from was boring. Julia's reasons were pretty boring, too. There was no great catalyst. It was the same in Percy's books. In *I Was Someone Dead*, he had created fictional lives that weren't overly saturated with drama, and yet his characters hurt all the same.

It was ironic then that Percy himself had experienced such great tragedy. What were the rest of them crying about? Look at what he had faced. It sucked for him, and she was sorry, and she wanted to tell him that. She wondered if anyone ever had.

Perhaps sensing that this could be the direction her thoughts were taking, Percy slapped his hands on his thighs and rose from the fountain. "I think I should be going," he said abruptly.

Julia protested. "Why? I've been enjoying this."

"Val can only get up to whatever Val gets up to for so long. It'll be easier if we call it a night now."

He began to walk away from her, then he stopped, hesitated. She thought he would turn, and it was a good hunch, as he was thinking of doing so, but then fear got the better of him and Percy went inside.

---

g.

The first time Iris let Percy know he could have sex with her was on their debut Valentine's Day. Percy organized a romantic evening at the university where his father worked. There was a patio area in the Literature department that wasn't being used, and so his father gave him access, allowing for an outdoor, candlelit dinner three stories off the ground and that much closer to the stars. He picked up the food from a fancy restaurant and had it there with flowers and chocolates for when they arrived. Iris was blown away. She didn't think boys did stuff like that anymore, and she thought it must have been particularly tough for someone who couldn't even drive yet.

Keith Mendelssohn left them unchaperoned for the night, and he gave Percy cab fare to take both of them home. He didn't want to hover around his son's romantic evening—though, he instructed the boy that if his mother asked, Dad was just down in his office reading through submissions for the literary magazine he edited. It wasn't a foregone conclusion that Gwendolyn wouldn't approve, but why risk it?

Percy pulled out all the stops, serving Iris himself, playing a special Depeche Mode mix tape of all the band's romantic songs on his small cassette player, toasting her with sparkling grape juice. "I am tempted to make a pun on your name, saying this blonde Iris is truly the delicious, golden apple of my eye."

For her part, Iris didn't bring him any fancy presents. Instead, she had a simple card. It was a crème-colored paper with "You're Invited" inscribed in gold, cursive letters on the cover. Inside, she had written in her own flowery hand, "...to any part of me—or all of me—as you wish."

When he read it, Percy blushed. It made him nervous, and his chest fluttered. But when he looked up from the card, and across the flickering candles at his true love, she was smiling at him, and it reassured him.

"Don't you think it's too soon?" he asked. "I thought most girls wanted to wait until marriage."

"It's not, and I'm not most girls."

"Wow."

"I want to be yours, Percy."

"We're kind of young."

"Since when is something that we know is right limited by age?"

"But what if I'm not ready?"

"Then you're not ready. There's no expiration date on the card, Percy. I just think there's no need to wait to go someplace we're going to end up eventually anyway."

They did wait, however. Percy wasn't sure it was a step he could handle. Truth was, he wasn't really talking about most girls when he was talking about waiting until marriage, he was talking about himself. Those damned stories were too ingrained in his head. He was scared of what would happen if he gave his purity, even if it was to someone he cared as much about as he did Iris.

Percy really enjoyed kissing her, though, and he wanted to kiss her all the time. And the more he kissed her, the more he wanted to move beyond her lips, beyond the explorations of the other parts of her face and her neck, more than the chivalric kisses on the back of her hand. He liked the feel of her skin, the taste of her tongue, the feeling of being connected in such a way that no one could ever pry them apart.

It confused him.

Part of him thought maybe he was being tested. The knights were always challenged. Was Iris there for him to prove his mettle, to show he had the courage of his convictions? As he later wrote, "*A muscle man can't say he is strong without lifting a weight or two to prove it; a man of virtue must be faced with sinful temptations before he can claim to be pure.*" (This personal struggle would become the center of his first published essay, "A Question of Lust," published in *New Thought*, a philosophy journal run by one of Keith Mendelssohn's friends. The title was a nod to the couple's beloved Depeche Mode.)

The logic of it irked him. He didn't like a system that suggested Iris was anything other than good. To accept that set-up was to cast a dark light on someone who burned brightly, to make negative a person who only added positivity to his life. That didn't seem right to him. These old stories that his mother had taught him, and the religion that provided the characters with their belief system, they were meant to be metaphors, to be guides. Sir Percival remained a virgin so he could quest for the Grail, for a holy object of purpose. There was no such object for little Percival Mendelssohn to quest for, so maybe his application of the lessons was too literal. He had only been required to avoid other girls so that he could give himself to the one girl, to Iris. It would be her first time, too, a mutual surrender.

That surrender finally came, like so many other teenagers, at the junior prom.

As per their usual course of action, Iris and Percy decided to put their own spin on the night. Rather than just go in the standard attire, they decided to go with a Jazz Age theme. Percy wore a tuxedo with long tails and a bow tie, and he slicked his hair back with a shinier pomade.

Iris wore a beaded flapper dress, the material a champagne pink. Her long hair was tucked up under a platinum-blonde wig, cut in a bob, and she had a headband, shoes, and long gloves that ran up to her elbows that matched her dress. Seeing her walk through his door was a revelation. Percy's body reacted in every romantic cliché it could imagine. He became shallow of breath, felt perspiration on his brow, developed nervous flutters in his stomach, and when he tried to speak, he stammered. "Y-you're beautiful," he told her.

Iris curtsied. "Thank you."

What had transpired when he had opened that door to invite her in? She had come to him, rather than he go to her, but in keeping with the mythology, he imagined that he had experienced what Sir Percival and the others must have experienced upon recovering the Grail, upon seeing the glowing spear of Joseph of Arimathea above their heads, when the angels descended in the court of the Maimed King. Percy almost didn't dare to think it, but he did: Iris was metaphor made flesh, an ideal that breathed.

He knew then that he couldn't carry on avoiding the question of sex, he would have to act, now probably sooner than later. As he would ultimately posit in his work, "*Is not the act of marriage really one of making a commitment forever? If so, then it must be that the promise is the thing, and not how one does it; once you know, the rest is superfluous. There is no stronger bond than the one you solidify in your own being, and unless you can tell yourself that you are in it for good, no man or institution can make it work for you.*"

And he did know. Percy never wanted to leave Iris. He wanted to be connected to her forever.

The prom was held on the *Queen Mary*, docked in Long Beach, California. Since Percy and Lance were both juniors, they double-dated. Lance took a girl named Laine, whom Percy found a little tedious. She was tanned and bubbly and he didn't find her at all bright, yet he couldn't deny she was attractive. He noticed she had nice breasts, small but firm, pear-shaped; her nipples had been activated by the air conditioning of their rented limo, and Percy couldn't help but focus his attention on her.

"That's a lovely dress, Laine," he said. It was black, cut across her chest, with a knotted, white ribbon over her cleavage. He gestured in its direction. "What would happen if someone tugged on your bow?"

"It would come undone," Laine giggled, "and then the whole thing would fall off."

"That would give us the answer to what you're wearing underneath."

Laine winked at him. "Oh, yeah? Who asked the question?"

Percy saw that his brother had noticed the flirt, and he saw Lance share a look with Iris, who seemed to be ignoring the whole thing. It was an odd sort of voyeurism. Percy was seeing the others see him, and it knocked the boy out of himself. It had been less than an hour since he had mentally given himself to Iris for the rest of their lives, and he was already contemplating forbidden fruit. Something had been uncorked inside him. He was a sexual creature now. No wonder religious leaders were always so scared of it. Sex was electric, dangerous, and controlling it one of man's greatest challenges.

There was no more outside flirting that night. Percy immediately returned his focus to Iris, and it never wavered. They danced together all night, lost in one another's embrace. It didn't matter what the music was, or if it was fast or slow. Percy couldn't even say what any of the songs were. Their arms were entwined, their fingers interlaced, their eyes locked.

"Do you know I love you?" Percy asked her.

"Of course," she replied, "but I never get tired of hearing you say it."

"I'm pretty sure you love me, too."

"It's the safest bet you're ever likely to make."

He took his hand from around her waist and lifted hers from off his shoulder. He kissed the underside of her wrist.

"You remember Valentine's Day?" he asked.

"Yes."

"I'm ready to redeem your offer."

Iris grinned, but then blushed, the smile turning shy. She glanced down at their feet, and then looked back up. "Really?"

Percy leaned in, pressed his nose against her cheek, kissed her softly. "Really."

Once the prom was over, the limo drove them all back home. Lance had lost his date over the course of the evening, and he was ready to be done with the whole thing. They had all been invited to an after-party, and Iris tried to get Lance to go along, but Percy was relieved when he turned her down. The plan wasn't to go to the party at all. Instead, they were going to Iris' house. She had no siblings, and her mother would be asleep, so it would be easier to sneak into her bedroom than it would be his.

At her place, Iris went in first, just in case someone was around. Percy entered her back yard through the side gate and went to her window. The night was slightly cold, but clear. The neighborhood was quiet, the houses all around them shut down until morning. Percy rooted around his mind for doubt, but he found nothing. He wanted this. He was ready.

A small light came on in Iris' window. She appeared at the glass and slid it open. "Mom's asleep," she whispered. "Come on up."

Conveniently, the gas meter was under the window, and Percy was able to step up on it to boost himself into the room. As he climbed into the frame, he saw that the light was from three votive candles on her dresser. A framed picture of the two of them was behind it. They were smiling at each other, a candid moment captured at some family gathering or other. The two of them in love, frozen, the image of forever he had desired.

Iris had taken off her wig and headband. Her shoes were lying lopsided on the floor by her stockinged feet. Once Percy was all the way inside, she approached him coyly. She placed a gloved finger in his mouth, and whispered, "Bite." He felt the cloth in his teeth, and she backed away from him, the glove sliding off of her hand and hanging there from his lips.

*

Of course, any of Percival Mendelssohn's fans who read "A Question of Lust" or the troubles of his nameless hero in his debut novel *One* know that his resolve didn't last. Wherever doubt had run off to on prom night, it came stumbling home the next morning, arm in arm with regret. For as much as the night had gained him, Percy would never be sure how to assess what he may have lost. He wanted a moral certitude, some kind of assurance that his choices were unimpeachable—much of his writing would be about that very thing, both in his theoretical musings and his allegorical literature—but when it came to the complicated world of emotion, that was impossible.

Part of the problem was how much Percy enjoyed sex. He hadn't really expected it to be as remarkable as other people made it out to be, and the fact that it was made him feel a little guilty; feeling good is an integral part of any sin. Even more, though, it made him feel betrayed. Why had his mother acted like it was so horrible? He was still young, sure, but maybe he could have enjoyed a relationship or two with girls before Iris, had experimented more, gotten a taste of what life was like before choosing one woman. That was probably what the flirting with Laine had been about in the limo. He hadn't really considered all the things there were to be tempted by. Percy wanted to know why he should deny himself any longer. He should fully rebel, toss himself into the world of women with lecherous abandon!

The only thing that was stopping him was Iris. He couldn't do that to Iris.

School wasn't the same after that. Things had changed inside of Percy, and it looked to him like the outside world could tell. In his calculus class, a girl named Megan who had never spoken to him before suddenly had something to say to him. "Hey, Percy, I saw you at the prom on Friday."

"You did?" he asked, wondering why she would have even noticed him. Unless it was to note that he was still a freak, in which case an insult was sure to follow.

Megan took her glasses off. Little freckles ran under her eyes and over the bridge of her nose. She had long, dark brown hair, pulled back in a bun, and she smelled fresh, like clean towels and perfume.

"Yeah, you looked like you were having a really good time. I wish my date would have danced with me the way you danced with that girl."

Percy swallowed hard. "Girlfriend," he said.

"What?"

"She's my girlfriend."

"So? What does that matter?"

"I don't know. Shouldn't it?"

"Not to me," Megan said, smiling. "Not if you wanted to ask me to dance."

She winked at him, the way Laine had, and then turned to face front. The teacher had come in. Megan had inserted a new question into Percy's internal debate, one that had likely already been there but that he tried to ignore.

Should it matter that Iris was his girlfriend? Or, to put a bigger word on it, his betrothed. Was there any room to move around in that distinction at all?

Percy tried to tell himself that he had always liked girls, had always been friends with them, they understood him better than boys—should that end now that he was in a relationship? He didn't think so, that didn't make sense. Fidelity meant the body. His body was Iris', because it was with everything else that he communicated with the world. That was personality. Personality can't be tied down.

These ideas weren't something Percy was ready to test immediately. It would be some time before thought was put into action. He was beginning "A Question of Lust," and once that was completed, a flurry of literary activity was to follow. He would follow that essay with several more, beginning the groundwork for his philosophical thought. Beyond questions of love and sex, he was fascinated by the core idea of metaphor versus reality, where the stories written to guide and teach stopped being object lessons and became actual modes of being. Religious parables and the Arthurian legends were just his starting point. He also began to reach out to more recent pop culture, to find modern connections to old ideas.

Which was exactly the sort of early criticism he received from many academics, that his ideas weren't anything new, he was just echoing many who had gone before, particularly Kierkegaard and Camus. Supporters saw that as positive, though, a way to put a new face on old philosophy and attract a fresh group of thinkers. It certainly wasn't one of the more popular disciplines amongst young people, so a new canon of references might invigorate the scene, someone like Percival Mendelssohn who was just as at home with pop music and James Dean as he was with Baudelaire and Nietzsche.

Others scoffed that Percy was just a boy and that his writing showed it. The prose was shallow and adolescent. The flip side was that if he was this advanced at his age, then a lifetime of new thoughts lay down the road.

Percy met his first minor controversy with an article he published in a liberal theological journal, *Progressive Pilgrim*. Entitled "Past Imperfect," his thesis was surprisingly simple: "*The wisdom of the ages is that God is perfect and man a flawed reflection of Him; however, if one really looks at the relationship between humanity and divinity, he might find this thinking is backwards. God is unchanging, consistent, stuck; man is mutable, adaptable, finite. And does not he who burns the briefest burn brightest? As people, we are able to change, to learn, and to grow. We are told anything is possible for us, and we believe it, and so we strive, we still have things to achieve. According to theologians, this is where humanity fails, where we fall short of the glory of God. This way of thinking is paradoxical; the acceptance of it as truth is the real barrier between ourselves and divinity. The essential element of living that hedonists and libertines have so readily grasped is the one thing that eludes religious believers: free will. Our ability to choose is God's most precious gift, as evidenced in Him bestowing on us the one thing He does not have. What kind of being sets out to create something lower than he is? The act of creation is to try to master something, to better the idea. God didn't set out to make a pale imitation of Himself when He created Adam and Eve; instead, He established us as a race that could surpass Him by giving us the room to roam.*"

For Percy, the evidence was in the central question of Christianity: do you or do you not believe in Jesus Christ as your savior? "*If choice isn't our most essential trait, then why were we not born a race that automatically believes in one God without fail? Instead, we have many gods, and we must meet them individually.*" In order to support his claims, Percy cited several Bible stories. The most obvious was one that also captivated his existential predecessors: the story of Abraham being asked to sacrifice Isaac. Abraham was confronted with a choice, asked to examine his doubts, and when he overcame them, he was rewarded. "*Blind faith is not never asking 'why?' Blind faith is asking 'why?' and going forward despite seeing the situation is absurd, giving yourself up to the idea that there is something more to be gleaned from your ridiculous reality.*"

More important to Percy was the one story he felt "*modern Christianity is afraid to attach meaning to*," and that's the story of Christ himself. He suggested that the real existence of a man named Jesus Christ was "irrelevant," that the overriding metaphor of Christ's story was its main reason for being told. God turned His son into a human being in order to teach the humans by his example. Christ embraced the imperfection of humanity, and his journeys on Earth illustrated the ability of the individual to transcend via personal life choices. By resisting the temptations of the Devil and questioning his forthcoming death in the Garden of Gethsemane but ultimately choosing to believe that he would come out the other side as a greater being, Christ reinforced the gift of free will. "*This is why Jesus has taken the lead position in faith, why believers accept him rather than his father into their hearts. The real choice is humanity.*

When we choose Jesus, we choose ourselves."

Many of the readers of *Progressive Pilgrim* were offended by Percy's reversal, and a healthy debate began in the magazine's letters column. Had the discussion remained there, it likely would have faded, but the article began to circulate, and Christian leaders who normally wouldn't even glance at the tiny liberal journal were now decrying it from their pulpits. Articles in more conservative magazines punched back at what one writer referred to as "this blasphemous upstart who seeks to put himself up on the cross in hopes of confirming he's as intelligent as he (falsely) thinks he is." Some ministers spoke out against "Past Imperfect" in their local papers, which lead to bigger papers and the wire services, and before he knew it, Percy was at the center of a snowstorm of words.

At the time, he was sixteen, a fresh driver's license in his hand, and attending his first year of college. He had his pick of schools when he graduated high school, and he settled on a small liberal arts college in Maine. As it was his first time living anywhere but home, he wanted to get as far away as he possibly could, and so he chose a university on the opposite tip of the country, a place where he could be a big fish in a small pond. Plus, Iris was planning to attend Wellesley in two years since it was the same school her mother had attended. This would eventually put them close together. There was nothing Percy could do about graduating ahead of her, so rather than ask her to give up her goals, he would just maneuver it so he would be waiting for her.

When the tempest finally hit Percy's teapot, he was amused. He had already moved on from "Past Imperfect," and he was more interested in the idea of putting his ideas into fiction. He wanted to stop explaining other people's metaphors and began to work on creating some of his own. He had written a story called "Deep End," about a man contemplating his own suicide. His goal was to capture the emotions raw, to create the palpable sense of despair that would lead a person to take his own life. He had spoken about suicide in a theoretical sense in some of his essays, enamored as he was of Camus' position that the only real action of 20th century man was to kill oneself. Percy had sought to dispel the misconception that Camus had been advocating suicide in a real sense, as opposed to a symbolic rebellion to eradicate the body. He found that by being in agreement with the theory, his own attempts to unravel it were automatically misconstrued, as well. Ideally, "Deep End" would lead to a greater discussion about the philosophical impact of self-extermination. Percy felt that people were afraid to discuss it because they didn't understand it, and so by opening up the interior life of the suicidal, maybe he could break down those walls.

Perhaps partly fueled by the religious fervor surrounding Percy, his agent—one of his writing teachers—was able to place "Deep End" in *The New Yorker*, and it was published on March 15, 1993. This gave the religious right more reason to flog their latest whipping boy. Not only had he suggested that Jesus was irrelevant and man was better than God, but now he wanted everyone to commit suicide—none of which he had actually said, but that didn't matter. He was a cause célèbre, and people were now paying attention.

The school's faculty was excited to have a literary *enfant terrible* in their midst, so they circled around him, formed a protective barrier that the media had to go through. It was more attention than the university had ever received, and they knew attendance would assuredly go up. They wanted to keep Percival Mendelssohn happy, keep him writing, and, more importantly, keep him at their school.

It worked for a while. Percy began early drafts of *I Was Someone Dead* as well as more essays and short stories. Mainstream magazines were contacting him not just to be profiled, but to see if he would write articles for them. The obvious zenith of this mania for Percy was when *Rolling Stone* hired him to profile Depeche Mode on their summer Devotional Tour. He even managed to persuade them to fly Iris out so that she could travel with him and the band as they entertained the East Coast. He made frequent trips to New York, as well, to attend literary events and be wined and dined by publishers who wanted to sign his first book, whatever it turned out to be. He refused all offers, choosing instead to write the book in private, free of outside influence.

He enjoyed the attention, though. He liked being able to walk into a room knowing that everyone was going to turn around and look at him. That in itself wasn't new. Being the youngest person in all of his classes had always garnered stares, but they were usually judgmental. These people wanted him to be there. They were impressed to see Percival Mendelssohn in their midst. Percy imagined himself as a hero out of Fitzgerald, one of Waugh's bright young things, and it didn't take long before he started playing the part. He developed visual affectations, like wearing a long white scarf and carrying a cane. His status also allowed him entrance to a lot of situations someone his age normally would not have access to. Champagne was plenty, and Percy discovered he had a taste for it. He liked the bubbles, which he had only heard about in old movies when ditzy blondes would giggle at how they tickled their noses. Those ladies had not been lying. It made him feel like he could walk across the bottom of the ocean without having to worry about breathing.

Champagne on its own was fine, but it became dangerous when combined with one of the other enticements that was now available to him. Despite being forthcoming in publicity interviews that he had found the love of his life, for the women at these galas, if Iris was not there, she did not exist (and even if she was there, it was a toss-up as to whether it would have made a difference).

In fact, pretty women and alcohol had nearly the same effect. He remembered the winks from Laine and Megan, and how they had made his head feel light, and he realized they were identical sensations. A bull could possibly ignore a single red rag, but two? No chance!

Initially, the contact stayed at the parties. It wasn't uncommon to find Percy sitting at a table where he was the only man, surrounded by young socialites in cocktail dresses and pearls. They would hang on his every word, and he would trot out amusing anecdotes about his childhood, his brothers, the whole routine. Tristan was also starting to gain fame as a musician, so stories about his younger days were often very popular; even better for Percy, though, were the ones where he himself came off as the better. Easy laughs were always available with a detailed account of Tristan's morning regimen, for instance. Percy would exaggerate the length of time he spent on his hair, Tristan's head bowed over as he blow-dried his bangs from underneath, nearly half a jar of pomade dispatched to give his pompadour its lift. He'd tell them that Tristan would usually be brushing and fussing as he himself showered, and when he stepped out, he would run two hands over his wet hair, pushing it back, and it was instantly styled—much to his older brother's chagrin.

Percy could spend the whole of a night in the company of these young women. Then, when the champagne ran out, he'd excuse himself, giving each one a good-bye kiss on the cheek, and strut on his own down to his waiting car. He was the mysterious untouchable. Jay Gatsby is here to entertain, but only Daisy can share his company outside of the party.

That all changed when he met Anne Persson. She was a Swedish-born stage actress who had recently wowed critics in a mediocre play by the previous year's Pulitzer winner. As the former wunderkind fell from grace, eighteen-year-old Anne stepped from the ashes. At the time of their meeting, she was in rehearsals for a revival of Strindberg's *Miss Julie* that transplanted the 19th century European story to late-20th century New England. The industry wags were already promising her a Tony, and rumor had it that Disney was sniffing around to try to load her into a treacley remake of *Pollyanna* and that 20th Century Fox wanted her to be in a period Jane Austen adaptation—despite Anne consistently saying she did not want to be in the movies.

All of which was very impressive on paper, but it was nothing compared to how impressed Percy was to be in her presence. "It's like I've been looking at the cosmos through a telescope," he told her, "but now I am in a space capsule and I had no idea how magnificent it all would be close up."

The gossip columns would write of the meeting of Percival Mendelssohn and Anne Persson as though it were an inevitable collision of fate, the two youngest artists on the party scene in a union befitting their beauty and creativity.

That much-talked-about meeting was at a shindig thrown to celebrate the release of the season's biggest novel, the name of which has been forgotten, though every thrift store in the country has at least one copy on its shelves. Percy had staked out his usual position: a table in the back with a view of the door. He was surrounded, as always, by several young women: an assistant editor from Knopf, an alternative rocker who was touring her first solo record since splitting from her noisy band that was massively popular among college students, the daughter of a hotel magnate, and two others who avoided explaining who they were the way party crashers usually did. Percy was telling them about the wildly divergent paths of the Mitford sisters, and of how their stories all winnowed their way into Nancy Mitford's novels, which were some of his favorites, when Anne entered the room wearing a strapless red dress, her hair pulled up on the back of her head and a cigarette pinched between two gloved fingers. Her arrival stopped him in mid-sentence. He found it impossible not to stare, and he had to meet her immediately.

Abandoning his table, Percy did just that.

A panther fearlessly stalking the jungle, absolutely confident in the scent he was following, Percy crossed the room, brushing aside the crowd to get to Anne. Quickly surveying the situation, he said to her, "You don't have a drink."

"I do not," she said. "I've been waiting to see who would step forward to offer me one first."

Percy smiled. "Well, here I am."

Retrieving the cocktail in question was the last time that evening Percy would leave her side. They spent the rest of the soiree talking. Strindberg was an excellent entry point, as Percy had read many of his plays and enjoyed talking about them. They also shared a love of the theatre of the absurd, and Anne dreamed of doing Pirandello's *Henry IV* with the gender roles reversed. "We now have a fantasy in common," Percy said. "I'll never read that play again without seeing you in the role."

Anne took a sip of her drink. "It's refreshing to talk to you, Percy. So often, I come to these things, and it seems like no one has actually read anything that's older than last week."

"I know! They purport to be a literary crowd, but they have no idea. Their heads are full of this modern fiction, with its tricks and its eye on the bestseller list."

Tearing apart their fellow partygoers became another favorite topic of discussion between them, and they would have plenty of fodder over the coming weeks as the pair was practically inseparable. Word of Percy's new friendship made its way back to California, but over that distance, it had grown to a full-blown affair. Iris called him, sobbing. "Why, Percy? You told me you'd wait."

"I did," he insisted. "You've got it all wrong. This tabloid stuff, it's not true. We're just friends."

"I want to believe you."

"Well, you should."

Iris took his word for it. It was all she could do. She had confronted him with the rumor, and he had explained it, and she thought it would be unfair to ask for his side of the story if she wasn't prepared to give him the benefit of the doubt.

What she didn't count on was Anne having other ideas. On the night *Miss Julie* was to open, she summoned Percy to her dressing room. She was wearing a silk bathrobe, untied, with nothing but her violet panties underneath. Percy was shocked by the sight. Her body was beautiful, curvy, porcelain. Anne had ample breasts shaped like fine fruit. Her navel was deep, and its darkness was drawing him in, beckoning him to find out what was hiding inside.

"Anne, what are you doing?"

She held out her arms to him. "Percy, I need you. I'm so nervous, I need you to hold me, to love me."

"I can't," Percy said. "I'm practically engaged, I—"

"Oh, don't talk about your Iris! Isn't it time we stopped playing around, Percy? We both want this."

"I don't."

"You're lying. Tell me you're not."

Anne had moved close to him now. She wasn't touching him, but a weak breeze could have easily pushed their bodies together. He could smell her perfume and the scent of that devil champagne on her breath.

"Tell me," she demanded.

He looked at his feet, but when he did, he couldn't help but see her panties and the soft bump of hair that lay inside, pressing against the silk. He turned his head to the side, away from her. "I can't," he whispered.

"You can't tell me you're lying?"

"No," he said, still not looking at her. "I can't do any of this, Anne. I can't."

Percy left the room without turning back.

But there was no turning back from what had happened, either. The loss of Anne Persson's friendship was as devastating as any love affair would have been. He missed her terribly, and he cried the entire car trip back to Maine. He enjoyed the company of women, he really did. As long as he went no further than spending his time with them, he was fine. There would be no betrayal of Iris. He tried to return to just the short-term fawning of the many, but it wouldn't be long before he was once again enjoying a long-term affection of a singular woman. This time it was a young folk singer with kitty-cat glasses and dark hair. And once again there would be the same exaggerations in the gossip columns, the same tearful conversation with Iris, the same defense, until it was no longer defensible and he had to move on.

It was a pattern that would go on for the whole of their relationship, even after they were finally married when they both turned nineteen, in the summer of 1995. It was a pattern that, when Percy wrestled with it, he told himself he could not break, as if it were beyond his control, so that he could cover up the fact that he didn't really want to.

Still, back in 1993, these new relationships, this new sensation of stardom, and Percy's many jaunts to New York and beyond began to make him aware of what a rarefied world he was living in. The protection of his own pocket of academia was starting to grow stifling, and Percy felt his prose was losing some of its life. Even *I Was Someone Dead* was suffocating under the limited experience. It was growing stale for him, so he shelved it before its completion, turning instead to a new idea that was formulating in his brain, the story of a prodigy jazz pianist who rejects his privileged lifestyle to go to a sprawling, unnamed metropolis. He works as an office temp by day and trawls the music clubs at night, but he refuses to return to the keyboard before he finds something new, a more grand mode of expression.

It would be called *One.* And it couldn't be written inside a classroom. He would have to join the literary world full time, bathing in words and all the enticements that came with them.

7.

If Val suspected that Julia and Percy had been meeting and speaking, he was not showing it. From Julia's perspective, he was no more dismissive of her than usual. Usually when he saw her, he would wrinkle his nose and scrunch up his lips as if to say, "Oh, *you're* still here." As if he could ever forget.

But the two had been meeting since that discussion of Kundera, and they had been meeting often. Percy never did anything as direct as come to Julia's door and knock on it, but sometimes she'd find him loitering in one spot, out in the garden or the library. A faint smile would appear on his face when he saw her, almost like he was smiling in spite of himself, the naughty boy with a secret. "I was terrible at games where you had to pretend not to have done something," she once told him, referencing that smile without his realizing it.

"What do you mean?"

"Like, did you ever play Thumbs Up 7-Up? It's the game where all the kids in the class put their heads down on their desk, but one hand is out and they stick their thumbs up in the air. Then a couple of other kids who are it walk around the class and each puts one thumb down. If your thumb was put down, you had to then guess which person had done it. If you guessed right, you switched places. Whenever I was it, I always got found out because I'd get this stupid grin on my face and start to blush."

Percy didn't leave her any more books outside her door, but he seemed to always have a question waiting to ask her when she arrived.

"Have you ever seen *Hiroshima, Mon Amour*?"

"Did you read *Brighton Rock* by Graham Greene? The Pinky character reads to me like a prediction of the confused white male of the late 20th century."

"What's your favorite myth? Are there any that represent your inner desires?"

Not all of the questions were about books or art. Sometimes he wanted to know about her.

"Did you ever reach a point in life where you wanted to test God, and so you demanded He show you He was there?"

"Did you have pets growing up?"

"What's the earliest dream you can remember?"

Julia wondered if the questions were loaded or if he was simply trying to gather information about her. Were they picked specifically to tell her something? If she had index cards, she could write the questions on them and move the cards around on the floor and see if she could find the right order, the message Percy was trying to send. Of course, when he asked her, he would answer, too, so the question might not have always been about her response, but about what he wanted to reveal to her. Like, it may not have mattered what she thought of *Hiroshima, Mom Amour*, he wanted to make mention of the notion of telling a story by extracting two people from all surrounding life, making them representative, and then watching as the two ideas try to merge into one.

Once again, it could be about the two of them, and Julia initially felt that must be far too obvious to be true, but then Percy explained, "We have a rare thing here. We are able to talk completely absent of social convention. We need not worry how we look or sound to other people. It's just us."

"And Val."

"Val is the tragedy that threatens to tear us apart. All great stories must have that!"

On Percy's part, he was just excited to be talking to someone again.

Like a groundhog that had spent far too long digging underground not being able to find his way to the surface, now he had broken through, and he realized how much he had missed fresh air. He saw no shadow, the clouds had lifted, and he wanted to stay out in the light.

There was a problem, though, in that Val wasn't the only tragedy waiting to tear them apart. There was also Iris, and the tragedy that had brought Percy to Beijing. It would come on them in a flash, never staying out of the room for long, like a heat wave that came without warning and stifled all breath. Julia would say something she thought innocuous, like "I've always had a secret love for plaid skirts," and Percy's face would screw up and he'd excuse himself from the room.

Once she asked him, "So, what was the first thing you did when you got to China?"

"Shaved my head," he replied. "I was in mourning."

This was not her crime exclusively. Percy led them to that point as much as she did. In the discussion of dreams, for example, he told her about a dream he had when he was a teenager. "I had been a passive observer in my dream life when I was younger. I was a watcher, an outside force in my own fantasies. The surreal dramas would play out for me, and I was ineffectual to change them. Then one night I dreamt of visiting a house made entirely of bamboo, and it turned out to be a temple of some kind. The monks there were of all ages, and they were preparing for a ritual mass suicide. There was a girl who couldn't have been more than eight or nine, and she had a knife she was polishing for the act. I got enraged and I grabbed it from her, and I asked her, 'Do you think this is a joke? Is it funny? Ha ha!' while I mimed stabbing myself in the stomach. Only I slipped, and the blade slid into my gut. I seemed to be the only one surprised, though. No one else cared, and the shock of it woke me up. I found myself turned over and hunched on my knees, with my fists under me and pressing into my abdomen. The pressure had caused me very real pain. Even so, I felt like I had saved the girl, and from then on, my dream self stopped letting events go by without getting involved."

As he finished, there was a pause. Julia had no response, and maybe if she had, he'd not have gone to the dark place he did. Percy's face went pale, his eyes widened, his mouth fell open. He shivered a little as a very real chill ran through his body. Without saying a word, he rose and he left her.

It usually happened without warning like that, and so when they would talk, Julia would feel rushed, like she had to say as much as she could because at any moment a bell could go off and they'd be stopped, and she was afraid that at any time, it could be the last bell. She had to make it count.

There were some times, of course, where there was no bell. They would talk until the discussion ran its course, or other less weighty elements brought things to a close. One such night, when Julia had entered the courtyard, Percy was sitting on the ground playing with a few of his cats. For her part, she had met Lancelot in the hall and had carried him out with her. Julia sat down next to Percy and held Lancelot in her lap. She stroked him from skull to tail, and he held his head high in the air and purred loudly, an occasional stutter in his revving, a snort to catch his breath.

"You're amazing with him," Percy said.

"He's not so bad."

"Oh, no, he is. It's impressive how you've gotten him to be so calm. You've soothed the savage beast."

As if sensing he was being spoke of, Lancelot jumped off her lap. He started to walk away, but then turned back and looked at the others. Pendragon was nearest to him, and the black cat hissed and swatted his claws at the Siamese. Surprised by the sudden attack, Pendragon jumped backwards onto Percy and dug his claws into his master's thigh. It was a chain reaction of events, as Percy cried in pain and grabbed the Siamese and tossed him away from his body. Julia then sprung into action, slapping her hand down hard in front of Lancelot, sending the one-eyed misfit running. Morgan and Roland, who had also been hanging around, scattered off in different directions, too, leaving the two humans alone.

Julia leaned across to Percy and felt his leg. She didn't really think about it, it was a natural reflex. "I'm so sorry," she said. "Are you all right?"

"Yes." Percy had frozen. He had not been touched by another human being except Val in nearly eight years. It was almost paralyzing, both hot and cold, like someone had twinged the nerve of his funny bone and locked him up.

Julia took her hand away. "I guess I'm not so good with restless creatures after all."

"Well, I had misquoted the cliché," Percy said, trying to cover. "It's really 'soothes the savage breast.'"

"True."

Percy slid a little away from her, but then lay down on his back, looking up at the sky. He rested his hand behind his head. He could feel her close, his elbow was now bent so that it was almost touching her knee. If she moved a couple of inches, she could hit that funny bone for real this time. What effect might it have to strike it directly?

"It's a clear night," he told her. "You can see every star. Look."

He pointed with his free hand. Julia followed the direction of his finger. He was right. The sky was bright with stars.

"Do you know the constellations?" Percy asked.

"Not really. I always found them confusing," she replied.

"Lie down," he said. "Let me show you."

Julia repositioned herself and then reclined on her back. Her head was near the top of his, but their bodies speared away from each other, like their feet were magnets and the common polarity was pushing them apart. Or maybe they were the two arms of a drawing compass.

"Amusingly enough, we can see some of the feline constellations tonight."

"Really?"

"I can only kind of tell you where the Lynx is. It's named that not because it looks like a cat, but because when it was discovered, it was so faint that it was said you'd need the eyes of a lynx to see it."

Percy extended his hand again. "Follow the tip of my finger," he said. "There are four points. That star there, that's the bottom, up diagonally to the next, bend slightly to the next, then bend again. It's almost like a car antennae bowing in the wind. Though if we follow it over, as if it were forming an arch, we land on Castor, in the Gemini constellation."

His finger traced across the sky, and Julia followed it. She imagined that as he pointed to each star, it grew brighter, illuminated by Percy's touch.

"Of course, the Leo constellation is the other cat figure, the lion. We can't see the main one here, but if we cut straight across from the bottom of Lynx, we can see the tip of Leo Minor. It's like the Little Dipper of the lion duo."

Julia laughed. "Okay, this is going to sound so stupid, but is there anything you don't know?"

"Oh, a great many things." Percy chuckled in response. "The funny thing about trivial knowledge is you can trot out little tidbits when the time is right, and it masks the fact that you let all these other things pass because you had no idea what they were."

"I don't think it's all that trivial," Julia said.

She was still on her back, still staring at the night sky. Percy turned slightly, now propping himself up on that same elbow that had nearly touched her, the arm he had used as his astronomer's tool. He stared down at the young girl. Her brown skin looked soft in the celestial light, her dark eyes appeared bottomless. He looked at her nose, its slope a straight line; her lips a tender pink, parted slightly, the white of her teeth exposed.

"You don't, do you?" he asked, the question catching in his throat.

"No. The stars are important. How old are the stories about them? Man has relied on them since the beginning of time. They provide us with directions."

"And they predict our fate."

As he said it, Percy's voice dropped down to a whisper. He was moving, leaning over, leaning into her. His lips touched her lips, and she didn't recoil, didn't seem too surprised, but instead parted them more to open her mouth to let him in. The flesh of her lips was soft and conformed to the shape of him, feeling like they were extending over the top of his lips so as to hold him there. He touched her tongue with his, and it was warm. His whole body was warm. His body became like the galaxy floating in the sky above them, a million hot points, sparkles of light, spreading over his skin.

When Percy stopped kissing Julia, he held himself in position above her, looked down into her eyes. They were still dark, but they were not bottomless, they were right there, right with him. In his mind, he let his other self extend his arm and reach out to touch them they way one would touch the surface of a polished stone at the bottom of a flowing river. In turn, in real life, Julia reached up a very real hand and brushed her fingers over his forehead, sliding them into his bangs. Every follicle was on high alert, and he thought the hairs may snap off, a defense mechanism like a lizard dropping its tail. Only he didn't want to escape like the lizard would.

For the first time in a long time, even from before the beginning of his exile, Percy did not want to escape.

He lowered his head again and kissed the bridge of her nose, felt the center of her that rested beneath her eyes. Her skin was salty, but nourishing. Percy felt as if he had new strength.

Then he rolled back over, lay down diagonal from her once again, but this time he let the top of his head touch hers. He felt the silkiness of her hair against his face. Her hair was a dock, and as long as he was touching it, he was anchored in this ocean of life.

Neither of them spoke until the orange edges of the rising sun began to creep over the edge of the hutong. "There will be breakfast soon," Julia said then.

"I suppose there will be," he replied.

They both stood and walked to the doors back to their parts of the quadrangle. Percy paused before entering, and he turned back to see the girl he had just spent the night stargazing with. He was pleased to find that she was also looking back at him, wearing a small smile that he thought must be the mirror image of the one he could feel on his own face.

As the sun set that evening, Julia took one of the first flowers she had brought back to life in the house and placed it outside Percy's door. It was a simple corn cockle, but a Chinese variety with a small purple bloom. Its scent was slightly spicy, but its hue was splendid.

Julia saw the gesture as her trade for the way he had left her the Milan Kundera novel to read. It was her signal to him that it was her turn to take the next chance.

*

Val had gone out on another of his incessant Val errands. That morning, Julia had tested him with one of her many requests, just to see if she could suss out what he was up to. "I made a list," she said. "You have to take care of me. It's girl stuff."

When he saw the various feminine products she was requesting, he screwed up his face as if the paper gave off an offending odor. "You really can't do without these?" he asked.

"No."

"Because I wasn't really planning on going to a drugstore or anything like that."

"It'll only take you a second. Unless you'd prefer I go and get it all myself?"

This last taunt was especially delicious, given what Julia had planned.

"Never mind." Val sighed. "I'll take care of it."

Julia stayed in the kitchen after Val left, waiting to hear him open and close the outer doors. Once she was suitably convinced he was gone, she went and found Percy.

He was in his room. Julia knocked on the door, and then heard him tell her to "Come in." He was inside, dressed in what had become his standard uniform—the polo shirt with the long T underneath. He seemed pleased to see her. "You look like a woman with an agenda," he said.

"You're perceptive as always. I need to get out of here, Percy."

"What? You don't mean for good?"

"No, no. I just need new clothes. You've got to be sick of looking at this outfit almost as much as I'm sick of wearing it. I want some skirts, I want to let my legs out. Besides, if I wash this outfit one more time, I think it will disintegrate."

"Val won't get you any clothes?"

"No, he's not that nice, and I wouldn't trust him to pick them out anyway. And he won't let me go back to my dorm. He won't let me go outside at all."

"You're going to sneak out?"

"Yes. If I go, will you make sure I can get back in?"

"Of course."

"I'm hoping to get back before Val does, and then no harm, no foul."

Julia needed to play the next move just right. It had to be natural, had to appear spontaneous. If it had any whiff of forethought, it might scare him. She turned to go, but then paused at the door, resting her hand on the frame. She squeezed the wood, felt the hard surface under the smooth paint. It was cold. Pushing herself off of it, she hoped its strength and the kinetic energy of her rebound from it would give her what she needed to make the words come out the way she wanted.

"You wouldn't want to come with, would you?" she asked.

Percy raised his shoulders and leaned his head back. He looked puzzled. "Me?"

"Sure."

"I don't see how I possibly could."

"Why not?"

"That's...I'd be going outside."

"You won't burst into flames."

"But I'd be on the street."

"I know. You don't have to go if you don't want to. I was just thinking if I was sneaking out, maybe you could sneak out."

"What if someone sees me?"

"I don't know. What are the odds, really? It's been a long time, and we're in China. Who's lurking out there?"

Percy paused, thought over what she had said. "I suppose it is presumptuous...."

"We can even give you a disguise. Sunglasses and a floppy hat, whatever is around."

Though he wasn't willing to commit completely at that point, Percy was willing to let Julia give the disguise angle a try. They broke into Val's room, a closet almost as small as Julia's. A plastic bin under his bed housed various clothing accessories. The required sunglasses were there, though not big and round and dark like most celebrities trying to conspicuously blend in would wear; rather, they were small, rectangular lenses with red tints. There was also no floppy hat, but Julia selected a black ski cap. She pulled it down over Percy's skull, and adjusted it, tucking his bangs back up under the rim of it, pulling out chunks of hair on the side so that he looked just so. She cupped his chin in her hand. "Look at me," she instructed.

He looked at her straight on, his eyes trained on her eyes a second before she scanned the whole picture. Her tongue was slightly out of her mouth, her eyes narrowed. She lightly flicked at the hair on his left side, pushing it back a little off his cheek. Then she reached around and feathered the hair hanging over his neck, loosening it up. Percy watched her every move. He could feel her breathing, could smell her toothpaste and a faint whisper of the coffee she'd had at breakfast.

"There, I think that looks good," she declared.

"Can I see?"

"What for? You're not one to judge."

Percy mocked offense, and Julia laughed. "I'm just kidding," she said. "In a sec'. First things first."

Taking the sunglasses in both hands, holding them by the arms, she slid them back over his ears, settling them on his nose.

"There. Now you can look."

A small mirror hung on the wall over Val's dresser. Percy went over and looked at himself. Julia followed, peering over his shoulder at her handiwork.

"My goodness, do I really look like that?"

"Yeah, I'm not sure the skull cap thing is for you."

"No, I mean, do I look so old? Look at those lines separating my cheeks and my mouth. I didn't have those before. I look like a puma gone to seed."

"Nonsense. You don't. It's the stupid sunglasses. You're a very handsome man, just more distinguished by life than the last time anyone saw you."

"Distinguished means old."

Julia slapped his shoulder. "Quiet. Look at the disguise. Is it good enough?"

"It certainly doesn't look like what I'd wear."

"Does that mean you'll go?" Julia was grinning. "Come on. You gotta."

"I'm still not sure."

"An old guy would stay, but a young guy would come with me."

Percy began a huffy exhale, but it turned into a laugh. He could see his cheeks flush red in the mirror, feel the heat of the embarrassment. He couldn't believe how easily that logic worked on him. "Fine," he said. "I'll go."

"Yay!" Julia squealed, and she threw her arms around his neck.

*

Nothing earth-shattering happened when Percy stepped outside the door. Neither in a literal sense, nor in a metaphorical one. The way was open, he moved through it, and he was out of the Chinese house for the first time since 1999.

"See? Wasn't that easy?" Julia asked.

Percy turned his face to the sky. It was really no different than the patch of sky he saw from his courtyard, and even here there was the front of his house and the tall building opposite to create a different kind of box for him to peer through. Plus, he had on Val's hideous glasses, and their lenses cast a crimson glow over everything. He felt as if he was viewing life the way one does an eclipse: the true power was removed by several protective filters.

They walked out to the street with their arms hooked around one another. Percy practically leaned on Julia the way a blind man would. Or maybe like someone who had been strapped down in a hospital bed for so long, his muscles had atrophied and he was having to rebuild his stabilizers from scratch.

No, the earth had not shattered, but it was definitely having an effect on the man.

Striding on jellied legs, Percy allowed Julia to lead him down the alleyway to the street. The siheyuan came to its end, and the building that overshadowed it gave way to the skyline of Beijing. There were barriers behind him, but the road was clear in front, to the left, to the right....

It would be a mischaracterization to say that this did the trick, to see the horizon going on forever, over the rooftops of China, distant clouds across Asia, to Europe, to oceans and America and family and home. While Percy still had the imagination to project himself and fly over all that distance, he wasn't yet ready to do so, not even in his mind's eye. Instead, it was more like the hospital bed again. Now that he was awake and the IVs had been removed and he was standing, Percy, who had been sick for so long, could not help but stretch. He no longer leaned on Julia. He reached his hands toward the sky above him. It wasn't a perfect blue, but if he could have, he'd have stretched himself far enough and swatted aside some of the smog to see the cerulean canopy in full.

Taking a deep breath, Percy looked at Julia. "I'm afraid I don't know where anything is," he said. "I only have your word to go on that I'm even in Beijing."

"I think you can trust me on that." Julia gave him a wink. "Don't worry, I know a market near here. It's not far."

Instead of hooking their arms again, Julia reached down and took Percy's hand, wrapping her fingers around his. With a gentle tug, she steered him to the left and up the street.

Small red taxis whizzed by them and honked their horns. Men and women pedaled by on bicycles. An old gentlemen had a giant metal barrel on wheels, and smoke rose out of a chicken-wire grating strung across the top. Percy took a sniff. "Are those sweet potatoes in there?" he asked.

"Yeah," Julia replied. "Chinese children chow on yams like candy. You want one?"

"No, I don't think so. It smells delicious, though."

"Is this freaking you out?"

"A little. Not in a scary sense, though. It's just strange, how familiar the sensations are. The noise, the sights—I'd say smells, but the sweet potato, that's uncommon for me."

"I'm sure we can find some roasted nuts. It'll be just like you're back in New York!"

The market was only a few blocks away from Percy's home. Another jog to the left, then a cross over to the right, and there between two unassuming buildings was a ramp going underground. From the street, passersby could see an eating area at the bottom of it—fiberglass tables and little stalls with brightly painted signs advertising the food they had to sell. "This is just the entrance," Julia assured him. "What we're looking for is down below."

Once they entered the food court, Percy's nose was assaulted by the smell. He wasn't ready for so many fragrances at once. There were plenty of spices in the air, but also a smell like cabbage, like rotting. There was meat cooking and buns baking. And beyond the smell, more physical in its assertion, was the sound of the talking, of the chatter. At first Percy recoiled from it, and he reflexively turned away, but Julia gripped his hand tighter and nudged his shoulder with her forehead. It was the perfect gesture, because it reminded him why they were there. They had come to the market for her, to buy her clothes. He had come with her on her shopping trip because he had wanted to. He wanted to do it for her, he wanted to *be* with her.

The actual market was through a corridor on the other end of the food court. The underground complex housed small individual stalls where sellers of various wares set up. It reminded Percy of swap meets back in America, but organized more like little shops with genuine product instead of just being a random selection of people renting out tables to sell old junk from their garage. The air down there was cold and musty.

Julia walked at a medium speed past the tables, slow enough to look but not so slow she could get nailed down by a salesperson. Some still tried. Percy noticed shoe sellers were particularly forceful, holding out gaudy pumps and saying, "Try on?" Some merchants ignored the two of them altogether, not wanting anything to do with the visiting foreigners.

There wasn't really any rhyme or reason to the layout of the market. A stall selling knock-off luggage was next to one selling cheap plastic toys, and one over from that was a man with all manner of radio and music-playing devices. Julia stopped at one booth that had books and magazines and little trinkets. She picked up a comic book with a blue cover. It had a picture of a blob of a white rabbit with a plunger stuck to the top of its head. "Have you ever seen this?" she asked.

Percy shook his head. "No."

"MashiMaro," Julia explained. "Say it out loud. 'MashiMaro.' It's like a variation on marshmallow. It's really weird."

She handed him the comic, and Percy flipped through it. MashiMaro got into a lot of trouble, usually involving things landing on his head or something toilet related. In one cartoon, he laid enough curly turds to form a heart pattern on the ground in an attempt to impress a girl rabbit. Percy showed it to Julia. "Romantic, eh? A metaphor for modern love. My brother Lance would find it hysterical."

"I think they're funny in a really bizarre way. I'm almost tempted to buy the MashiMaro underpants," Julia said, pointing to a pair of girls panties hanging on a peg. They were purple and had little pictures of the rabbit, plunger in place, printed all over them.

"I'm not sure I could respect you if you did."

"Oh, like you'd be so bothered!"

Around the corner from the bookstall, they found a merchant who was selling women's clothes. Julia began to go through the dresses, looking for darker patterns. Most of them were sleeveless and the skirts went mid-length. "Women make these in their apartments," she said, "so you actually are getting hand-sewn quality. The funny thing is, they put fake tags for designer labels in the dresses to make them seem more fancy, and if you didn't know better, you'd think they were just some assembly-line, factory-made product."

Percy nodded. He watched Julia hold the dresses over herself and look in a full-length mirror. There were no changing rooms, so she was just going to have to eyeball the sizes.

"When you mentioned Lance, it was the first time you've brought up either of your brothers since I've been here," she said. "Do you miss them?"

"I don't know. I stopped thinking about everyone for the most part. I look at pictures occasionally, but you know, memories fade, needs go away."

"Don't you think they'd be happy to see you?"

"It's hard to tell. I felt bad for a time, thinking how worried or angry they might be, but now, maybe they've forgotten me, too."

Julia nodded. She had three dresses now—a plain black one, one that was more gray, and a black-and-white checked number. She asked the woman working the stall something in Chinese, and the woman showed her to some stockings in the back of the booth where she picked out some plain black tights. Percy listened as she haggled with the salesperson, not really understanding the numbers being tossed around, but the nature of the conversation was clear to him. Julia eventually settled and handed over some bills to the woman. Her garments were placed in a plain white, plastic bag. "I got a pretty good price," she said. "I think I'm going to have to make due with the undergarments I have, though. Or go back to get the MashiMaro panties. We'd have to go to something more like a department store for that stuff."

"Do you know where one is?" Percy asked.

"Not really. We should be getting back anyway."

Percy knew she was right, but he wasn't particularly happy about it. He had actually liked coming here. It was nice to be part of something so simple, so common. Even before coming to Beijing, when he had stopped going *anywhere*, Percy hadn't really had a regular shopping experience in quite some time. Fame and wealth had meant that he hadn't had to.

Even so, that wasn't really what the excursion was about for him. It wasn't even about being back among the living. He realized it was more about being with her. Shopping was no big deal; it was following her around while she looked at everything, being alone and free with Julia. That was what he had liked. It was so obvious, why hadn't he noticed it? She had made it so easy to forget everything else. Even back at the house, the more he was with her, the less he brooded on the past. Breaking through the forcefield of exile, being out in the open like this, being free, it was all her doing. Julia had a subtle power that had been taking him over inch by inch, until he had ended up here, and when it came right down to it, he was actually pleased.

Heading back out the way they had come, Percy smiled to himself. As they passed an older woman wearing a hooded parka on the rampway back to the street, he absent-mindedly flashed that smile at her, giving her a tiny nod. Apparently that was all the incentive she needed. She had a cardboard box filled with bootleg DVDs, and she gestured wildly at it. "DVDs!" she cried. Her voice was loud. "CDs! PC!"

The woman waved her arms out at Percy, blocking his way. He stopped. "What?" he asked.

"DVDs!" She said something more in Mandarin and grabbed a

handful of movies in thin cardboard packages out of her box. She began shoving them at him, trying to get Percy to take them from her. He held up his hands, tried to tell her no, but she kept pushing. "DVDs!" she insisted.

She was on him before he had realized what was happening. Percy had been lost in his reverie, and it had all taken him by surprise. He was trying to push her hands away, but she wasn't backing down and he was getting flustered. He looked to Julia. "Why won't she go? What is she doing?"

Inserting herself between Percy and the woman, Julia said something angrily in Chinese. The woman barked back, but Julia said it again. That seemed to do it. The bootlegger turned away from them and was going back to her box while casting a scornful look over shoulder at Percy and muttering under her breath.

The flare-up had rattled Percy, and he was shaking a little. "What did I do?" he pleaded. "I didn't do anything."

Julia put her hand on his shoulder and started to direct him away from the woman. "You're right, you didn't," she said. "I think she just though she could peg you as a sucker."

"That was absurd. What was she selling? Movies?"

"I guess DVDs were pretty new when you left." Julia laughed. "Really, don't worry about it." They were at the top of the ramp now, back on the street, and Julia could see that Percy was still agitated. She placed a hand on his cheek. "Seriously, are you all right?"

He liked her touch. It was warm. She was looking him straight in the face again, and it focused him. He couldn't help but think how beautiful she was. "Yes," he said, almost whispering. "It's just...you know."

Julia winked. "Yeah, I know."

There was a man nearby with a metal cart with a glass display case. He was selling candied fruit on a stick. "Why don't we get something sweet?" Julia suggested. "Sugar will set everything right."

Percy sat down on the curb while Julia bought four miniature apples on a skewer. His brothers had been on his mind since she had inquired about them. The three boys used to have a ritual. Once a year they would disappear together, meet someplace out of the way where no one knew they were going. Sometimes it was just for a couple of hours, sometimes for a whole weekend. It was for them to get away and reconnect, to shore up the bond they'd had since childhood. Only, they had missed it in 1999, let it pass without too much fanfare. "We'll just have to make it a long one in 2000," Tristan had said, with none of them knowing that reunion would not happen either. Percy had forgotten how much he cherished those times. It was the rare moment he could stop being Percival Mendelssohn and just be little Percy again. No one else can cut through the bull the way family can. It had been his fault the ritual hadn't happened. He wished he could say he had missed it for a good reason, that he had stayed home and been with his wife, but the truth was, there was no good reason, he just hadn't felt like making the effort, and he ended up just puttering around in his study and reading. He wasn't even working on a manuscript. How easy it had been to forget the important in order to indulge in the trivial.

Julia approached with the candied fruit snack. They looked like little rubber balls. As she sat down next to him, she took a bite out of the first one. He could hear the sugar coating crack. "Oh, my," she said. "Sweet is right!"

She handed the stick to Percy, and he took the remaining half of the first apple. It was oddly crispy and chewy, and very sweet on top, sour underneath. Each sensation was overwhelming, exaggerated. He almost wanted to spit the fruit out. "It makes my teeth hurt," Percy said.

"I know! I'm not sure I can eat any more of it."

"Haven't you had this before?"

"No. I've always seen the vendors selling this kind of stuff, but I never got around to trying it. The school always told us to watch out for street carts."

"Oh, great. You just got us the Chinese version of Montezuma's Revenge, probably."

Julia laughed. "I doubt it. I think they meant the meat skewers, anyway. They were mostly concerned about dodgy beef. Besides, I always wanted to try the fruit snacks. I wouldn't have bought it otherwise."

"Look at us," Percy said, smiling. "Trying new things together."

Julia tapped his nose with the end of the snack stick, and then she wriggled her own nose in his direction. “It’s a regular adventure.”

“Oh, no, it’s a highly *ir*regular adventure, Julia. But I like it. Thank you.”

“Any time.” Bravely, the girl moved her face in close to his, and she gave him a small kiss on the mouth. It was his turn to accept, and he did. Julia felt his surrender, felt his lips warm and wet. She repeated the words. “Any time.”

---

h.

Following Percival Mendelssohn's disappearance, a morbid ritual came into existence. Though many people now claim that they were the first to throw a Percival Mendelssohn Halloween Party, the truly dubious honor belongs to Scab Calloway, the ridiculously monikered lead singer of the cartoonish, low-level goth band Splinter of Our Discontent. While neither of Splinter's two albums had ever been reviewed in *Rolling Stone*, their October 31, 2000 bash landed them in the front section, with a picture of Scab and his then-boyfriend dressed in the Halloween costumes worn by the doomed Mendelssohn couple at their last public appearance. Scab was Zorro Percy and his significant other was Burnt-Barbie Iris; additionally, there was a photo of former Like A Dog bassist Emery Powell and his girlfriend Medea Stahr—a model and the bassist for Splinter—as the couple's zombified corpses (never mind that Percy was not believed to be dead), she decked out in a dress matching the one Iris was buried in and he in a dilapidated Zorro outfit, full of wormholes and moss stains. They used make-up that made them look like they were decaying, their flesh rotting away, and Medea sculpted exaggerated wounds on her wrists. The article tastefully reminded people that Emery Powell's former band was fronted by Percival Mendelssohn's oldest brother, Tristan Scott, and lamented that such ghoulish bad taste would likely put the kibosh on any long-rumored Like A Dog reunion. Music fans, after all, have no problem keeping their perspective on what's important.

By 2001, the idea had mushroomed, and multiple Percival Mendelssohn End of Existence Halloween Parties (as they would eventually be dubbed) were held all over the world. The majority of them were on college campuses, thrown by young fans who felt this was the best way to celebrate the life of their tragic hero. By this point, the range of costumes had expanded from distasteful depictions of Percy and Iris' sad end; people were coming dressed as a young, healthy Percival in the black-and-white suits he was known for, or as characters from his books.

It was in her second year at Lewis & Clark that Julia Jiménez found herself attending such a party. That year, a new literature professor had joined the campus and had taken over the Percival Mendelssohn Society as faculty advisor. She was Professor Kestly Edwards, and it was her first posting as a teacher. She was attending the Lewis & Clark graduate program to finish off her doctoral thesis on the works of Percival Mendelssohn. She was considered to be in a unique position to do so thanks to an alleged proximity to the author. It was her aunt and uncle who had thrown the Halloween bash that would inspire the later ones, and Professor Edwards had the distinction of being one of the last people to have seen Percy; these facts somehow leant a lot of weight to her opinions on his writing, despite the fact that she had only been reading it since his vanishing. The End of Existence Party, or EOE, was her attempt to introduce herself to the larger student body and show them she was still one of them, and not yet a faculty automaton.

Julia liked Halloween and relished the idea of dressing up as one of her favorite characters. Because the first person to go costumed as Iris was a boy, cross-dressing became a regular fixture of the EOEs, and so Julia chose to attend as Horatio from *The Other Side of the Street* in his boarding school outfit. In the book, Horatio is the poor boy whose father is killed while traveling on a business trip. Horatio's father was friends with his boss, and Horatio was friends with the boss' son, Terrence. Terrence's father arranges a scholarship fund under the name of Horatio's father, and it's used to shepherd Horatio into the expensive school. The whole affair makes Horatio suspicious, like maybe Terrence's father had something to do with his trusted employee's death, and this scholarship is not a distinction of honor, but some kind of bribe to make the abandoned son look the other way. In protest, Horatio dyes his blazer from royal blue to the darkest black and shaves off all his hair. Committed to the project, Julia had shaved her head, as well.

Professor Edwards came dressed as herself, wearing the same outfit she had worn to her aunt's party on that fateful evening. Julia overheard her explaining this to a group of students, and she felt it sounded horribly self-serving. You go to a party to honor someone else by wearing costumes that pertain to his life and art, and you show up in a costume of you? It made Julia wonder just what this woman had really been up to that night. She and Percy had been seen dancing, and there were actually some photos of them, but there had been a lot of speculation that they had moved on to other athletic activities before the night was through, and some people went so far as to say it was she who was the real cause of Iris' death. Julia's snap judgment was that none of the rumors were likely true, this woman was not nearly important enough to warrant such a place in literary history.

Perhaps she sensed Julia's distaste for her, and that was why Professor Edwards approached her later that night. "Are you having fun?" she asked.

"I suppose," Julia replied.

"I like your outfit. You don't go halfway, do you?"

"Not when it's important."

Julia tried to sound cold and dismissive, because then maybe this woman would go away, but it didn't seem to be working.

"You know, I have this theory about Percival's female fans," Professor Edwards said. "I think they're far more intense about their feelings, and so much more immersed in the books. We understand it better than the men do. I'd posit that Percival gravitated to them as a result. I don't believe that all these stories about his philandering are true, at least not in a carnal sense. Rather, he was just giving attention to people who understood him."

Was she admitting to not sleeping with Percival?

"Really?"

"It's just an idea right now, but that's part of my graduate study.

I'd like to talk to Percival's readers and get a broader sense of why—and how—they react to his writing and see if I can chart any differences in gender."

"That sounds pretty cool."

"You think? Because I'd really like you to be a part of it."

"Me?"

"Of course! How can I resist someone willing to stand so firmly in Horatio's shoes?"

Julia blushed. She had snapped to judgment too fast. This woman seemed to have more of a sense of humor than Julia had given her credit for, so maybe she wasn't remotely as bad as she'd tried to make her out to be.

*

The interviews took place in Kestly Edwards' office, a small space in the English department. She enquired ahead of time as to what sort of beverage Julia would like to have when she answered the questions, what might help her relax. Julia asked for a red chai tea, and it was waiting there when she arrived, the water already boiled, the tea bag steeping in the mug.

There was only the desk between them, the teacher on one side, the subject on the other. Julia was given a large, upholstered chair. It had wheels and leaned back. Professor Edwards' chair was wooden, stiff-backed, it didn't move.

The first session was very basic. Julia was asked how she had first discovered Percival Mendelssohn, her first reading experience, etc. What was her favorite book, what character did she like, what themes did she identify with, was there anything about the style that appealed to her, etc. As she spoke, Professor Edwards shuffled papers around on her desk. There seemed to be no end to the documents that were placed in the wrong spot and had to be moved to the right one, a system that only the professor knew, based more on instinct than structure. As soon as she was done asking each question, though, she was immediately focused, scribbling notes on a slab of foolscap, attentive to every word.

There was also a miniature tape recorder running. It stood up straight in the center of the desk, and occasionally it would get rocked by tremors neither woman could feel and would look like it was going to topple over. It never did.

"Today was just an overview," the professor told her when it was all over. "Next time, we'll go deeper."

Their next meeting was a week later, and although Professor Edwards had asked her not to worry about it and just show up fresh and answer off the top of her head, Julia did worry about it. To her mind, this was an important bit of research, and it could be her part of the Percival Mendelssohn legacy. If the resulting report ended up being a touchstone in the study of the Mendelssohn bibliography, then her opinions could end up influencing how other people interpreted the stories. She had to make sure she could do them justice.

Neglecting her studies, she spent the next seven days re-reading everything by Percy that she could. She started at the beginning, with his earliest collected work, and read straight through everything in chronological order. She had never tried it that way before, and it was a real pleasure seeing his ideas grow, following the line of his logic that led Percy from the initial seeds of his ideas to the final product. *The Other Side of the Street* was his longest work, his most complex, and it was breathtaking every time she immersed herself in it.

But beyond the pure enjoyment of reading, Julia found something else in Percy's books: clues about what had happened to him. He had written them long before Iris' suicide, of course, before he went missing, but Julia became convinced that anyone who had spent any time reading his words would not have been at all surprised that his life had taken the path it had.

There were echoes of it everywhere. In *One*, there was the preacher who could not save the life of his daughter, and so he renounced his church, claiming he was going to make amends by spreading the gospel around the world, only to be found dead shortly after, possibly from suicide, possibly murder. Or his short story about the man who wanted to build a rocket ship and go into space to find out if there was a better life beyond our planet, only to blow himself up when the police came to his door to find out what had happened to his girlfriend, whose body he had hidden in the basement. And, of course, all the essays about finding enlightenment in solitude and transcendence through suicide—though Julia could see that it was quite clear that the latter was all metaphor and found it was impossible to think otherwise. Anyone who had thought he really meant that everyone should leap into a self-made grave obviously had missed the point.

Most illuminating, however, was *I Was Someone Dead*, the novella that had run in *Playboy* and had been reprinted in book form some time after Percival had disappeared. When it had run the first time, the author's popularity had seemed limitless, and the story came off as a fable about modern life. Reprinted after the tragedy and departure, it took on a nuance of prophecy. The story of Hieronymus Zoo had been a precursor of the turns his creator's life would take: a man faced with a life he could not handle disengaging from it, establishing an existence beyond all human interaction. There wasn't a catalytic event in the same style of Iris' suicide, but Percival was too much of a romantic to imagine such a fate befalling the love of his life. In fact, it was rare in his stories for true love to reach such a disastrous end. Even in the one about the rocket ship guy, the point was that the man had not understood love, he only thought he had. Part of his mission was to maybe find a race who could explain to him where he had gone wrong.

No, in Julia's mind, Iris' death was a chaos element, the unforeseen monkey wrench that threw off Percival's carefully manufactured plan that would allow him to retreat to a monastic existence later in life. His essays dreamed of a peaceful withdrawal, his fiction of an eventual build-up of heartache. Something so drastic must have blindsided him, knocked him off his feet and right out of common acceptance and understanding. It all made sense.

And yet, there was one riddle from his fiction that, as far as anyone knew, life had not provided an answer for.

Hieronymus Zoo eventually had his Nadya, the woman who showed up and surprised him back into full consciousness, into real living. She invaded his exile and inspired the man to conquer his fears and re-engage with the world beyond his island.

Who would there be to do the same for Percival Mendelssohn?

*

EXCERPT FROM THE TRANSCRIPT OF THE SECOND INTERVIEW WITH JULIA J.
Conducted by Kestly Edwards 11/12/2005

Q: Your theory about Percival's later life being foreshadowed in his early work is an interesting one, but what does it say about you?
A: What do you mean? Like, does it say maybe I've devoted a little too much time to thinking about tiny details?
Q: Ha-ha! No. I mean, you're looking at Percival's writing and you're telling me how you see the author in it, and what I'd like to do is try to talk about where we'd find you in it. How does Julia J. fit into Percival Mendelssohn's world?
A: She doesn't. I'd love to, trust me, but come on! I'm not nearly glamorous enough, or smart enough, or anything enough.
Q: Really? You don't think his writing is inclusive of all types? I think he's generally fair to consider all classes of people.
A: Oh, his writing, sure. I thought you meant, like, the world he lives in, like hanging out with him.
Q: No, you didn't. You're toying with me. That was a joke, wasn't it?
A: Yeah, it was a joke.
Q: Why did you make that joke?
A: I was just being funny.
Q: Are you sure? Because I don't think that's it. I think you're deflecting. Is there something about how you relate to Percival's books that you're scared to talk about?
A: Not scared exactly. [pause] More embarrassed.
Q: About what? There's no one here to judge you, no right or wrong answers.
A: Well, the thing is, when I agreed to do this, I thought I'd have a lot to say about everything, like I was some kind of expert on Percival's books, but when I read everything again, I realized I wasn't. Because if I had

never thought about his work in the context of the choices he has made, then how many other ways did I not think about it. I started to consider your thesis and what you were looking for, and I asked myself, where am I amid the philosophy? It's not that I don't understand it, it's that I am not sure I understand all of it.
Q: All of it? No one understands all of it. Not even the writer.
A: That's the wrong way to see it. I think what I mean is I understand it in the abstract, but not in the practical. I get how his stories are supposed to be what I aspire to, but I don't get how to implement the concepts.
Q: You see the things his characters achieve, you see the ideals he points to, but you don't know how to make yourself in that mold.
A: Exactly. I mean, I know that a whole part of his deal is that we should be ourselves and set our own path and all that, but obviously he has established these examples that are supposed to be the top, you know, like the peak of the human mountain, but it's like he left before giving us the last piece.
Q: You've got an engine but no fuel.
A: Yeah! [pause] But maybe the other way around.
Q: Okay.
A: It's like, if you read One, and then you read the essays that he did right around the same time, it's like he's giving you the key to understanding the novel. It's not explicit, but it's like, he told us the story, and then he told us these other things, and I realized that the other things can be linked up to the story and kind of explain what he meant and what we can do with all of it every day. Then I read The Other Side of the Street and I Was Someone Dead, and he's really gone beyond everything he's done before. It's all incredible. Yet, when I look to him to illuminate these things for me, he's not there. He's just not there. I've got all these tools and yet he left me in the dark and I can't see how to use them.
Q: That's interesting. But don't you think he wanted you to go out on your own and become your own person? Maybe that's his example. He left us to show us how to stand on our own two feet.
A: I don't know. Maybe. But it's all starting to sound a little too much like he's Jesus or something for my taste.
Q: Sorry. [pause] So, what do you propose?

A: Propose?
Q: Yeah. How do we put your two sides together? How does Percy's real life and fictional life collide so you can understand how to make your real life reflect his fictional life.
A: I don't know. That's what we need a Nadya for. To go get him and make him clean up this mess he made out of me.
Q: Maybe that's the message. Maybe you need to be a Nadya. Don't sit and wait for life to happen to you, go to life and happen to it.
A: [pause] Yeah [pause] Maybe.

*

Kestly Edwards turned off the tape recorder. "That was very good," she said.

"Thanks, Professor Edwards."

"No, please. Call me Kestly."

"Okay."

"I'm not trying to shine you on our anything, Julia, but you're definitely one of the more unique Percy fans I've talked to."

"Really?" Julia scrunched up her face. She couldn't see how it was possible.

"I'm not kidding. I've been getting a lot of the standard responses, very shallow interaction with the material. You've dug deeper, you've spent a lot more time analyzing instead of just clinging to the surface emotions."

Julia felt her face get hot. She had probably turned several shades of crimson. She crossed her arms, pressing them against her ribs just under her breasts. "Thanks."

Kestly was smiling. She looked like a little girl who had a secret to tell. "You want to see something cool?"

"Okay."

The professor rose from her desk and crossed the room to the door. She motioned for Julia to follow. They went outside and down the hall, to another office door. Kestly pulled a set of keys out of her pocket and unlocked it. A puff of stale air came out as soon as the door was open, carrying with it the fragrance of dust and old paper. Flipping a switch on the wall, Kestly turned on the light.

Inside the office, the walls on either side were lined with metal shelving units filled with file boxes. The far wall had a desk with a light box and a lamp on an armature poised above it. There were all sorts of writing tools and scissors and things scattered about. Kestly went to the shelves on the left and pulled down a box. It said "Edwards" in marker on the outside. She hefted it over to the table.

"Come in," Kestly said, "and shut the door."

Julia did as she was instructed. She watched over Kestly's shoulder as the professor pulled some papers out of the box. "These are some of Percy's letters," she said. "His family sent them to me. They're trying to do more to preserve his legacy, so they've been showing me a lot of material no one has ever seen before. It's been fascinating, because it's practically uncharted territory, and it's rare to get an opportunity to study a writer whose effect on his audience is so immediate. Not to mention, ongoing."

Kestly held up a pink folder. "These are fan letters he received. Interesting stuff, some of it. You'd be surprised what girls would offer to do for him. Guys, too. It's like, they missed all the religious connotations of his work, ignored all the articles about chastity."

Next she brought out a purple folder. "This has letters he wrote, some in response to fans, some were fan letters of his own. He'd read something he liked and he'd drop a note to the author. He never stopped being a fan himself."

She reached deeper into the box, but before pulling her hands back out, Kestly looked back over her shoulder at the door like she was making sure no one else was there. Then she took out a manila envelope. "This," she said, "this is something totally different. I don't think I was supposed to get this. It must have ended up with the other letters by mistake."

"What is it?" Julia asked.

"You have to promise me you won't tell anyone about it. You're the only one I'm showing, so I'll know if you did."

"You don't have to worry. I promise."

"Okay."

Kestly unclasped the envelope and pulled out a single piece of paper. She handed it to Julia.

On top of the paper was Percy's letterhead, which seemed normal enough, but then Julia saw the salutation and knew instantly why this particular missive was so precious. "Dearest Iris," it read.

Julia stopped reading there. She instantly felt uncomfortable. "Is this a love letter?"

"Uh-huh. I think he wrote it on a book tour. It's all about how he's traveling and he misses her."

"I don't know if I should be reading this."

"It is intensely personal, but he was a writer. Some would say his papers are fair game."

"I know, but still...."

"It's really fascinating. He brings up his old fixation on the knights and calls himself her champion and how he feels like he is fighting his way back to her. He paints this whole picture of her living on a solitary island of splendor, and the rest of the world is a vast ocean full of monsters and perils that he must face to get back to her. He feels guilty having left her alone, because who will stop the beasts if they find her and he's gone. You can feel that he just aches for her."

"You've got to wonder why he ever left her, then," Julia said, handing the letter back to Kestly.

"Well, it's the whole Percival Mendelssohn conflict in a nutshell. Why is he following his body if his heart demands otherwise? To make money? Why? Because he needs to eat?"

The presence of the letter was making Julia nervous. She wasn't going to feel comfortable until it was back in the envelope, sealed back in the box. "What are you going to do with it?" she asked.

"Nothing," Kestly replied. "Send it back when I send back the rest. I don't have the strength you had, I couldn't resist reading it, but you're right, it's not for sharing."

Julia could hear paper scraping against paper as Kestly returned the letter to the envelope. The girl exhaled, only just then realizing she had been holding her breath. Kestly put everything back in the box, put on the lid, and returned it to its shelf. Everything felt safe once more.

---

i.

"DEEP END"
by Percival Mendelssohn

Sometimes I stand on a bridge and look out over the water, and I wonder, if I dive in and sink to the bottom, where will my body surface? And how long will it take?

*

You step out through the side door. The path is familiar and tedious. You take it every day. The opening and closing of the door time after time weighs heavy on the hinges, pushes them toward the point where they will break and won't work. You can't help but sympathize with their plight.

It's a cold day, but you are prepared for it. You have your big coat to keep your body comfortable and your umbrella to keep the sprinkling rain off of your head. You've also dressed light under the coat, just in case. The conditions can be so schizophrenic here, no weather report is to be trusted, you must be ready for anything. The flimsy metal of the umbrella irritates the palm of your hand as you slide the device open. Somehow, the sensation travels through your body and into your mouth, where you taste the metal between your teeth, on your tongue. It's jarring, like biting down on a current of electricity.

You hear meowing from across the sidewalk. It seems to be coming from some trash cans over by the wall of the apartment building in front of you. You go over, and there is a cat under one of the cans, in a little square vent cut into the concrete. It must have been sleeping there when the trash was put out and become trapped. The feline's squeals are shrill, horrid. Immediately taking pity on the poor creature, you move the garbage pail and let the kitten out. From what you can see, the cat has somehow hurt itself. There is a shocking stain of blood on the white fur of its back leg. You move to help it, not even knowing what you can do, but it swipes its claws at you and dashes away. You realize that, being in pain, it was probably embarrassed by your charity.

You adjust the collar of your coat and look around you. Which way will it be today? North? South? Right? Left? Does it matter?

*

It rains nearly every day here. I think once someone told me that we get at least a drizzle 300 days out of the year. It drives some people nuts. They move up from the South all fresh and tanned, and after a few months of getting less sunlight than they are accustomed to, they get depressed. Even people who have lived here their whole lives hit winter and find that sadness is their only friend. It makes you wonder why evolution let humanity work hibernation out of its system.

Personally, I never get tired of the rain. I like to take long walks in it, just to relax. There's something soothing about the gray going on forever, something comforting in the sound of its drops against the canvas of my umbrella. I like wearing a heavy coat I can hide in.

Today, though, today I wish I had someplace to go.

Cars rush by, splitting puddles, spraying water everywhere. Cars full of smiling, laughing people, all of them with a final destination. Well, maybe not all of them. Maybe some of them carry hearts that house a loneliness that can't be shared, that the driver never speaks of, never tells anyone. How easy it would be for me to step in front of one of those cars, to let it take me away. If all were lucky, I could choose someone else who wants to die and we could go down the same drain.

I know it's melodramatic. At least, it would be to someone outside of it. To voice these sorts of feelings somehow renders their gravity meaningless. No one wants to know about them, and they certainly don't want to believe them. Yet, it's just something I have come to live with. It seems that, for me, these things are inevitable.

When I was younger, I learned that if things weren't going my way, if life was really doing my head in, I could scratch the hell out of my arms. The ensuing sting gave me something else to focus on, and whatever other weight I was carrying didn't seem as heavy. I stopped cutting my nails, letting them grow long so I could dig in deeper. I think it was just a simple step from there to see that as problems increased, so could the physical pain. Ultimately, I'd hit that last threshold and...well, it's pretty obvious where I'm going with this.

I've thought about the possibility of slitting my wrists. It seems to be the most soothing way to move on. Take some pills, draw a warm bath, and slice open a couple of veins. It's the closest to what is already familiar, a simple, flowing movement up the arm. I'd lie there, head tilted back, the warm, warm water. I'd begin to remember things.

"We're going to have so much fun together," she told me. "We'll go to the movies, and we'll see things neither of us have ever seen before. We can do anything."

"It's limitless," I said, and I placed a kiss on her cheek.

"I like the way you hold me," she said.

In the morning, I kissed her forehead to wake her up. She had the blanket pulled up to her neck, and I brushed the hair away from her face with my hands. I had already gotten up, showered, made breakfast, but she hadn't been roused from her sleep, hadn't noticed I had left the bed. It hadn't mattered to her that I had been gone, but still, to see her wake, turn, look at me, smile....

There in the warm water, aware of every escaping bead of blood, every drop of sweat, every cell in my body that is letting go. Slowly falling asleep. This way is ideal. It will be days before I am found, before anyone realizes something is wrong. I'll be long gone, no way of getting me back. Besides, where was everyone anyway? When they ask how I could do this to them, how I could run out this way, will they ever realize they weren't there, that I was all by myself, and this is why things moved the way they did? Will they recall that there was no one around the first time I was beat up? All alone, walking home from my summer job, jumped by some punk who'd decided I was a little too different to leave alone. The kicking I received was unbelievable. I never saw who did it, but I'm sure he was the bully who decided to make my life hell when school started. And who stepped forward then? In a school full of people, how did I get messed with nearly every day, and not one person ever stopped it or punished the bastard? Where were they when my mom was telling me I was trash and had ruined her life? Where was my father? Where was my brother?

Nodding off, drifting into sleep. Don't tell me we all suffer. If everyone feels this way, then let's all go together.

The warm water, so warm you lose everything to it. Not like this rain. It blows in under the umbrella and the cold slashes against my face. Reminds me I'm still here.

I see these streets every day. I walk to and from the bus stop, board the bus, ride over them to get to work. Trudge through the day, and then trudge back. If I'm lucky, there are a few pieces of mail in the mailbox and the light blinking once or twice on the answering machine. If I'm more lucky, the mail isn't all bills and the messages are more than hang-ups. I catch a few programs on TV, maybe read a thing or two, get a few hours of sleep—pray to God that my dreams aren't against me tonight!—and get up to do it all over again tomorrow.

Yes, I know. This is everyday life. But why must I be forced to accept it? Why should it just be taken for granted that it's the same for everyone? Maybe I just wasn't cut out for it....

I wish I could keep walking until I was able to turn around and not know the way back.

Jeez, it's really coming down. It's true what they say, that the heaviest rain hits just before the downpour stops. Duck into a shop, wait it out, and it'll usually clear up after a few minutes. Still, how optimistic should I be when there is only a one in sixty-five chance that tomorrow will be clear all day? Besides, when it's this nasty, it tests my strength. I can feel it pushing against my umbrella, each drop slamming into it like a tumbling bullet.

*

There's a homeless man ahead of you. You have seen him nearly every day since you have lived here. At first, he was lucid and spoke clearly. The only thing that distinguished him from any other in your mind was his supplicating manner, the way he would cup his hands together and hunch over when he asked for change. Since then, he has gotten progressively worse, to the point where he wanders the street wailing, bemoaning his fate, stopping and sucking up the tears just to ask for money, only to begin crying to the heavens when he is turned away empty-handed.

You lower your umbrella so as to block him from your view. Are you afraid of what you might recognize in his madness?

He asks you if you can spare any change, and you ignore him. He curses you, but you've been cursed before. They're just words in the end. Words themselves are a nuisance, but like flea bites, they don't really hurt. You spend your time avoiding them now. An old college friend called last night and you didn't pick up the phone. He just wanted to know how you were doing, but knowing that wasn't a question you could answer to anybody's satisfaction, you chose not to accept it. Deaf, dumb, and blind—that's the best policy.

The puddle in the gutter on the corner doesn't look very deep, but you feel foolish when you are in water above your ankles.

*

A dramatic flourish may be a better answer. After a life of quiet stumbling, to go out loudly could be more worthwhile. This would require not only an extreme method, but timing as well. Here's a scenario:

I run into her somewhere. One of my ex-girlfriends. It could be anyone. It could be today. I am walking, and I happen to bump into her—quite literally—as she emerges from her office building. "Oh, gosh, I'm sorry," I say, before actually catching on to who it is. When I realize, I laugh stupidly. "Sorry. Hi. How are you?"

"Good, good," she says, smiling falsely. "It's good to see you."

"I doubt that," I laugh.

"No, it is," she says. "I've been wanting to get in touch with you."

"You have?"

"Yeah. I'm getting married, you see, and I want you to come."

"Really? Married? To who?"

"Oh, this wonderful guy that I met after you. He runs a floral business. You've probably seen his vans. They're the ones with the flower pot with wheels painted on the side."

"Really? Wow! That guy."

Of course, I go to the wedding. I can't help but torture myself. Plus it begins to dawn on me, moments after we part on the street, that she was the one. She's the gaping hole in my life, the pain that has been haunting me. Ever since she left, ever since that morning where we ate bagels on my bed and laughed with each other and caffeine-bombed our hangovers. She never came back after that morning, only called to apologize. I got really bad, really stupid. I yelled, showed up at her office, just couldn't get the hint. That was the last glimmer of hope in a slipping-down life, the last spark to fade.

So, I go. I get a tux, a haircut, new shoes, and I go to the wedding. I buy them a lavish gift, one beyond the call of duty, beyond reason. She kisses me on the cheek and whispers her thank you in my ear. "Just my way of showing there's no hard feelings," I say. "I'm happy that one of us found goodness in this world."

She looks at me. Her eyes are full of tears. "You'll find it, too," she says. "You *will*."

I don't answer her. My face says it all. I wish it were true. You don't know how wrong you are.

I leave before the reception is over, walk out during the big dance between the bride and groom. I have been drinking heavily and openly. Not obnoxious, not making a bigger ass of myself—being there, the gift, all that made me ass enough. No, I drink very casual, but continuously and without skulking around about it. I do it out in plain view of her and all the friends we share. And I walk out right as the band kicks in and the pair steps onto the floor—the jilted lover retreating to his four walls and his broken heart.

I go home, pull out the gun, and erase my memories.

*

You are halfway across the bridge over the freeway when a huge wind comes up and turns your umbrella inside out. All the cars have created a force you did not expect, and the thing slips out of your hand and goes sailing across the four-lane highway. How simple it would be to follow it.

*

What of all the broken hearts created by my ending my life? Are any of these hearts more important than mine?

The guilt of death can't in any way compare to the guilt I feel at being alive. I just can't escape the fact that it seems everything I get involved in goes haywire. What good have I brought to anyone's life, much less my own? I'm nobody's hero, and I don't feel obliged to keep fighting.

I stopped going to school eventually. It was just clear that I would never win, so why keep walking into the fight. I never could get stronger because whatever energy I could recharge, the bully would just beat out of me the next day. I would spend a lot of time in parks, or I'd buy an all-day bus ticket and ride all the routes until it was time to go home. After a couple of weeks, the school called my folks. My dad took off work and spent the day driving around looking for me. He found me playing video games with my lunch money, and he dragged me out of the arcade. He didn't say anything—not the whole ride home, not when we were in the house. He just took me to my room and started hitting me. When I saw my face again, one whole half of it was blue. Looking in the mirror, I realized that life was bigger than I was, and no matter what, it would step on me.

The next time I went somewhere with my parents, I threw myself out of the car. It was a suburban street, and we weren't going very fast, so it was a stupid place to do it. I broke a couple of bones, but there was never any chance of me actually succeeding at dying. My father barely spoke to me for two months, and I think the only reason I didn't try something like that again was because his anger scared me so much, I was frightened he'd sense if I even thought about it and would beat the daylights out of me.

It seems strange now, taking anyone else's anger into account. Let them be mad at me. Yeah, I lost it for the team. I dropped out in the last leg. Rest assured, the defeat is all mine.

*

Your head is heavy now, and your clothes are soaked through. The streets are no longer familiar. You aren't lost, but you are someplace you have never been before, and that is subtly comforting. Tired, you sit down on the curb. The rain rolls out of your hair and down your face, over your nose, into your mouth. There doesn't seem to be anywhere else for it to go.

8.

Val was waiting for them when they returned to the hutong. He was sitting in the kitchen with the lights turned out, drumming his fingers on the table, listening to a static-filled transistor radio. He had been scanning news stations for any mention of his employer. Percy had gone in alone at first, and Val had turned off the radio the moment he arrived. On the other side of the house, Julia went straight to her room to put her clothes away, only to find her space turned completely upside down. She wasn't sure what Val had been looking for; she had only come to the house with the clothes on her back, and she was still wearing them. The things he had scattered over the floor were books from their library and toiletries that had been purchased by Val on her behalf. She hadn't smuggled anything into the building concealed in a hollowed-out book or immersed in a bottle of shampoo. He had overturned her mattress, as well, and that was about the end of his futile terror. There was barely room for her in the space, so the contraband wouldn't have been hard to find had it existed.

When Julia reached the kitchen, the men were sitting in silence. Percy had taken a chair opposite of Val, and he was holding the stocking cap and sunglasses in his hands. He stared at the objects like he was willing them to speak up and explain what had happened. Seeing her, Val flipped on the light. "There she is," he said, his voice dripping with contempt. "The culprit."

"What's going on around here?" Julia asked. She made a point to look at Percy, not at Val; Percy did not return her gaze.

"Really, don't you think that's a question I should be asking of you?"

Julia crossed her arms, but more out of defiance than nervous habit. She didn't really see a point in answering, so she didn't.

"You were expressly told not to leave the house," Val said.

"I kept telling you I needed clothes."

"You were *told* not to leave the house." Val leaned in toward Percy. "What were you thinking? What if someone had seen you? And what did you expect me to think when I came home and found you gone?" He pointed an accusing finger at Julia. "For all I knew, this girl had kidnapped you. She could be a plant, sent here by people who want to take you back, and she could have called in the goon squad to smuggle you back to the States."

Percy looked up now. He looked at Julia. "No," he said, shaking his head. "She wouldn't do that."

"You don't know that for sure. I keep telling you—"

Julia snorted. "Are you really that paranoid? Do you know how ridiculous you sound?"

Val stood quickly, nearly knocking his chair over backwards. "This is serious. Have you any idea of why we're here? Have you even thought about it?" He whipped himself around, turning on Percy now. "Better yet, what about you? Have you forgotten? Has the smell of a new girl made you that insensitive?"

That last bit made Julia angry. "Hey!" she shouted. "What the hell is that supposed to mean?"

"Exactly what it sounds like." Val turned back to Percy. "It really is 1999, isn't it? What did this one do, huh? Have you kissed her yet? Maybe a small peck on her hand?"

There is no reason to assume that Val had chosen his words for any other purpose but to be cruel. He knew that point would sting, and he was right. It was a fatal blow, stopping Percy dead, reminding him of the indiscretions that had sent them running to China. His face turned ashen, and he put the hat and the glasses on the table, sliding them to the center.

He stared at them. "You're right," he said. "I should have kept my head, remembered all you've done. I've been callous."

"What? Percy, no—"

Percy held up his hand, silencing Julia. "I put everything at risk. I placed body over mind," he said. "It's like a second betrayal."

He got up from the table, and without looking at either of them, Percy left the room. After he was gone, Val collected the remnants of his disguise. "I take it you found these in my room?" he asked.

The nonchalance in his tone enraged Julia. "Wow," she said, "you're really something. Is that really what you care about? That we went into your room? What about mine?"

Val smirked. "Oh, is that what *you* think about?"

"Gimme a break."

"No, why don't you give us a break? You ask me what I care about, but what do you care about? I've worked for that man for a decade now. I've given up everything for him. How easy it must be to waltz into the middle and start taking what you please."

"Taking—? Is that it? Do you find me threatening? Are you *jealous*?"

"Not at all. Merely annoyed. You don't understand what he needs, Ms Jiménez. You're out of your element."

Julia groaned and held her hands toward the ceiling, shaking her arms in surrender. "Then fill me in, Val. Make me understand."

Laughing, Val crossed the kitchen and dropped the hat and sunglasses into the trash. "There's no need," he told her. "I've taken the liberty of contacting your school and letting them know you are here. They in turn promised to contact your parents. I imagine someone will be around to collect you at some point in the near future. Once you're gone, I can take care of securing passage for us, and I'll take Percy somewhere even more remote, ensuring no knob-kneed schoolgirls ever show up on our doorstep again."

The way he said it, it was definitely a threat, but Julia was unsure where it lay. Was he giving her a warning, or was he promising something more dire? How deep could he bury a personality so that it might never emerge again?

Before she could ask him to clarify, Val left the kitchen.

*

The confrontation had disturbed Julia. When Percy had left the room, he looked deflated, a far cry from the man who had gone out with her. Who was working for whom here? Val really knew how to push his buttons, knew just the right pattern to completely shut Percy down. As she returned to her room, she wondered how much of the wound of his wife's death remaining raw was directly due to Val's influence.

Lancelot was stepping amid the mess Val had made on her floor. He found a tampon still in its wrapper and he was batting it around like it was the most fascinating of toys. Despite the gravity of what had just happened, she couldn't help but laugh. The mangy black cat half-yawned, half-meowed in response. Julia closed the door and began to pick up the debris. The cat wandered around her ankles as she did, investigating each object just before she picked it up. "You're a good little supervisor," she told him.

The last item to be returned to its rightful place was the mattress. It took a bit of effort, but Julia was able to slide it back on the metal frame and adjust it to its proper placement. With that done, she closed the door and removed her dresses from the bag. She lay each one flat on the mattress and looked at them. She had gotten them cheap, but she had also thought they would be the down payment for buying Percy his freedom; now it seemed they would cost her the whole shebang. How long before someone came looking for her? Had the school even noticed she hadn't been around for several weeks? With the semester already paid for, they probably didn't care. The problem was, she had come looking for answers, and she hadn't gotten any. Instead, it was like she had joined a stage drama already in progress.

She tried on each dress to make sure it fit. The gray was baggier than the others, but she could probably do something about that. A belt might do the trick simple enough. She opted to keep wearing the black one. It fit the best and seemed the least ostentatious for her setting.

Sitting on the bed, she ran her fingers over her new stockings. The softness of the material was refreshing. The house was significantly lacking in soft things, and she hadn't realized how deprived she had felt. Julia loved wandering through clothing stores and touching the various fabrics. Sometimes she'd go to department stores and feel the sheets and the curtains. She had always believed her sense of touch was the most direct connection she had to the world around her.

This made her think of putting the stocking cap on Percy, of touching his face and tucking his hair back. Such a little thing, but it made such a big difference. It brought calm to the room, it put them at ease. Just touching had connected them.

Julia thought maybe she should go find Percy now, maybe just having someone put her arms around him would make a difference. How lonely life must have been for him, and Val definitely wasn't helping. But before she could go, she heard some rustling outside the door. Lancelot heard it, too, and the cat raised his back, his tail sticking straight up in the air, and hissed. His reaction made Julia think it was Val pulling some kind of trick, so she leapt from the bed and flung open the door to catch him in the act.

Only no one was there.

At least, no human. The gray and white cat with the tiny green spot was standing in the hallway. Gawain. He wouldn't have come with Val, he'd have come with Percy. In front of him, just outside the door, there was a book. Yes, it must have been Percy.

Julia crouched down and picked up the book. It had a white cover with a pink design of three delicate flowers, two with the center of their bloom facing out, the third turned away, hiding its face.

Snow Country by Yasunari Kawabata.

She had never read it before, but if Percy had left it for her, then there must be a reason. Julia immediately went back inside and cracked the novel open.

*

Percy spent the night in his room. He barricaded the doors with the little tables and boxes he used to house his books. He didn't want anyone coming in. Having removed all his clothes, he lay on the floor in the dark listening to Wagner's *Parsifal.* Its story was familiar to him, even if it was different than the regular story of his namesake he had grown up with. Wagner hadn't looked to the Arthurian legend, but to a poem about a strange manchild written by Wolfram von Eschenbach. Unlike the knight Percival, the odd boy stumbles into his destiny rather than actively questing for it, becoming the keeper of the Holy Grail by being in the wrong place at the wrong time. It's only by the power of fate that this happens, because Parsifal grows up as a sheltered child. His father is killed in battle, and so his mother doesn't want him to be a warrior. Her name is Herzeleide, which translates as "Heart's Sorrow," a rather nasty symbolism to pin on the mother figure. She tries to hide Parisfal's destiny from him, but it nabs him anyway.

Percy felt maybe he had more in common with this literary figure than the one he had been raised to emulate. His own mother's name had its origins in Wales, where a Gwendolyn was said to be the wife of the wizard Merlin, and perhaps there was something in that, also. Too cognizant of magic, she had left her child ill-suited for reality. Maybe that was the tragic irony of his existence. His mother had tried to instill in him the belief that anything in life was possible, her hope being that she would show Percy that he could pursue his high-minded goals without becoming a bumbling recluse completely cut off from his fellow man; only, by doing so, she had also provided her son with the blinders that caused him to trip over his own feet right into the heart of that fate. He was too caught up in the magic and thus oblivious to the gravitational pull of emotions and the way his actions could drag others down. He had received his Grail, taken charge of his sacred duty. He was tied to one person, and it was his responsibility to protect her. Iris. For a boy so attuned to symbolism and what names mean, how could he have been so oblivious to his own dear Iris? Named for a flower that time had given the distinction of standing for faith, wisdom, hope, and the wonderful promise of love. Like a little kid dressed in the armor of a much older, stronger, bigger man, Percy had run out to be her champion, but he was poorly equipped to use tools he had never grown into, and he trampled all of her virtues underfoot.

That he had trampled on her promise of love was the destruction that hurt most of all.

Both the care of his mother and the passion he had shared with Iris put Percy's head in the clouds, and it wasn't their fault that he hadn't appreciated the rarefied gift they had given him. Maybe he was being too easy on himself by saying he tripped and fell off that pedestal. Really, he had divebombed toward his fate like a kamikaze. In the Parsifal myth, the idiot boy is seduced by Kundry, an evil temptress. It's with her kiss that the sleeping warrior awakens, and it's from there that Parsifal knows real suffering. Only by denying the carnal and accepting a holy mantle does Parsifal redeem himself. The things that Herzeleide had given him—the things Percy's mother and his wife had also provided—were all he had ever really needed.

There was no Kundry for Percy, though. No one had lured him out. He went looking for it. Parsifal was enlightened by compassion, but Percy had none. He pursued his lusts, blind to the pain he was causing, blind to the life that was slipping away. He was no longer the special boy his mother had raised him to be; he was all too common a man.

As Wagner's orchestral swathes weaved through the room around him, Percy reminded himself of this. How could he have let himself forget? How could he dare step out again in pursuit of a kiss? He must always remember the dark consequences, the chain of events that had driven him here.

*

Dawn had not yet broken when Julia finished reading *Snow Country.* When she closed the book, she was infuriated.

Kawabata's novel was the story of a rich gentleman who spends several seasons visiting a mountain resort to be with Komako, a somewhat reluctant geisha who lives there. Yet, for all the devotion Komako shows him, he will not commit to her. He's more drawn to Yoko, a young girl who flits in and out of his life, occasionally entering his sphere of reference though rarely giving him the time of day. Komako wastes what is left of her youth pining for the man, while he also makes empty promises to Yoko about helping her establish life in the big city. In the end, the man chooses neither, and his indecision is the symbolic catalyst for Yoko's eventual demise in a fire—the passion, maybe, that he has denied her—just as much as it was responsible for Komako being caught in a state of being she did not intend.

Snow Country was a good enough book. In fact, Kawabata's writing was beautiful. In other circumstances, Julia would have gravitated to his story about love denied, of this dilettante who hides from his own heart. Under these circumstances, however, the book was baffling, even enraging. Why had Percy chosen to give this to her? Did he mean for her to be the young girl who intrudes on what should have been the real relationship? Or was she the deluded geisha throwing her life away on a cold fish, and the ghost of his wife was the thing he could never catch?

And either way, was Percy trying to tell her he was chickening out? Was he going to be Shinamura, the self-exiled, rich academic who lets desire go cold, who lets life pass him by? In the climactic scenes, the man sees himself separate from the cosmos while the women are a part of it, and he's scared to bathe in the starlight.

If this were the case, then how disappointing. This was the state of the man she had searched the world for? She had already tested the limits of his strength, and sneaking out of the house for a quick shopping trip was all he could handle. So much for the guru who would have all the answers.

Then again, it wasn't the first time she had been disappointed in people she had previously afforded respect. Ironically, it wasn't that dissimilar to what had led her here. It was just that Percy was the last person Julia was convinced she could count on.

---

j.

After they had shared the secret of the misplaced love letter, Julia and Kestly had established a kind of friendship. Julia had come to realize that Kestly had a genuine interest in Percy's work, and though she had originally thought otherwise, Kestly's having forged that interest through a personal experience with the man was not a drawback. Rather, the connection lent an emotional honesty to her studies. She really wanted to do right by him.

It was spring break Julia's sophomore year, several months after the Halloween Party. Kestly offered to give Julia a ride down to Stockton. She was on her way to Los Angeles herself, and so not only would Julia get back home, but it would give Kestly some company for a good portion of her trip.

Unfortunately, the drive turned out to be pretty miserable. A wicked storm had moved in off the California coast and was pushing up through Southern Oregon. Sheets of rain fell down on them, slamming into the professor's car nonstop until they finally found the tail of the weather pattern just over the California border. To make it worse, conversation seemed to run its natural course after an hour or so. The confined space and the unhealthy condition of the sky seemed to drain both women of their ability to communicate. Julia was more than content to sit in the passenger seat and watch the passing scenery. The dark skies were almost magical at that speed. The car was moving one way, and the clouds were moving another, giving Julia a weird perspective on the world. It was like they were pushing against the waves of the ocean. Or fighting to climb through an avalanche.

Even if the natural flow of their conversation had petered out, Kestly didn't stop talking. It was almost as if she were afraid of silence. She told Julia about her rich uncle and the rages he would go into. "You think famous men have it together," she said, "but they don't." She said the whole key to their success was appearing to be in control. It didn't matter if they were or not as long as everyone thought they were. As a little girl, she'd spend vacations visiting him and her aunt, and that was when she'd witness him losing his cool. Norman Jones was an infamous boozer, but when he consumed the wrong amount, his temper would start buzzing and he'd stalk the hallways with a cloud of invisible gnats swarming his head. He'd carry a poker from the fireplace, and he'd hit things with it. Uncle Norm would smash a lamp here, knock over a statue there. Kestly never saw him hit another person, but he would shout at whoever got in his way with such fury, he might as well have struck them. "The force of his booming voice was like a giant foot stomping down on you, an angry god punishing his subjects."

This line of talk naturally led her to Percy. "The thing was, when I met him that night, I think that having seen behind the façade of my uncle was what allowed me to see past Percy's, as well. His position as a dispenser of truth, that was his true mask, not the Zorro costume. The man behind the words was flailing, and he was looking for something to hold on to so he could steady himself."

Kestly didn't say it outright, but Julia could tell she was trying to say she was that fencepost Percy could lean on, the railing to protect him from being tossed from the ship into an angry sea of his life. Julia tried to tune her out. She couldn't bear to hear her picking over the carcass of that evening again. In social situations with other people or in a classroom setting, that was one thing, but here, when it was just the two of them, it just seemed unnecessary.

"I think part of what makes me want to write about his legacy," Kestly continued, "is that I want to preserve it. I want to protect him the way I couldn't that night. At the same time, I want to be the first to take everyone else past the outer layers, to see the true man, the one I saw. It puts me in a very unique position. I can build my name on it, you know?"

"Build your name while preserving his?" Julia asked.

"Oh, well, yeah. Of course. I have to serve his words first and foremost. Any other benefit, that's just the whipped cream on top."

This was a new side to Kestly that Julia had not seen before, and she found it offensive. Sure, there might have been some truth to her perception of what Percy was going through, but any helping hand she was retroactively extending was coming with strings attached. She'd help as long as she got something in return.

Now that Julia was thinking about it, it was always the same. It didn't matter how Kestly began talking about Percy's writing, whether it was about a specific essay or one of the novels, it always led to her stories about having met him. It was the one story told in an infinite number of ways. Kestly Edwards was exactly the icy opportunist Julia had originally judged her to be, but Julia had allowed her to charm that judgment away with a few well-placed compliments and the bribe of shared secrets. Julia felt her face grow flushed with the shame of her easy seduction.

Watching the roadside landmarks whiz by—a billboard, a street sign, an abandoned car—Julia began to wonder about Kestly's notion that Percival Mendelssohn was a man looking for a shoulder to lean on. There was a tragic irony to the idea. Here was a man who had provided support to so many, whose work had inspired and uplifted millions of readers, but what kind of support had those readers ever given back, Julia included? All that time she had been thinking he had abandoned her and left his fans standing on their own with the discussion unfinished, an anecdote hanging in the air without the punch line, but maybe it was the other way around, and Julia and all the others had failed Percy. What if he really had been reaching out to Kestly that night, and instead of taking his hand and pulling him to his feet, she had let him drop in order to grab a meal ticket?

"What about your father?" Kestly asked Julia. "Is he in control?"

"Of course," Julia replied. "Papa works with his hands. He actually gets it done. He's not like those guys that tell everyone else what to do, he really knows how to do it."

Julia wasn't sure who she was lashing out at with the answer. She didn't really mean it to be about Percy, but it kind of sounded like it. Kestly was her most obvious target—those who can, do; those who can't become graduate students. Julia didn't even really believe it about Papa, when it came right down to it. A lot of his life was taking orders. Nor did she believe it about herself. What was Julia Marie Jiménez in control of?

No, when it came down to it, Percy was still winning out. At least he had been able to pull himself out of the mire, to hide himself. That was control. Maybe he was still blazing a trail after all.

Julia soured on Kestly even more once the bad weather passed. Without the clouds to focus on, Kestly was all that was left. The farther down the freeway they went, the more the older woman's insecurities began to show. She was smoking like a fiend. She claimed she only smoked on long trips, but it was like she was making up for the rest of the time by lighting up one after the other, as if she could suck down all the nicotine she had abstained from since her last road trip. "The other professors, they frown on smokers," she explained. "If they catch you, you're out of the club."

Kestly's standing with the other faculty was something she fretted over constantly. The usual debates over the validity of Percy's writing dogged her. She was constantly in fear that the powers that be would come down with the final word that his philosophy was not worth studying after all. She even made a joke about Percy's disappearance. "I almost wish they would find a body so he can join the ranks of the dead white guys and gain some credibility."

As the sun rose, Julia could really begin to see how the all-night trip had affected Kestly's appearance. Normally an attractive woman who knew how to put herself together well, her skin had grown sallow and the dark rings under her eyes were almost visibly expanding moment to moment. It was like a little piece of her veneer had exited at each off-ramp the women had passed. First it was a bit from the mental image she presented of herself, then a matching piece of the outside appearance followed. No one could have survived such an erosion across two states.

The true lesson was that Kestly Edwards was no more fabulous, no less human than the rest of the world's population. Without her pile of research materials and her surveys and her encounter with Percival Mendelssohn, she aged and she smelled bad just like anyone else. University professors weren't special people. Who were they to guide young minds? They were mortal, too.

Once they pulled up outside of her parents' house in Stockton, Julia was to discover that the road trip had opposite results for Kestly. Before Julia could open the door to get out, Kestly was leaning across the seat and hugging her. "This has been so much fun," she said. "I feel like I know you heaps better."

The embrace lasted a little long for Julia's tastes, and eventually she wrestled out of the older woman's grip. When she had done so, she felt like she had broken the hold that all of academia had on her. If she had glimpsed behind the curtain of how higher learning was run, Julia wasn't all that impressed with the cogs and levers.

Little did she know there would be further consequences of that hug. Someone else was watching the exchange and preparing to distort it to his advantage.

*

Without Julia knowing it, her parents and the Villagrans had decided it was time to push the marriage issue once and for all. They left her out of the machinations partially because they thought it was Arturo's job as the man to spearhead the endeavor, and partially because he played the good boy around them and he was seen as more taken with the idea of the union than Julia was. Of course, that was all a ruse. He was only going to play along as long as he had to. He was biding his time and waiting for Julia to do something he could use to bring it all tumbling down and pin the whole fiasco on her while doing it.

When her parents called her into the room to talk, Julia could tell it was about something serious, that they were displeased with her again, probably her hair, which was shorter than ever thanks to the Halloween buzz. She would have never guessed it was because they were going to accuse her of being a lesbian. She had been wiped out from the drive and after a quick meal had gone straight to bed, sleeping all through the night. This gave Arturo time to go to work.

He had been sitting up the block from the house the day before. His mother wanted him to greet Julia when she arrived, but he had decided to hang back rather than get spotted by Mrs. Jiménez and be forced to wait inside with her. He had seen Julia get the hug from Kestly, and it sparked something devious in his brain. Instead of saying hello like he was supposed to, Arturo went straight home and told his mother that he had seen Julia in the car kissing another woman. He had told her what Mrs. Villagran would later tell Julia's mother, that he had heard about this happening when girls were allowed to go away to college. "They get into all-female dorms, and they start being made to read weird poetry, and the next thing anyone knows, they decide they're gay. She'll grow out of it, though, don't worry."

Julia had Arturo to thank for introducing her mother to the term "L.U.G.," Lesbian Until Graduation. Luckily for him, even if Julia did grow out of it, no one would expect him to marry her now. It was a bittersweet reward. Sure, now Julia was free from having to weasel out of the proposed marriage on her own, but at the same time, a little of her died that day when she was forced to confront some of the things about her parents that she had always made excuses for.

Most people make concessions when it comes to their folks. They'll give them a bit of a pass for being from a different generation, and in Julia's case, there were cultural and religious reasons for them to feel the way they did about certain types of people. It had never been personal, though, it was always—well, she didn't want to use the word "bigoted." She much preferred "antiquated." The Jiménezes had antiquated opinions about certain things, but it had always been directed at people they didn't know.

Now, thanks to Arturo, those opinions were directed at their daughter.

Julia tried to protest. She told them Arturo was wrong, and then she upgraded it to say he was flat-out lying. "I'm not having an affair with that woman," she insisted, "she's my teacher. Come on! Don't you remember when Artie slighted me back in school? You never believed me, but do you see it now? This is all *him*."

Unfortunately, they didn't see.

In all fairness, Julia was not kicked out of the house or disowned. Her mother and Papa did make it clear, though, that they were severely disappointed, and they were going to have to formulate some kind of strict regimen to save her soul. More church was required, and perhaps they would have to consider taking her out of that school. Yes, it had become "that school" in the way things always lose their identities when they are on the outs, just as Julia would become "that Jiménez girl" to the people to whom the Villagrans would spread the juicy gossip. Just as Arturo had exposed the ugly side of Julia's parents, he'd done the same for his own. They were proving once and for all what kind of friends they were.

By the time the argument was over, Julia had denied everything and agreed to nothing, and neither tactic had shaken the acceptance of Artie's false report. Julia was now their dyke daughter with the shaved head who had been corrupted by a liberal education, and her parents no longer believed in her. On the flipside, she no longer believed in them. It had only been a day since she had lost her faith in education, so losing her belief in her parents was quite a blow. There had been no warning signs, the crisis had hit and she was left with nothing: college and teachers, family and friends, none of it could be counted on. If religion had steered her parents wrong, then it was fallible, as well.

So, then, what was left?

Julia needed an answer, but the source she normally went to was no longer available. Percival Mendelssohn was gone, and she had found herself once and for all in the spot he had abandoned her. She had gotten as far as she could go with the tools he had left behind, and to go any further, she needed something more. She thought back to the conclusion she had come to in the car, that maybe his leaving was a statement. In going, he was showing how in control he was. She needed whatever answer Percy had gleaned from that. Was there salvation in the departure? Was it in the isolation? Did Percy see some truth that made him do it?

Julia had to know.

It was then that she decided to actively look for him. She didn't know how she would find him when no one else had, she just knew that she must. She would find him and ask, "Why?" No qualifiers, no parameters. She'd just ask "Why?" and let him choose why what.

9.

The story had come back to her in a flash, remembered in the space of time it took to walk from her bedroom to Percy's. At the end of it, she instantly saw the hypocrisy of her own reactions. What had happened to the guilt of never having been there for Percy the way he had always been there for her? Oh, the fickle stance of a fan! It had been so easy for her to justify it back then. "Surely, he must have it together. He doesn't need me, because he's already ahead of me and waiting for me to catch up."

Now, confronted with the reality of the grief Percy lived in, it was no longer so easy to pass the buck back to him. She needed to face up to the role reversal that had occurred: she had come there looking for him to bail her out, and he was in need of bailing himself. She wasn't so full of herself to think that she was any better off than he was, that she would be his savior. They were merely struggling in the same personal labors, and it was her turn to put her back into it.

When Julia had first gotten involved in Kestly Edwards' research project, she had wondered who would play the role of Nadya, the woman who changed the course of life for the banished hero of Percy's novella, *I Was Someone Dead*. The main character, Hieronymus Zoo, had run from life and the pain that came with it, and the surprise appearance of this woman hadn't erased the fact that there was suffering; she had just shown him there was a reason to keep kicking against it.

Julia had become Percy's Nadya, and it was time to lace up his boots.

*

She gently knocked on Percy's door. There was no answer.

She knocked again, this time harder. Still, nothing.

The third knock was more of a pounding, using the bottom of her fist. He could continue not to respond, but he would not be able to ignore her. "I won't be kept out," she shouted.

There was no lock on the door, and the knob turned in her hand; yet, when she pushed, it would not give, there was something behind it. Pressing her shoulder against the wood, she pushed with all of her strength, digging her heels against the floor. The door slid in a little. Julia could hear something crash behind it, a piece of Percy's barricade. Now she had a crack. She could feel the stale, warm air of his bedroom, the smell of ginger and sweat. It wasn't much, but it was enough, a measure of proof: even he was incapable of escaping fully.

"What are you going to do?" she asked, pushing as much of her face into that crack as she could. "Are you going to stay in there forever? How will you eat?"

Julia thought she could hear music. Classical music. A full and melancholy orchestra was going through its paces. It was dark in the room, and the rest of the house was quiet. She hoped Val was in bed, and then thought for a second that maybe Percy was actually asleep, until she heard rustling from inside. He was awake, and he was moving.

She pushed again. She was still in her new dress, and so her shoulder was bare. The wood was rough against her skin, and she could see out of the corner of her eye that the flesh was turning pale from the pressure. It wouldn't surprise her if a dark bruise would be waiting for her in the morning.

The door gave a little bit. Just a little, but enough. Julia heard another crash. She let up on the pushing, and the door came back in her direction, but when she pushed it again, it immediately went back to her point of progress.

This was it. She couldn't give up now. She was almost there. One more shove with everything she had, and the whole thing came crashing down. Several cats shot past Julia as she stumbled through the door. She thought she recognized Gawain, Tristan, maybe Pendragon himself. She turned her head to watch them go and immediately tripped over the various objects Percy had used to fortify his hiding place. There was a small end table, now lying on its side, and a chair upended a few paces from it. Various books now littered the floor, and a small Buddha vase smiled up at her from the ground, its dirt having spilled from its bald head. Her own purple flower lay there in the trampled mess. Julia had to turn away from it, and she peered around the room, trying to focus her eyes, to see if she could see anyone in the light that now came in through the opening she had created. "I'm sorry," she said aloud, though she still hadn't found anyone there.

Then, in the blackness, a head rose up. Percy had been on the floor by the bed, ducked down out of sight of prying eyes. Julia only knew it was him because she recognized the shape of his silhouette. "Who's there?" he asked. He sounded panicked.

"It's me. Julia. What are you doing?" Her voice cracked. Seeing him there had made Julia a little less sure of herself.

"Julia?" He tossed the name back at her. "Oh, I thought...."

His voice trailed off.

"Were you asleep, Percy?"

"No."

"Then answer my question: what are you doing lying here in the dark?"

Percy disappeared again. "Leave me alone," he said, his voice coming from low in the room. He had slipped back down into his murky hole. "Can't you see this was a mistake?"

Julia crouched down. She had been holding *Snow Country* in her hands, and she placed it on the floor by her feet. Cupping her palms, she scooped the soil back into the Buddha vase. "Which part?" she asked, as she slid the purple flower back into the dirt as best she could.

"All of it," Percy moaned.

Julia picked up the book again, and she tossed it into the black where Percy's voice had come from. "All of it? You mean like giving me this book?"

She could hear him reaching for it, the movement of his body distinct from the music in the background. "You didn't like it?" he asked. His voice had changed. He almost sounded perplexed, as if her disapproval of Kawabata was the last thing he expected.

"I liked it fine," she replied. "I'm just not sure what kind of bullshit move you were pulling giving it to me."

He sat up again. The book was visible in his hands, the white of the cover and the pages standing out in the shadows. "It's a lovely story. It reminded me of you."

"In what way?"

There was a pause. "Just that you'd like it," he said.

"You weren't trying to tell me something with it?" Without her willing it to, Julia's tone had risen to angry.

"What do you mean?"

Julia pointed a damning finger at the book. "Who am I supposed to be in there? Are you Shinamura?"

"No," Percy replied defensively. "It's not like that. I just wanted to share it with you. I didn't mean anything more by it."

"No way." Julia stood up. "Don't try to kid me. You don't do anything without meaning. Every gesture you make is indicative of something. I refuse to believe you would drop a book outside my door without intending to say something with it. All I know of you is through books. You communicate to me through them. First your own, now those of others. You started with *Unbearable Lightness of Being*, with romantic connections that could not be broken, with women who come together over the common bond of the man who wreaks havoc on their hearts. In the end, though, they don't abandon each other. Not even Tomas.

"But this...what is this? Am I meant to be a whore who is too ignorant to realize her unattainable John is using her? I can never replace the mercurial child who won't succumb to your attentions?"

Percy tossed the book back at her. He rose up higher now, balancing on his knees. "That's not fair," he said. "You shouldn't say things like that."

"Why not?" Julia asked. She realized she had hooked into something, and she wasn't going to let him wriggle out of it. "We can't bring her up, is that it? I'm tired of dancing around the issue, Percy. In the books, the women never discuss the mistresses their men take. Tereza silently endures their scent, Komako steers the subject away from Shinamura's prying questions, but I'm not going to let you do it.

"I get the code, guy. It wasn't that hard to decipher. Shinamura goes to the mountains to get away from people and recharge his batteries so that he'd be prepared to face them again, but then he gets stuck there because he's not really looking to engage. He's more caught up in his fantasies. He doesn't let his women be real, he keeps them at arm's length rather than give in to his heart.

"But you know what? Our lives are not these books. I am not either of the women in *Snow Country*. I couldn't be them any more than you're the insect Shinamura sees dying on his hotel floor, a victim of a slow, creeping death brought on by changes in the weather that are beyond its tiny control. That's right, Percy, I know how to read these things. I am your student after all. I'm just starting to wonder if the teacher remembers his own lessons."

Julia moved across the room, looking to the small sliver of light to restore her bearings. She knew the room. If she had come in through the outside door, then the door that led to the kitchen was to her left, and by that, a lamp.

The brightness bathed them both. Percy didn't so much as blanche from it as he dropped his gaze in shame. It wasn't very dramatic, more an act of resignation. Julia went back to him, sat down on the floor in front of him. Here they were again, sitting cross-legged on his bedroom floor. Only now she wasn't in awe of him or scared of him the way she was the first time. Now she saw him for what he was. How unfair it had been of her to give him such superhuman status. Like she had seen that Kestly was a real woman, she had to remember Percy was just a man. His gift just happened to be ideas, and for the first time, she realized that was his weakness, too.

"Listen," she said, speaking softly, removing the edge from the words the way a mother would remove crusts of bread from a sandwich. "I know that the novels you gave me aren't supposed to reflect us exactly. You'd be the first to say that stories are signposts, not full explanations. We still have to find our way to where we're going. Even so, you wouldn't have given the books to me unless you were trying to say something. I'm trying to listen, Percy, but you have to help me out."

Percy lifted his head and looked at her now. His eyes were stung through with red, his lips were dry. Only half a day had passed, but he looked like it had been much longer. Julia thought she was seeing the full weight of eight years manifested on his face.

"Tell me."

He shook his head. "No, it's mine. I can't. That's the price."

"Price? There is no price, Percy. It certainly wouldn't be years of your life spent in banishment. You really think Iris would have demanded this of you?"

The mention of her name caused a jolt to run through him. His complexion grew more pale, something Julia would have thought impossible a second before it actually happened. Seeing that reaction, seeing it in his eyes, she understood, like the name Iris had been a cover over a picture, and now it was lifted and she could see what was in the frame. She reached out and touched Percy on his knee, keeping her eyes locked on his. When she saw that it was okay, that he was going to allow it, she reached further and grasped him by the wrist. "I know it's about Iris," she whispered. "It's okay. You can tell me."

Julia extended her other hand and put it over the top of his. She was now cradling it in both of hers—one above, and one below.

"What happened on that night that you're afraid I'd find out?"

*

Percy began the story slowly....

---

k.

The November 1st, 1999 issue of *The New Yorker* began to circulate a couple of days before its release. The lead review in its "The Critics" section was an overview of Percival Mendelssohn's career, precipitated by the release of his fourth and most recent book, the sprawling novel *The Other Side of the Street*. The review was entitled "To Get to the Other Side," and subtitled "Why the Self-Obsessed Cross the Road in the World of Percival Mendelssohn." It was not kind.

Percy was not prepared for such a backlash. He saw *The Other Side of the Street* as a culmination of his work. His other books—*One*, *Divine Plight*, *The Ballad of Strangelove*, and even the long-gestating novella *I Was Someone Dead*—were all dry runs for this narrative. He had adopted an approach he saw as a tried-and-true classic: two friends, one rich and one poor, the son of an employee of the other boy's father. The book followed them through childhood and their teen years and on into adult life where their fortunes changed and both boys now had the lot in life previously denied to them. How someone might choose to adapt to these twists of fate was a true test of the measure of a man, Percy believed, and so his story would provide unique opportunities for him to explore the existential crises of modern man. The central metaphor of the title was a variation of the cliché about the grass always being greener. As a child, the poor boy, Horatio, went with his father when the man had to deliver some news to his boss. The boss had taken his family to the theatre for the evening, and Horatio and his father had to wait outside for the patrons to emerge. They parked across the way from the theatre, and Horatio sat in the car and watched as all the rich men and women, in their tuxedoes and their fancy dresses, stepped out onto the sidewalk. Even his friend, Terrence, was all decked out for the evening. "*Seeing his playmate in a bowtie was possibly the oddest thing Horatio had ever witnessed. He realized that he himself did not know how to tie one, and so he could not wear one even if it was given to him by some benefactor. Was the thing that separated his family from Terrence's really that simple? A bowtie? Or was it the great expanse of concrete that existed between the curb where his own father had parked and the curb where he met Terrence's father? Horatio realized that his dad had not stepped up onto the sidewalk when he spoke with his employer, he stayed in the gutter. He was not permitted to cross the street fully and join the crowd there. His brown suit looked drab and ratty when pressed up against the women with their jewels and the men with their orange-glowing cigars. It was as if Horatio's father were standing in front of a movie screen, a member of the audience, and though the theatre-goers appeared to be close enough to touch, they were just figures of light reflected on a wall.*"

Over the years, Horatio and Terrence would cross that street several times, often passing each other in the middle, and they'd each find that life wasn't about where you expected the journey to come to rest, but it was tied up in perpetual movement. There was no stopping, only going forward. Existence was a never-ending process, and no one position was permanent.

The *New Yorker* review made its way into Percy's hands the day before its cover date. The main exception that the reviewer seemed to take to the material—and, in fact, *all* of Percy's writing—was that, to his mind, it was all surface and no substance, more feeling than thought. "*One has to wonder at the popularity of such simplistic fables,*" he wrote. "*You would think their very lack of complication would divest them of any believability, as surely Mendelssohn's rather large audience leads more complicated existences than the fictional characters he sells them. Perhaps the idea of 'selling' is the operative here: these stories are cynically devoid of deeper meaning, like a band-aid that doesn't stick so tightly that it hurts to remove. It's philosophy in a can, and you don't even need to add water. Forget the stove, too. A microwave will do for such disposable points of reason.*

"*The real problem*," the piece continued, "*is there is no real problem. For all of Mendelssohn's protagonists, nothing much really happens. We are told that No Name and Hieronymus Zoo and the two boys in* The Other Side of the Street *feel heavy emotion, almost too heavy for them to carry it all, and they often attempt to escape the burden. But a careful reading leads one to ask, 'What burden?' Their lives simply aren't too terribly bad. I can think of things that happened to me this morning that, comparatively, are worse, and one is that I was not given a paper jacket for my to-go latte, and it was so hot I nearly dropped it. A small trifle. Perhaps these books are reflective of the apparent ease that Percival Mendelssohn has come to such prominence: he has not had to struggle, and so his work takes it just as easy.*"

It wasn't necessarily new criticism for Percy. All of his books had received similar charges from various corners. It was that this time he had thought he had beaten the doubts. He believed *The Other Side of the Street* to be his best work. It was meaty and important. Surely he had reached depths his writing had never gone to before!

And yet, the first major review of it played to his worst insecurities—that the book was shallow, and by implicating his entire bibliography, so was Percival Mendelssohn. Like most writers, he feared that he was uninteresting, that his writing lacked resonance. The last thing Percy wanted to be was shallow.

He showed the review to Iris. She glanced over it. "He's an imbecile," she said. "He doesn't get it. How can he not see that your very point is that not a lot has to happen for things to hurt? I've always liked that about your stuff. The tragedies are normal, they aren't overblown."

"I know!" Percy exclaimed. "A pain felt is still pain. There's no scale to measure whose is worse!"

Iris handed the review back to him. "You just need to laugh it off, darling," she said.

"How can I? You didn't even read the whole thing. You don't know how bad it is!"

"I don't have to read it all. I've read it before. This idiot isn't saying anything new, and we know it."

"Iris, that doesn't make it better. The criticism isn't new, which means it keeps coming up, which means it might just be *true*."

Iris put a hand on his shoulder. "Except we know it's not," she said.

"My point is, by now, it's a lie you should be used to. You have to stop letting it affect you."

These words were not what Percy wanted to hear, and he shrugged Iris' hand away. "You just don't understand," he declared and walked out of the room. "I'm going to get dressed for the party."

It was Halloween, and the couple had someplace to be.

Percival was going dressed as Zorro. He liked the simplicity of it: the mask, the hat, the short cape, the blackness of the clothes. He didn't like in one sense that it was sort of borrowing a childhood chapter from his brother Lance's book, but the spiteful kid in him took pleasure in the knowledge that he carried off the chivalric nature of the swordsman far better. He liked imagining himself as the mysterious stranger, and tonight, the mask could take on an added layer, hiding the morbidity that lurked within him. He was feeling worthless and superficial, and the mask would do the work of presenting a courageous front. Once it was on, Percy arched an eyebrow, just to see how it looked. Perhaps he wasn't chivalrous after all. Perhaps he was a scoundrel. "Time will tell," he said to himself, a wry smile delivered through the mirror.

Iris' costume was much more creative. At its base, it was a princess costume. She had a pink dress with satin and tulle, a star pattern on the skirt and a lighter pink underskirt that showed out the bottom. A gold belt was tied around her waist in a bow. The sleeves cut off just under the shoulder, and the neckline scooped down just above the bustline. She accessorized with a gold necklace dotted with green jewels that looked like jellied candies and a golden tiara with a pink heart at its center. Her long blonde hair had been set so that it fell around her shoulders in waves.

Then came the twist. Iris had taken lumps of black charcoal and rubbed them all over the left side of her dress, creating big dark smears on the pink. She used a less abrasive goo for that side of her hair, also adding chunks of Vaseline to knot some of it up and add a sheen to it. Next came a make-up kit to simulate burn scars. She applied it to the left side of her face and neck, and a little on her left arm, adding more black and bubbling it rather than making it look like the mottled pink of burnt flesh. She wanted it to look like plastic that had melted.

When Percy saw her, he looked disgusted. "What the hell is that get-up?" he asked. He had realized then that he hadn't yet inquired about Iris' costume, not even when he told her what costume he had wanted and sent her out to get it. That was rude of him, he knew it, and he was sure that callous fact had not gone unnoticed by her.

And he was right.

"Isn't it obvious?" she replied. "I'm a doll who has been set fire to by a mean boy."

Percy put his hand over his mouth. "That's *grue*some, Iris."

"That's Halloween, Percival." She stepped over to him and kissed him on the cheek. "My only regret is that I couldn't find anything to make me smell like smoke. I thought about rolling around in the fireplace, but then thought again."

She smiled. She was laughing. Maybe he wasn't as in trouble as he thought. Which was good, because having to deal with that kind of domestic strife would take him away from his selfish brooding.

The car ride over was silent, the two of them in the backseat staring out windows in opposite directions.

*

The host for the evening was Norman Jones, a media mogul with his hands in various forms of mass communication, including both television and publishing, among other things. His Vermont estate was one of several around the country, and he also had a house in Spain. To be invited to one of his shindigs was a special thing, signifying that you had made it into an exclusive echelon of society. He liked to have a wide variety of people from all fields—art, science, industry, and anything in between—they only had to be the very best. The affairs weren't as large and grandiose as those of other men with the same kind of money he had. His largest gathering would tap out at under a hundred people. The line for who was the best and who was not had to be drawn somewhere, after all.

When Percy and Iris entered the house, the husband was instantly removed from the care of the wife. Though older than Percy's usual demographic, the hostess was a fan of his books. She was known as a bit of a self-help fanatic, a public relations sore spot that caused her husband no end of consternation. Percy had encountered her type before. These kinds of women were what Percy felt lent credence and fuel to detractors like the critic from *The New Yorker.* They gravitated to the positive message at the core of Percy's ideas—self-definition, love, spiritual contentment—while skipping over the harder bits—the struggle toward perfection, the fallibility of man. In some ways he viewed them as jailers. Their money, which helped keep him riding high on the bestseller list, locked him in a prison of disrespect.

The woman at the party insisted that Percy call her by her first name: Marian. She was dressed as Eliza Doolittle in her ball outfit, when she is first presented to high society in *My Fair Lady.* Her blue hair was done up on her head, fastened tight with a tiara. Marian placed a gloved hand on Percy's shoulder and whisked him away from Iris. Percy wasn't particularly happy about this kidnapping, and judging by the glare in Iris' unmelted eye, she wasn't either. Truth be told, though, he also wasn't that eager to stay with his wife. She hadn't wanted to understand how much the review of *The Other Side of the Street* had bothered him. She used to be there to cushion him when the poison pens delivered their stabbing blows, but time had made her indifferent to his plight. If she had comfort to give him, she was keeping it to herself.

So, in its own way, Marian's one-dimensional admiration was an escape hatch. Or, to stick with the jailer metaphor, Marian was taking Percy from maximum security to minimum.

"You have to meet my niece," Marian told him. "I gave her your books last summer when she graduated from Brown. She studied literature, she's going to be a teacher, and can you believe she went through all four years without ever reading you? For the money Norman paid—my husband, he took care of her, the dear. Her father is my brother, and between you, me, and the marble tiles, he's *useless.*"

"Oh, come now," Percy said, knowing the exact sort of thing Marian wanted to hear, "no one is useless. They might be wasting what God gave then, but they *could* be useful if they so chose."

Marian gripped his shoulder tighter. "Darling, you *know,*" she said. "But then, you would, wouldn't you?"

She laughed at her own discovery of the obvious.

Percy could file away this experience with so many others of its kind, ones largely ignored by those beyond his immediate circle. For all the noise made about his adolescent fanbase, there was none made of the society matrons who wanted to form a chorus of angels around him. It was probably for the best, as they would easily be turned into a throng of bored, rich housewives wanting to possess the young and handsome professional intellectual, much like how tennis trainers and golfers had for so long been the illicit treasures of upper-class women on television soap operas.

Marian led Percy past a throng of luminous guests: a sitcom actress he had met twice before, a physicist he had read a profile of in a magazine, an author of comic books and legal thrillers. The house was massive. Percy thought they could probably fit the populations of several public schools in there. The ceilings, he guessed, were at least thirty feet high and paneled—was it more marble? Regardless, it was black, and every fifth panel was replaced by a light, the green glass of their coverings cross-sectioned with thin gutters in diamond patterns. The individual glare of each lamp was soft, but when added up, they illuminated the room as if it were the most intimate of summer afternoons.

The walls were noticeably absent of decoration—no paintings, no photos of the family, not even decorative carpets or foreign tapestries. There were, however, statues, one every few feet on alternating sides of the corridors. Percy was particularly struck by one of Saint Jude. He had a flame burning on the top of his head, and in either hand, he held an object. In the left hand, he had an axe, and he cradled it in the crook of his arm as if it were a baby. In his right hand he had a plant frond, and he gripped it like a harpoon, like he might throw it any second. His face, however, was blank, as if he had grown bored of the eternal pose he was trapped in. He was now his own lost cause.

Along his walk with Marian—how far away *was* this niece?—faceless people seemed to hand Percy drinks. Was it champagne? Must be, if only for the way it went to his head. How long had they been traveling? How many empty flutes had he left on their trail? Iris could find him if she wanted to, just by following the glasses. If she chose to look.

Later on, looking back at the night, Percival wished to blame none of what happened that evening on the demon alcohol. His actions were his own; but he also understood the sensation of the time was important, because at that moment, he knew with complete clarity what the phrase "my head is swimming" meant. The spirits imbibed on that Halloween evening left his body feeling leaden, as if trapped at the bottom of an unnamed sea, and his cranium had become dislodged from the body, was floating free, attached to his shoulders by a lengthy chord, bobbing around on the ocean currents.

This was important because it was in this state that he met Kestly.

Marian's niece was the thing. The quarry. *L'objet d'art*. While Marian quoted predictably from some text that Percival would have never felt comfortable resting on the same shelf as his oeuvre, Kestly was something unexpected indeed. They found her sitting on a divan in a remote room with dark statues of Egyptian cats in every corner. She rose to meet them.

Kestly was young. As her aunt had said, fresh out of school. Her brown hair was tacked back on one side with a barrette. It was adorably girlish, but with a practical air that said it was just business that was pulling it out of her face. Percy himself was only twenty-three, so he was really closer to Kestly's age than he was to anyone else at the soiree.

The girl's blouse was made of a sheer silver fabric with the see-through appearance of gauze, though Percy was sure it was much finer to the touch. She had a black suit coat on over it so that one could just see the edges of her shoulders and breastbone. The outfit gave the illusion that Kestly had nothing on underneath to bar one from her lightly tanned flesh. On closer inspection, however, Percy could see that she was wearing a black halter top just on the right side of tasteful, a carefully planned fashion sleight-of-hand.

At that moment, as the girl looked at him with her dark brown eyes and smiled, Percy felt he had fallen in love. He also knew, in that flash of the heart, that if he counted all the times he'd fallen in love this way, these mini romances, he'd be dealing in imaginary numbers.

When he moved to greet her, Percy reached up to remove his Spanish hat the way a proper gentlemen should, only to discover that he had lost it on the journey from the front door to here. Kestly noticed this gesture, aborted halfway through, and asked, "Are you missing something?"

"Apparently," Percy replied.

"Well, at least you still have your head."

"Yes, there is that."

Percy smiled and dropped the hand that had been arrested in midair. "I'm Percival Mendelssohn," he said.

"Kestly Edwards."

She took his hand, and hers was cold and small in his. Not exactly small, actually, but thin, longer, the meeting of the two hands being rather like a triangular peg being slid into a round hole.

"Kestly here is doing her masters thesis on the Ophelia complex in literature," Marian informed him.

"Oh, really? Now I'm scared of you casting an eye toward my books. You might decide I'm a ghastly fiend."

"Well, from what I hear, Mr. Mendelssohn, you've suggested to many a young girl that she should hurl herself into a watery grave."

"You can call me Percy, and I don't think I've ever been so specific as to insist it should be watery."

"My, my," Marian clucked. "The young are always too morbid for my tastes. I'll leave you two here to fight over Yorick's skull."

Marian touched Percy's shoulder once more as she began to exit, but if he noticed, he made no indication. His attention was now focused on this creature in front of him.

"So, tell me, Kestly, is it the new thing among college kids to go to costume parties without a costume?"

"I don't know, Mr. Mendelssohn. I try not to pay attention to what college kids are doing. I've got more important things on my mind. Besides, this is a costume. I'm here as a respectable young lady."

Percival took another sip of his champagne. The length of time it took for it to reach his mouth after the glass had been tilted told him the quantity was dangerously low. "Well, as far as respectability goes," he said, "I think you overestimate mine with this whole 'mister' business. I already told you, skip right past Percival and take Percy between your jaws."

"I don't know. It seems a little odd. My mother told me to always show respect to a masked man because you never know who is hiding underneath."

When she said that, Kestly reached out and touched the tip of Percy's nose with her finger. He felt her skin, and the light brush of her nail. Her hands smelled like pecans. As she pulled her hand away, he felt himself start to follow it. He may have even lurched forward a little, as if being pulled by her scent. He wasn't sure, and he hoped if he did, it wasn't noticeable. To cover, he stepped into the lunge, spinning on his heel and plopping down on the divan that Kestly had been sitting on when he and Marian entered the room. A little champagne splashed from his glass, landing on his thigh. Thankfully, Zorro always wears black, and a little wet spot was not noticeable.

Kestly laughed. It was a miniature laugh, and it was mainly in her nose. "Make yourself comfortable," she said.

Percy pushed a hand up under his mask and rubbed his right eye. "I'm sorry," he said. "Sometimes these things...well, don't you find this is just a lot of kerpuffle?"

"Maybe," Kestly replied, sliding into the spot next to him. "But I don't think you've been here long enough to be tired out already."

Percy gave a conciliatory nod.

"Which means you dragged the tired in here with you."

"Maybe the mask is there not to hide who I am, but merely to conceal the bags under my eyes."

"Maybe. Or maybe it's there to present a sturdy front on behalf of an indecisive prince."

"Ophelia, is that you?"

Kestly pulled the champagne glass from Percy's hand. "Hey, nonny nonny," she said as she put it to her lips, her words echoing inside the damp chute, her breath forming condensation on the glass. She drank the last of the alcohol down.

Percy believed that their breath now smelled the same. It led him to think dangerous thoughts, of leaning in to kiss her, of tasting her tongue on his, champagne vapors passed between. He quickly tried to block such notions with a question: "So, what was it that led you to write about

Hamlet's betrothed?"

After setting the empty glass on the floor, Kestly straightened her neck and back. She smoothed her skirt over her knees, and then left her hands on them. She didn't look at Percy as she spoke, but instead at a spot where the direction of her fingers met, as if a small ball of energy was being balanced by invisible beams emanating from them. "Well, it kind of started out of annoyance. I was noticing a tendency for you writers—particularly in movies—to tell stories about very shy boys who are rescued from their doldrums by wild girls who force them out of their shells. Only these girls end up being crazy, or at the very least, troubled, and by the end, the tables are reversed and the boys have to save them with their oh-so-male stability. I started to wonder where this archetype came from, and it led me to Ophelia."

"But Hamlet wasn't a shy boy."

"No, he wasn't. But it's this notion of the female driven insane by her emotions that I ended up being more curious about, and the need to neutralize her."

"Interesting. And how many boys have you saved in your time?"

Kestly's mouth dropped open in an expression of shock. She lightly slapped Percy's chest. "Mr. Mendelssohn, are you saying I'm crazy?"

"Not at all. I'm just making a guess as to where your annoyance with these characters stems from. My conjecture was that many a young man has looked at those eyes and thought if they looked back at him, he wouldn't die having wasted all of his time."

"Flatterer."

"No. If I were to flatter, the implication would be that I'm lying. I'm telling the truth."

"Ha! Nice save."

"Oh, I do believe you called me Mr. Mendelssohn again."

"I did. How I address you will change based on what you deserve at the moment."

"Goody. I do so like to get what I deserve."

As Kestly pulled her feet up off the floor and tucked her legs under her on the couch, Percy could feel the movement vibrate through the cushions. She turned her legs sideways, her knees pointing at him. Her skirt was a silvery gray, and Percy could see now that she was wearing black stockings that stopped just under the thigh. They stretched with her bending, the fabric turning white, making her kneecaps pale moons in a dark sky. Just above them was a hint of flesh, a sliver between the tops of the stockings and the bottom of the skirt. He watched closely, as if hypnotized, as she slid her shoes off with her feet. He wished they had been pointing in his direction, so that he could take them in his hands and caress them.

"What about when you think you're being treated in a way you don't deserve?" Kestly asked. "Do you sulk?"

"Hmmm? Why do you ask that?"

"It's something about your carriage. I've never met you, so this is just a guess, but I wasn't joking when I made the comment about the brave face. You strike a dashing pose, but there is a slight slump in your shoulders."

"Oh, yeah?"

"If you don't want to talk about it, that's fine, you just have to say so. But I think you're bothered over something."

This was all the invitation Percy needed. Sure, he was shocked that he was wearing his heartache so openly, but he was also impressed that this girl—he kept thinking of her as a girl, and given their ages, if she was a girl, then he was a boy—was empathic enough to notice; not to say a little bit relieved, as well, to be asked to unburden himself.

So he told her all about the review, the unfairness of it. "Doesn't he see that there being no cataclysmic event is the point?" and similar defenses. The ultra-secret admission that for all his posing as the outsider, his defense that it "doesn't matter what the bitter academics say about me as long as real people read it and understand" was a sham. Of course he wanted critical acceptance! How could he not want to be put on the shelf next to his idols? He wanted to be rated as *one of them*.

The only element he kept to himself was Iris' reaction. In fact, he didn't mention Iris at all. He told himself that it was because he didn't want to badmouth her, but even as he formulated the excuse, he knew that an excuse was all it was. The real truth of the matter was that he didn't really want Kestly to know he was married. If she already knew, that was fine, nothing need change; if she didn't...well, one never knows how a young lady would react. Even though he never went any further with his female friends than he had already gone with Kestly, it was their attention he was after, and it was their attention that could change.

When his sad tale was through, Kestly's brow was furrowed and her lower lip had just the hint of a pitying pout. "You poor dear," she said. "I would think you'd be used to such things by now, but I guess that just means it never gets any easier, does it?"

"No, it doesn't."

"Well, I know this probably sounds empty, but you know what this writer says isn't true, and that's the only real fact here."

Her hand was on his chest, just under his shoulder and just above his heart. He bent his face forward, brushing his cheek across her knuckles, feeling her skin on his. Ever so faintly, he extended his lips and kissed her there. She probably heard it more than felt it, the familiar smack of a kiss distinctive above all other sounds. He wanted to keep kissing, to move up her arm, over her shoulder, her neck, her chin, her mouth.

In response to his gesture, Kestly lifted her hand from his chest and placed her fingers on his face. The index was touching the corner of his mouth. He could almost taste the salt of her skin. She was smiling at him now. Was it motherly? Or something more? He hoped for the latter.

Which made Percy ask himself where he was. Was he standing on the precipice of his first real infidelity? God, no, he had to push those thoughts away.

Except he didn't want to push *her* away. He didn't want to. She *understood*. This girl—and he a boy—she felt what he felt, she knew how it hurt. Was that such a bad thing? Everyone wanted to make sense to someone else.

Just as desire fuelled these rationalizations, guilt dragged him back down. He was in danger of being lost, he had to find a diversion.

The whole time they had been talking, Percy could hear big band music being played somewhere inside the house. "Do you know where the music is?" he asked. "Do you think there's dancing there?"

"I wouldn't be surprised if there is," Kestly replied.

"Enough of this maudlin wallowing, then," he said. "We should go there." It was a snap decision. He would stay with her, interact with her, but this way their behavior would remain totally appropriate. There would be too many eyes spying for there to be any more. Percy stood up from the divan, bowed, and held one hand out to her while using the other to lift the Zorro mask away from his face, exposing his eyes. "Would you care to dance with me?"

She smiled. He saw her eyes as they fixed on his, felt them like two sharp hooks. "I'd love to."

Once more she placed her hand in his. He wrapped his fingers over them and around her wrist. *You've grasped me, now I'll grasp you*, he thought, knowing that he wasn't pulling himself away from the temptation at all; rather, he was pulling her to her feet, closer to him. Percy let his mask slide back down.

Kestly took her shoes from the divan and slipped them back on using simple and quick movements. For some strange reason, the slap of one of her ankle straps against the back of her foot made Percy think of a bra unsnapping. This was reinforced when he placed his hand on her back to guide her out of their hidden chamber, and he felt her actual bra strap through her shirt.

For as long as it had taken Marian to lead Percy back to Kestly, they seemed to enter the ballroom directly. The band was in full swing, and the couple took the dance floor with a grace and ease that would have suggested they had known each other all their lives. Percy was correct when he assumed that there would be spying eyes in attendance, but it might have been a good idea to consider all the people those eyes may have belonged to.

*

No one knows what really happened to Iris that night. She was gone before anyone had any reason to inquire. All we can do is piece things together from the scant facts available and try to fill in the holes.

Percy did ask about his wife. He wasn't completely coldhearted to her. Unfortunately, it was only her absence that had piqued his curiosity.

From what anyone could tell him, she had parked an elbow at one of the bars. There, the drinks had kept flowing, as had the male suitors, and while she took every drink that came her way, she rebuffed every man who approached. As Percy would imagine it later, in the many times he rolled the night around in his mind, Iris would show each prospective beau the side of her face that was not made-up for the occasion, luring them to her with her beauty, and then turn to show them the charred remains of the other half, a test to see if they were men of substance or just more dogs hunting out a quick sniff.

The part about the drinking is probably unfair, though. Or, at the very least, exaggerated. Iris' blood alcohol level was not very high. .04%, half of what it would take to be declared legally drunk. This is a detail Percy had been spared in his exile. He could still tell himself that her judgment was impaired, and she hadn't entirely known what she was doing. The truth was, she most likely had.

In the first hour the Mendelssohns were at the party, Iris is remembered to have been genial and charming, moving through the crowd with a smile that belied her ghastly make-up. One partygoer, a neighbor of theirs who had also been invited by the Joneses, recalls asking her where her husband was. "She laughed and waved her hand," he said, "and told me, 'Oh, you know, probably chasing down mice in some lonely corner somewhere.'"

The only existing photo of Iris from that evening has taken on an eerie hue. It's in black-and-white and was taken from Iris' "good side." In it, she poses like the regal princess she was dressed as, perfect posture, her chin up, the light falling over her. Her face is seen in three-quarter view, her delicate features toned with velvet, passing over into the dark shadows of the burnt side. It looks supernatural, the flash of the camera having the same effect as lightning in a horror movie, the momentary illumination revealing death walking among us.

The photo was most likely taken in the first hour, before Iris moved into the ballroom. She did sit at the bar, as Percy had learned, drinking champagne and listening to the music. She was hit on, both innocently and not so innocently, asked to dance multiple times, and despite her love of dancing, Iris refused all company. We are reasonably sure that she did know that her husband was tucked away with another woman as Marian Jones has said that she passed by Iris shortly after leaving the pair and told her so. In her mind, it was an innocuous revelation. "I left your darling husband with my young niece," she recalls saying, "and the two of them are getting on swimmingly." Percy's reputation as a gadabout never crossed the hostess' mind.

Iris was still at the bar when Percy and Kestly Edwards entered the ballroom. The bartender at that station recalls seeing Iris watch them dance, and adds, "The entire room had its eyes on them. It was like they were the stars of the night or something, and everyone had been waiting for them. I asked the woman at the bar if she knew who they were, and she said, 'One of them is my husband. I imagine looking at our marriage from the outside, it would be hard to decide which of us had a bigger Cinderella complex.' She didn't sound bitter or angry or anything. More accepting, really. Or maybe defeated."

Of course, what Iris did not know, what she could not have seen, even if she had stuck around to watch, was that Percy's mind did not stay focused on his dancing partner. Sure, it had at first. He was caught up in the blush of her flattery, the girl's devoted gaze more powerful than any alcohol when it came to fermenting his brain and pickling his sense of self. Had Kestly acted fast, she may have stolen him. A kiss on the lips, a tug on his hand, a giggle aged a decade beneath her own—Percy would have melted, relented, gone with her wherever she asked.

She did none of these things. Her reasons are her own, and not for others to know. Perhaps she didn't sense what was before her, perhaps she could not believe it was true. It would have been keeping with the state of the evening if she, like so many others, failed to see the breadth of love that lay before them. Whatever the reason, she and Percy merely danced.

Or, at least, they did so in body. As the pair twirled around the floor, Percy's mind began to careen off in its own directions, snagged on the fishing line of memory.

It led him back to when they were very young, to the night Percy and Iris had gone to the prom together—the double date with his brother Lance. For Percy, the story held different things than may have been previously related. It was one of the first times Percy had worn a tux, for instance, and he relished it. It wasn't vanity, per se. He just enjoyed dressing up, of playing the role. On that night, he was designated the romantic lead. The best part: he was already in love. He had been dating Iris for several months by that point, and he already knew.

She was the one.

Percy had high hopes for that evening. He knew that proms were silly, and he hated himself a little for being so into the idea. Yet, they were fifteen, and opportunities were few to have a real night out, special nights like in the old movies they both admired. Clark Gable had the advantage of already having graduated high school. Percy was, at that time, limited by his age.

Besides, if he had bought into the notion that this was cliché and somehow meaningless, that would be no more noble than buying into the event outright. Either way, he was letting others—people whom he did not respect—dictate how he lived his life. Who cared what they all thought of the evening, the point was not where he was at, but the person he was with. If this was his and Iris' night to get dressed up and go out dancing, then it would be the most romantic night the two of them had ever known by virtue of the fact that they were together.

Everything he was supposed to do, Percy did. He bought the corsage so that it matched her dress, and the same with the cummerbund. He rented a limousine and made sure it was stocked with chocolates. It was to be a grand night.

In a stroke of luck midway through the night, the DJ played Depeche Mode's "A Question of Lust," a song more tender than its title might suggest. Iris and Percy couldn't help but think fate had put it on for them, and so they danced as if there would be no other dances for the rest of their lives. Percy kept his eyes locked on hers for the entire song. How they managed to not bump into other attendees was beyond him. It was as if the entire world took several steps back to let the couple do their thing, and the sparkle in Iris' eyes and the flock of butterflies in his stomach made Percy a hundred percent sure that he would spend the rest of his life with her.

How long ago had that been? Not long. How quickly one can forget the rest of his life!

He had heard the cliché of angels dancing on the head of a pin, but only that night had he understood it. Their patch of earth seemed so small, the air rarefied. Nothing could touch them.

So, where was he now? Out in the open, exposed, spied on, touched by another. He would have thought he could never have gotten here from there.

But he had.

"I'm sorry, Kestly," he said, pulling away from her.

"What?" she asked. The girl looked bewildered.

"I have to go." Percy lifted her hand, kissed the top of it. "I hope you'll forgive me."

He thought of adding, "I hope we'll talk again sometime," but he let it go. Better to make a clean break. It was all about the gesture. He was returning to Iris.

Only she was already gone.

*

As soon as he got through the door, he could tell something was wrong. The house was dark and still. The stillness was unnatural, like someone had somehow removed all time from the building. Whatever may have been happening in that area, it was going nowhere. Any action was like shouting into deepest space—all motion, no effect.

Iris' shoes were in the doorway, kicked haphazardly to the floor about a foot apart from each other. Her stockings lay just beyond them, and her dress dripped over the bottom step of the stairway leading to the second floor. Percy thought it was almost like she was setting down a trail.

Then he thought, "What if it isn't almost like she is, what if she really is?"

This was only another in a line of strange occurrences since he had broken from Kestly. First, Iris not being there and the things people were saying about how she had been behaving. Second, his car was not on the premises when he tried to leave, so he had to wait for his driver to return—which itself wasn't so strange, as the driver would have been the one to take Iris home. The odd part was that as soon as Percy got in the car, the driver raised the glass partition between them and got on the phone. When he had hung up, Percy lowered the partition and asked him what was going on.

"Mrs. Mendelssohn asked that I call her as soon as I started back with you," the man said.

That meant that Iris knew he was coming. And she had *wanted* to know he was coming.

So, where was she?

As he approached the top of the stairs, Percy's reflex was to reach for the light switch, but he stopped himself. The hallways were dark, and though he knew their every inch and could navigate them blindfolded even in his drunken state, a dread had come over him that there were things now in his home that he did not know. He was scared to illuminate them, better to have them illuminated for him.

A small sheet of light crept under the door of Iris' bathroom. Percy approached the door and put his ear to it. He couldn't hear anything, but he could smell the scented candles she liked to burn while bathing. Orange spice.

He knocked on the door.

There was no answer.

"Iris?" He thought he had said it loud, but it came out quiet.

His heart was sinking. He no longer could say if he really knew for sure before he opened the door, but in his memory, Percy knew right then, right when he said her name, and that somehow made it easier to turn the knob.

Iris was in the tub. The water had turned red. Sticky strands of skin and blood dangled from the cuts on her wrists, swaying in the water like crimson algae in a stream. Candles were burning all around the tub. He was right about that. The room was hot, the mirrors fogged over. Steam was visibly undulating up from the tub.

Her head was under the water. Her eyes were open, staring back at him. For a second he almost laughed, thinking it a ghoulish Halloween trick. Iris was joking with him, giving him a fright...but no, this was no joke.

Spotting the envelope on the wicker hamper next to the tub, Percy wondered if he should go to that first. It had his name on it, it was for him. Get the explanation, then examine the consequences. But something seized him and Percy lunged forward, tossing his whole body into the water, spearing his arms around his wife's form, pulling her up out of the water and to his chest. He could hear himself wailing as if it were someone else. How could this have happened? How could she have done this? How?

Some of the time after that was lost to him. Percy no longer knew how long he held her, wasn't sure when he drained the tub, how long he sat on the floor with his back to it, staring but not seeing. Eventually, he took the note and he read it. It was in her handwriting, and it said:

My beloved Percival,

I envision you finding this, and it fills me with dread. I am afraid you will not understand. But then, if anyone should, surely it must be you?

There are times when I wonder if you know how much I love you. Do you? Most days, I feel like it is too much. I am so full of emotion I think it will cause me to explode. Other days, though, I think that it must not be enough, because if my love for you was as great as I thought, you would see it and you wouldn't let it burn on its own the way it does. If I loved you more, I could encapsulate you in its light and keep you with me and you would never have need to look at another.

Please understand, this is not your fault. I have made my choice to move on. I wanted a romance between us that was pure and forever, and the more time passes, the further away that truth becomes. The passing of our desire for one another—or more specifically, your desire for my desire of you—is not something I can bear to watch. I don't want to be around the day it ceases to exist, fizzling out like a match in a jar.

I envision you finding this, Percy, and though in one scenario it fills me with dread, I confess that in another I dream of you bursting through the bathroom door and scooping me from the water and carrying me to safety, rescuing me at last from my despair.

That's what our love is supposed to be, and that is what it's not.

So, I'm leaving you, and in my stead, you have this, my last testament to how much I care for you. If I could remove my heart and let it beat in your presence until the end of time, I would do that. Unfortunately, like so many other things, this is not something I am capable of.

"I love you," then, will have to do.

Yours always,
Iris

He had done this. His wanderings, they had finally caught up with him. Iris wanted to shock him back into loving her, her actions a defibrillator to get his heart beating the way it should.

Iris hadn't meant to go through with it, not all the way. He was supposed to find her, just like she had said in the letter. He was supposed to burst in and save her before it was too late—only he was too late. He had stayed away too long.

*

The autopsy bore out Percy's belief. It indicated that Iris Mendelssohn died from drowning. The wounds on her wrist were not sufficient to have taken her life. It was noted that the incisions were made across the wrist rather than along the vein, a common error that sometimes suggests the action was more of a cry for help than a serious suicide attempt. It is believed that the combination of the alcohol in her system and the heat of the water caused her to fall unconscious, and she slid under the water, never waking up.

10.

He told Julia about the bad review for his book, and the fight it had caused. He told her about Kestly and dancing and realizing he had been a cad. "I had always thought that I was saving the best for her, you see. I thought if I kept my body for her alone, that it meant I was being faithful in the way that was truly important. I understand how wrong I was. I was sharing myself, I was giving away my time, that was what she wanted from me. It's what should have been hers."

He explained this epiphany, and then told how he had gone looking for his wife only to find Iris gone. He described the car ride and the horrible climb up the stairs to her bathroom. He managed to remain calm up until then, but when it came to the detail of her body and the state of the bath, he could no longer hold it back. The grief surged in him. His whole body seized, and the sobs came, loud and heavy. Julia clutched his hand tighter. She put her face next to his, her mouth to his ear. "Shhhh," she cooed. "It's okay. You don't have to describe that."

Percy audibly choked. "No," he said, trying to collect himself and sit up straight again. "I do. It's the ugly part, and that's what makes it important. I can't hide from it."

"I can still see her," he said. "When I lifted her, her eyes stayed open, and her mouth fell, and it looked like she was going to say something. She looked like I had startled her, and she couldn't believe she was seeing me.

Of course, she wasn't, it was just the reaction of her body to being jostled like that. I understand what's rational even now. That doesn't take away the chill, it doesn't erase what I saw.

"In that instant, I knew. Even if she could have spoken, she didn't have to. It was my fault. I had my last chance to save her, to be her champion and fight for her, and I had lingered. While I had danced, she had waited for me to return. While I dawdled, she died.

"There were no options left to me. She was gone, and that meant I had nothing left, because what did anything else matter? It's pathetic, but we really do have to lose something before we can learn to fully appreciate it. For me, the sun had gone out, and I could continue to send my world on blindly through its orbit, but it would still be dark and empty without her.

"So, I took the only action that seemed logical."

As he said it, Percy pulled his hand away from Julia. He twisted his body at the waist, turning from her. Without saying anything, she took his wrist again. She didn't have to ask, she knew. Julia pulled his arm over to her lap, and with two fingers, she gingerly lifted the cuff of his T-shirt. Percy flinched slightly, but he didn't resist.

The scars weren't nearly as ghastly as she had expected. There were two. They were a pale pink and they ran up the length of his arm. The inside scar was more jagged than the outside one. It was probably made second, and so with a shakier hand. Without her having to ask, Percy brought his other arm over and lifted the sleeve himself, and he held both his arms there so that each was on display. The right arm only had a single cut, and it didn't reach as close to the elbow joint as those on the left.

"I passed out when I was on the third cut. I hadn't intended to mess it up. I sliced up the vein, just like I was supposed to. The police had been and left, and I didn't want to face another minute of it, I didn't want to know any more of what it felt like for her to be gone."

Percy began crying again, and he bent forward, placing his face against Julia's shoulder. She wrapped her arms around him and held him there, rocking him back and forth. "It's okay," she said. "You've been waiting years to share this with someone. Don't be frightened of it."

They sat there together until all the tears passed. When Percy was certain there were no more, he separated himself from her. He pulled his sleeves back down over his scars and then used the fabric to wipe his eyes. "I'm sorry," he said.

"Don't be."

"I must seem ridiculous."

"Not at all."

"Val found me. I don't really remember much about it. He bandaged me up, got me as awake as was possible while still doing what he could for the pain, and that's when he took me out of there."

Julia raised an eyebrow. "Was that his idea?"

"No, it was mine. I wanted to go. If I couldn't be dead, I would rather be far, far away." Percy stood up, looked around the room like he was trying to figure out a way to go, to get away. The old escape mechanism was kicking in again, but seeing nothing, he was forced to sit down again, this time on his bed. If he was stuck, he'd have to continue explaining himself:

"I had wanted to be dead, but I failed. I tried to take my life, but I was rescued in the way I could not rescue Iris. Here I was, Mr. Suicide, supposedly telling kids everywhere that if they thought about jumping, then to go ahead and do it. Then I turned around and tried to kill myself, and I couldn't pull it off. I was a fraud. I wrote about personal responsibility and fidelity, and then I was so blind to my own actions, I drove my soul mate to her death. So, leaving was my only option. I couldn't snuff out my life, but I could make sure I didn't really live it."

"It seems a harsh punishment for your mistakes."

"Was it? I had made it impossible for Iris to go on living, so was it really so harsh to accept the same fate for myself?"

"But that doesn't make any sense." Julia was growing excited now, raising herself up on her knees. "You didn't drive Iris to do anything that wasn't her own choice. The decision to take her life, whether it was to prove a point or not, was her own. That's, like, the most basic Percival Mendelssohn tenet. Our lives are our own, and only we can decide what to do with them."

Percy laughed. It was equally derisive and exhausted. He pinched the bridge of his nose. "That all sounds fine on paper," he said, "when it's just words being pushed up a hill, but it's a whole other matter when they roll back down and crush someone."

"No, that's not true." Julia was getting even more insistent. She had traveled halfway around the world because of her certainty of the concepts Percy had developed, and she was not prepared to let him tear them down. They were all that remained of her belief system. Defending them was no different than defending herself. "By this logic, then nothing is anyone's fault. If you're responsible for Iris, then she is responsible for inspiring your decision to flee. And then what? Who ever picks up the pieces?

"Maybe you should read *Snow Country* again yourself, because I think you have it wrong. Shinamura's downfall was his denial of his feelings. He kept love at arm's length. Like how he wrote about ballet without ever seeing one. But you're different. You wrote about love and tried to make it real, and that you failed doesn't make you evil, it just makes you like the rest of us. It makes you human. At the end of the book, Shinamura still doesn't act, and he's shoved aside. You have the opportunity to be different than that. If you're right and Iris was sending you a message, then the price you have to pay is to learn it. You were supposed to wake up, not go to sleep forever."

Percy's brain was pulsing with energy. There are times in a man's life when he stops and wonders if his heart is really the center of the body, if it's not really the brain that is pumping his blood. It was a little disconcerting, a little like being seasick, but it was exciting, as well. Julia was right, they had been communicating with books, but they had also been communicating with story. She would tell him about herself, and now he was sharing, too. He had been stopped up for so long, stuck on the same thoughts, rewriting what had already been written, but he was starting to feel clear again. Could it be that the things he had just told her, the story he had been avoiding telling anyone, had been the clog? Now that he had dislodged it, shared it, he was feeling like everything else could go forward.

Even so, with that also came new fears.

Looking at Julia with absolute seriousness, he asked, "But how can anyone believe a word I write ever again?"

"Personally, I can believe you more because now I know you have lived it."

"How can you say that after what I just told you?" he wanted to know. "You've gone to great lengths searching for something, only to discover that it doesn't exist."

Julia stood now to be more on level with him. "That's not true," she told him. "If the question had only one answer, I wouldn't have had to ask it. I found what I was looking for...just not how I expected."

*

As the sun was rising, Val came into the kitchen to find both Julia and Percy already there. Julia had made coffee, and she was at the counter pouring her second cup. Percy was still on his first. He drank in slow, measured sips. His body had not stopped racing, and his mind was moving so fast, caffeine would almost have slowed him down. He was still amazed by the sensation, this fortifying of his spirit to prepare for the next volume of his life. He had told Julia, "It's like my cells have been redeployed to take back an occupied country."

Julia was careful in how she looked at Val. Part of her felt like being smug, like making a smartass comment and winding him up. She was good at it, and given the victorious circumstances, she would have enjoyed it, but it really was not the time. Percy had asked her to take it easy, explaining, "I've let Val handle everything for so long, I don't remember what it's like to do things on my own. To not rely on him will be like disabling my reflexes. And what about him? This has been *our* life."

"It's no life," she had replied. "For either of you."

So, she maintained her distance. It was Percy's show.

For his part, Val was remaining surprisingly calm. The look he gave Julia was one of interrogation, but whatever question he was thinking, he did not ask it. Instead, he turned his attention to his boss.

"I'm glad to see you up and about."

"Thank you."

"Can I ask what's going on here?"

"I'm preparing a farewell."

Val smirked. "Really? So you've come to see things my way after all?"

"To a degree," Percy said, clearing his throat, "yes."

Stepping over to Percy, Val crouched down next to him. His knees were bent so far forward, it would have been a short drop for him to be kneeling, but he steadied himself by putting an elbow on the kitchen table. Julia worried that he wasn't actually about to prostrate himself in front of Percy, but he was getting into the same position as a jungle cat just before he strikes.

"To what degree?" Val asked.

"I agree with you that we can't stay here any longer, Val—"

Now Val did drop to his knees, and he nearly fell into Percy's lap. "I've got it all worked out," he said excitedly. "I don't want to say what I'm thinking while she's still here, but I think you'll be really pleased."

"No," Percy said. He held up his hand, waved it just a little. "You're not getting it. I appreciate all of your hard work, Val, I really do. You've been devoted to me for a long time. It's over now. I'm not going to hide again."

The words had the effect of tranquilizer darts. Even as he rose, Val's limbs appeared to grow heavy, his back slumped. Somehow, though, he still managed to raise his chin. He looked down at Percy through slanted eyes. "So that's it, then? After all this, you're dismissing me?"

Percy got up from his chair. He placed his hands on Val's shoulders. "No, Val, not at all. It's not like that. I'm going to figure this out, and when I do, don't think I'll just drop you."

"Sure." Val shrugged him off. "Let's go back, you can keep me on the payroll, and I can watch it all over again. The girl, the press, all the heartache. It'll be like we never fixed it, like we never got you away, and you'll be torn to pieces once more. And then what? I'll be necessary again because someone will need to gather you up?"

Percy was hurt. "Val, do you really think I could do that?"

The man didn't answer him. Instead, he turned away from Percy and turned his scorn on Julia. "This is because of you," he said. "You got what you wanted, didn't you?"

"What? To see him happy? To get Percy healthy? If that's what you mean, you bet."

Julia raised herself to her full height. She was much smaller than the man, but she wasn't going to let herself be intimidated by him. Not now.

"You might have him fooled, but you never had me," Val hissed. "I know what your game is, and I know what you'll do with him when you get him out of this house. Don't think I won't make sure everyone knows exactly what you are."

"Fair enough, but this isn't about you or me, Val. If you try to make it that, it won't work. People will see through you."

"Do you think you know what he needs?" Val was finally exploding. His hands were balled into fists, his arms were in the air, and he was waving them wildly, gesturing without purpose. Julia raised her arms defensively. He wasn't close enough to hit her, it was more of a reflex action. "Are you going to be able to handle it when he teeters off the edge again? He's not like other people. He can't last!"

Stealthily, Percy slid a hand on Val's shoulder from behind. "She doesn't have to know what I need," he said, "because it's what *I* need, and I have to start acting like I know."

Val stood still, his arms at his side. He was silent.

"Did you think this would last forever? At some point, it had to stop. Better this way than on someone else's terms, don't you think?"

Julia steeled herself for another flare-up—she was sure he would attack her, and not Percy, he would never attack Percy—but it didn't come. Whether Percy had found the right combination of words or it was something in his touch, or if logic had just taken over, Val maintained his composure. No more outbursts. Instead, he quietly left the room.

Later, when Julia and Percy would go to look for him, he would be gone. "I have to admit," Julia would say, "I was a little worried. I thought he might go all crazy on us like the maid in *Rebecca* and burn this place down."

Percy perked up. "*Rebecca*? The Hitchcock film or the book by du Maurier?"

"Both, but I saw the movie first, and it's what got me to read the book, so I have to admit, I'm partial to it." She cast a curious eye Percy's way. "Do you like Hitchcock?"

"Are you kidding? I *love* Hitchcock."

Julia winked that curious eye. "I should hope so."

As they walked from Val's room, they went by the front corridor. Percy saw that the door to the outside was ajar, and he motioned to it with his head. Julia followed him to the open doorway, and they both stepped over the little barrier that was there to protect them from ghosts. Percy looked back and tapped it with his foot, like he was testing it. Together, they stood there on Percy's front steps and felt the sunlight on their skin. The sun was off to the east, and the shadows it cast were slanting toward the opening of Percy's alley, to the street and beyond. An easy wind was drifting down from the south.

"So, what next?" Percy asked.

"We go home, and you face whatever is waiting for you."

"Is it really that simple?"

"You forget that people have been looking forward to the day you'd come back. They want to see you."

He looked at her again the way he had back in his bedroom, like he was considering her for the first time, surprised by what she had shown herself capable of. "No, really. Who sent you here?"

"No one. I just came."

"A creature of your own design. No wonder I'm in love with you."

Hearing him say it, Julia gave a tiny laugh.

"I'm sorry," Percy said. "Was that a silly thing to say?"

The girl smiled. "No, it's sweet, it just might not be true. You may only think you are, and that's lovely of you. It is. I think I love you, too. But let's hold on that. Let's get back and see what the world looks like first, and if we're right, all this love will still be hanging around. You never know, I may not look so great when you have the rest of the world to compare me to."

She bumped her shoulder against his. It was playful, telling him that if he was thinking of taking it hard, not to. Percy bumped her back.

"Maybe," he said. "Or maybe we'll discover that wherever I look, you're all I'll see."

A few moments passed, and both of them were perfectly content to let them. Then Julia stuck a hand out and tapped on the door. Her fingers drummed over the fading red kanji painted there. "I bet you don't actually know what this says, do you?" she asked.

Percy craned his head around to see what she was pointing at. He chuckled. "I didn't even know there were letters on my door, so you're right, I don't know what they say. What is it?"

Julia shrugged. "I'll tell you one day," she said. "You might find it interesting."

The girl spun around and went back into the house. Percy took one more look at the painted lettering, and then he followed, leaving the door open so the breeze could flow through.

-. a coda

The small black cat nudged at an overturned cardboard box with his nose. Once it had been upended, he crawled inside. It was empty. He sat down in it and looked around.

The house was dark, and it was empty now except for some garbage, things that had not been needed and were left behind. He only had one eye, so as he surveyed what remained, everything was cut off on the right side. Occasionally, he would twitch his head in that direction, distracted by phantoms of vision. From what he knew, the people were gone, but other things remained.

The cat hadn't been abandoned, per se. They had tried to take him with. The other cats had gone, climbing obediently into plastic carriers, but crying out as soon as the doors were shut. He avoided the girl as she called his name, eventually hiding behind a bush where she could not see him. Eventually, when all the other stuff had been removed, she gave up and left, too.

Now, sitting in the box, he licked his front paw and ran it back over his face, round his skull and past his ears. The cat did it again and again until he felt his fur had grown sufficiently clean.

* * *

ACKNOWLEDGMENTS

Jennifer de Guzman, you were the first to start reading this, and you were incredibly helpful with advice. I totally bit your style for Julia, too, and you were very gracious to let me do so. I hope no one confuses her with you, though, as you are far different, far more of a unique flower.

Maryanne Snell was second, and she gave me her usual brand of care. Thanks for consistently letting me toss ideas your way.

To the first respondents, those who took time with the earliest draft: Catherine McCullar, Ian "Speckled Eggs" Shaughnessy, Mason West, and Christopher McQuain, thanks for helping me find my way.

The list of friends and inspiration: Lara Michell; Chynna Clugston; Stephanie Donnelly; Kelly Sue DeConnick; Sarah Grace McCandless; The Who; Geneva (the band); Suede; Marc Ellerby; Kristan Strong; Greg McElhatton; Laurenn McCubbin; my editors at Viz, Tokyopop, and Hye-Young Im for keeping me in work; Jamie Bluhm for keeping me in coffee; Geoffrey Kleinman for keeping me in DVDs and providing all the support any writer could require; Terry Blas; Christopher Mitten; Ben Abernathy; Renée French; Mike & Laura and the Allred clan; Matt Wagner; Randy & Rocky Bowen; Jen Van Meter;

Diana Schutz; Stan Sakai; Andi Watson; Eric Stephenson; J. Torres; Jennifer Simmons; Brad Meltzer; Judd Winick; Greg Rucka; Jason at Floating World Comics; Richard, Barry, and the rest at Zeus Comics; Stephanie and Reese at Twenty-Third Avenue Books; Amanda at Muse; Jennifer at Dragon Comics & Games; Denny Haynes; Jason Anderson; the Criterion Collection; Travis Fox; Eliza Cowgill; and, of course, Steven Birch. Also, the Historic Fairmount courtyard, which gave me a table to sit in and write the ending of the book in the cool night air while my apartment boiled, and also gave Sadie the opportunity to explore its plant life. Sometimes it's all about the environment.

My father, and the childhood that gave some of this odd story its foundation.

All the people at Oni. You guys have stood by this whole trilogy and really taken care of me. Joe Nozemack, James Lucas Jones, Randal C. Jarrell, Douglas E. Sherwood, Jill Beaton—these are some of the most important people in comics. Really. They let me work with Keith Wood on design, and he's the only reason any of this is readable. Lynn Adair also bends my grammar to her will in ways I desperately need.

And though my agents, Bernadette Baker and Gretchen Stetler from Baker's Mark, signed me up as this project was wrapping, it was based on their faith in this stuff that they are now helping me plan the future.

Joëlle Jones, you drew my cover, but you also did so much more. Your importance to my life while I worked on this cannot be diminished (though I know you'll try). In so many ways, your constant presence, our chats, and our collaboration reminded me of where I was going with this story. Sometimes, when the scene was particularly rough emotionally, I imagined I was having to write to you and tell you these things, and it all made sense. And let's not forget that the Suede epigraph is because it's one of your favorite songs, and Kundera's prose is invoked because you wanted me to read your favorite novel. That is why this book is dedicated to you. As a collaborator, you have pushed me in directions

I never thought I'd go and helped me form a bond I never imagined a grump like me was capable of. That's why I consider this as much your book as it is mine.

It's nice not having to dedicate another novel to my cat. Even if Sadie resents being edged out.

— Jamie S. Rich,
who knows that he is like the rain

June 1, 2007

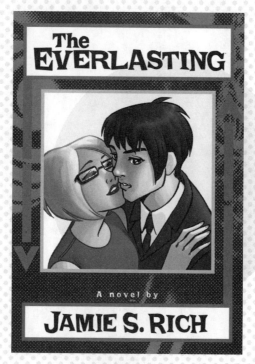

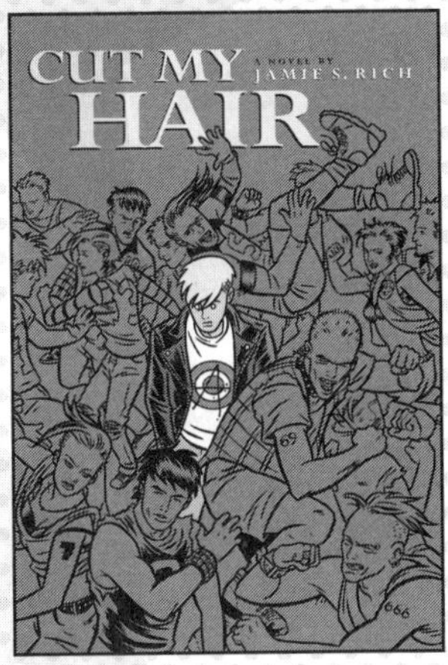

CUT MY HAIR™
cover by Mike Allred
illustrations by Chynna Clugston, Renée French, Scott Morse, Andi Watson, & Judd Winick
236 pages, prose with black-&-white illustrations
$15.95 US
ISBN 0-9700387-0-4

Praise for *Cut My Hair*

"Beloved by those lucky enough to have heard about it...Highly recommended."

- Bookslut

"High Fidelity *written by a young punk outsider instead of a 30-something music snob."*

- Alternative Press

"[A] lyrical elegy to lost youth, the death of modern rock, and the search for something authentic."

- Willamette Week

I WAS SOMEONE DEAD™
illustrations by Andi Watson
136 pages, prose with black-&-white illustrations
$9.95 US
ISBN 1-932664-26-2

Praise for *I Was Someone Dead*

"...allows you to think about the story in greater detail; examining everything from all sorts of different angles, even after having finished it. It sticks in your mind, playing out those scenes over and over again as you try and figure out 'is that what the author meant?'"

- Gotham Lounge

"...engrossing...causing the reader to think a little about not only the story, but also how it is told, and who is telling it."

- Cellar Door Publishing

Praise for *Love The Way You Love*

"A comic that not only has a twinge of real heart to it, but also makes you feel like the coolest kid in the room for reading it." – Comics Waiting Room

"This is what Archie comics should be, gripping love stories about realistic teens with exciting occupations." – Comics Worth Reading

"Marc Ellerby's art…is simple without being simplistic, and it has a comic-strip feel without losing the seriousness of certain moments." – PopMatters

LOVE THE WAY YOU LOVE™
by Jamie S. Rich & Marc Ellerby
64 pages, black-and-white
$5.95 US

Vol. 1: ISBN 1-932664-52-1

Vol. 2: ISBN 1-932664-53-X

Vol. 3: ISBN 1-932664-56-4

Vol. 4: ISBN 978-1-932664-67-6

Vol. 5: ISBN 978-1932664-68-3

Vol. 6: ISBN 978-1-932664-77-5
(available October 2007)

"I pretended to be somebody I wanted to be, and, finally, I became that person. Or he became me." - Cary Grant

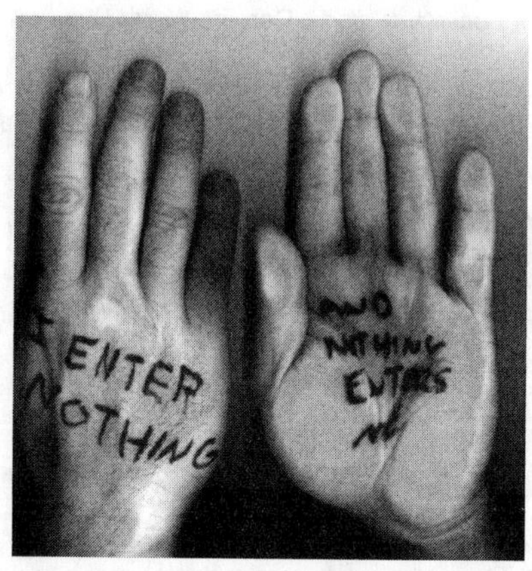

Jamie S. Rich is an author of both prose (*Cut My Hair, I Was Someone Dead*, and *The Everlasting*) and comics (the ongoing series *Love the Way You Love*, drawn by Marc Ellerby). He has worked for publishers as diverse as Image Comics, Tokyopop, Ice Kunion, and Dark Horse. In comics, he regularly collaborates with artist Joëlle Jones. The pair released their debut work, *12 Reasons Why I Love Her*, in 2006 to great acclaim, and they will be following it up in the fall of 2007 with the hardboiled graphic novel *You Have Killed Me*.

In addition to all that, Rich has written extensively for local, national, and online publications, critiquing music, books, and film. He currently reviews several movies a week for DVDTalk.com. He indulges in all of this cinema from his home in Portland, OR, U.S.A., where he lives with a grouchy, headstrong feline and more junk than he can possibly enjoy in his lifetime.